LOGAN COUNTY PUBLIC LIBRARY

I0540185

the NIGHT
WE SAID YES

the NIGHT
WE SAID YES

LAUREN GIBALDI

HARPER TEEN

An Imprint of HarperCollinsPublishers

HarperTeen is an imprint of HarperCollins Publishers.

The Night We Said Yes
Copyright © 2015 by Lauren Gibaldi
All rights reserved. Printed in the United States of America.
No part of this book may be used or reproduced in any manner
whatsoever without written permission except in the case of
brief quotations embodied in critical articles and reviews.
For information address HarperCollins Children's Books,
a division of HarperCollins Publishers,
195 Broadway, New York, NY 10007.
www.epicreads.com

Library of Congress Control Number: 2014949450
ISBN 978-0-06-230219-9

Typography by Michelle Gengaro
15 16 17 18 19   CG/RRDH   10 9 8 7 6 5 4 3 2 1

First Edition

To my parents for encouraging my dreams.
And to Samir, who held my hand as I pursued them.

CHAPTER 1

NOW
8:00 P.M.

Meg is in front of my house in ten minutes and twenty-seven seconds.

"You're late," I joke, sinking into her car's leather seats.

"Shut up," she says, smiling. "You ready?"

"Sure," I answer, somewhat hesitantly.

"It'll be fun, I promise. Rumor has it there may be a bounce house. And if I know you, I know you can't resist a bounce house." She tosses her blond hair over her shoulder, perfectly flipped as if she styled it to stay there. She knows I'm not much of a partier, not anymore at least, so she's clearly trying to be as enthusiastic as possible and hoping it rubs off on me. I can't help but laugh at her efforts.

"You know all my weaknesses," I say, crossing my arms over my chest. She grins, knowing she's won, and pulls the car out of the driveway. I watch the streetlights pass by, illuminating our drive, guiding our path. It's silent out, a normal Friday night, one in which I'd rather be home than going to a college party. But here I am. As we approach the University of Central Florida, the streets get louder, more crowded. Cars honk, voices yell. College students aching to stretch their legs—and livers—are out in full swing. Meg loves this. I . . . used to.

We were here just a week earlier for graduation. Our senior class was so large that the ceremony had to be hosted at the university's basketball arena. As we sat waiting for our names to be called, many of my classmates, Meg included, looked around, taking in their future campus. I, on the other hand, had nothing to get attached to; I'm moving four hours north to attend Florida State University. I need to get away and try something new. You can only be hurt in a town so many times before giving up on it. Meg still kind of hates me for my decision, in that best friend sort of way that makes me feel loved.

"We're here," Meg says, parking her car not on the crowded street like everyone else, but in the driveway. Being the sister of the host, she has a designated spot.

"Here we go!" I say in the cheesiest, peppiest voice possible. She rolls her eyes and gets out of the car.

2★.✩

"El, we have three months before college. Let's *try* to have some fun, okay?"

"Yeah, yeah, yeah," I say, following her to the house. Okay, she was right, I guess I could try.

Inside, the living room is already crowded, a mess of sweat, booze, and skimpy clothing. Meg is next to me, moving her body to the beat of the music. The thump, thump, thump of the bass, blasting off an iPod in the corner, is irresistible to her. I notice a few guys already starting to look; it's hard not to—she's five foot nine without heels, and stunning. I stand next to her, basking in my invisibility. I tried the center-of-attention thing before; it didn't go as planned.

"Shall we do a walk-around? Find Evan?" she yells over the music, looking at the room instead of me.

"Sure," I answer. She grabs my hand and leads me through the living room, snaking around a few people too absorbed in one another to notice us.

"Meg! Ella!" Evan calls out as soon as we walk into the kitchen.

We wave, smiling, and walk over to him. Meg and Evan have always been close, ever since I've known them. It probably stemmed from all the times she stood up for him while growing up, which was actually how we met. When a sixth-grader called Evan a princess, Meg punched him in the face. Hard. I ran to get her ice for her fist, completely in awe of her. I'd never gotten into a fight, much less started one. I was more of the cry-into-my-pillow type of girl. But after years of being picked on for my giant glasses, I understood why she'd do it. And we've been inseparable ever since—the amazing Wonder Woman and her sidekick, Ella.

Evan greets me with a giant, all-consuming hug.

"So glad you guys came. Isn't it amazing?" he asks, looking around the room. He has the same natural platinum blond hair as Meg, and is just as tall. I used to joke that their biological parents were Swedish giants. He used to get back at me by saying my parents were carnies because I'm so short.

"New record?" Meg asks, referring to Evan's ongoing count of how many people he can fit inside his tiny, two-bedroom house.

"Not yet, but the night is still young," he answers, brushing his hair back.

"Hey, where's the new boyfriend? I need to meet him," Meg demands.

"He's on a pizza run," Evan says, a smile playing at his mouth. "I'm starved. I spent all day cleaning and forgot to eat."

"No drinking for you then," Meg says, taking his cup away. "But for us . . ."

"Yeah, yeah, little sis," he says, rolling his eyes at her, and then reaching back to hand a second filled cup to me.

"Now, who can we meet? Anyone interesting? Who's, you know, not gay?" Meg asks, sipping her stolen drink.

"Go roam. I'm sure you'll meet someone up to your very

high standards," Evan answers, leaning against his counter. "And Ella, try not to have *too* much fun," he adds.

"Ha ha," I say, offering him a nice fake smile. "See? Fun."

"Meg, get her drunk or something. I'm tired of mopey Ella."

"Mopey Ella was promised a bounce house. *That* will make her happy," I say.

"Bounce house is coming later, with the boyfriend. Which reminds me . . . I'm going to check on him. He's been gone for, like, forty minutes. I'm beginning to think he's run off with the pizza guy."

"Good luck," Meg answers. He gives us both a hug and returns to the party. Since the house is packed, we head to the backyard. The humidity hugs my skin as soon as I step outside. The air is thick, a wall I have to push through. It's a typical Florida summer, and I'm instantly grateful I'm wearing a loose tank top and shorts. I pull my hair into a ponytail, exposing my neck to the stagnant night air.

Outside it's less crowded. Pockets of people are littered throughout the yard, but we can talk without yelling and hear without pressing our mouths to each other's ears. I breathe out, more comfortable in the open than jammed inside.

"Oh, hey." Meg jumps, turning to me. "Are you working tomorrow night? If not, there's a band Jake likes that's playing downtown. I forget the name, but we should go."

"Yeah, totally," I answer, my mood turning around. I do love a good show. "I usually like Jake's recommendations.

Speaking of, is he coming tonight?" I ask, still holding my drink. I don't really feel like drinking, but I grasp the cup anyway. At least no one bothers you when you're holding something.

"Nope, the guys are recording," Meg answers, tossing her hair back. Her lips purse, and I know she's thinking about Jake, wondering if any female groupies will be crashing their recording session. Clearly, I shouldn't have asked.

"Hey, let's go check out the tiki bar," I answer, changing the subject. Unofficially she may be in charge of protecting me from bullies, but I'm in charge of protecting her from herself.

"Yeah, cool."

The bar, which Evan constructed himself, has a deep brown hardwood surface, a thatched roof, and matching tiki torches. Behind it is the appointed bartender. He's muscular, with sandy blond hair and a wide mouth. His eyes are a little glazed over, like he's had two too many drinks, and there's a sly grin plastered on his face. He's wearing a tight T-shirt, and though he's not my type (too bulky), it's obvious Meg is instantly attracted to him. She's walking taller, and her eyebrows are cocked. This probably won't go well.

"Hey, you're Meg, right?" he asks as soon as we approach.

"Yep, and who are you?" she asks, with a tilt of her head and a wry grin.

"Anthony, a friend of Evan's."

"Well hello, Anthony, friend of Evan's. This is Ella, a friend of mine."

"Hey," I say, shaking his slightly clammy hand, and I can tell Meg is wondering what kind of "friend" he is to Evan. "So, do you go to school here?"

"Yeah, just started. Majoring in business. What about you?" he asks Meg, not me.

"Acting," Meg answers, despite the fact that she's not exactly in college yet. Minor detail.

"Well, that's not boring at all." He smirks, leaning closer to her, across the bar. Clearly not gay. I smile to myself, knowing what will happen next. There's no way of saving him now. "Have I seen you in anything?"

"Not yet, but you will soon." She puts her hand on her waist authoritatively.

"I look forward to it."

My phone vibrates against my leg.

At recording studio. Jake already hit on every girl here. It's been 10 minutes.

I bite the side of my lip, closing Barker's text message before Meg can see it. I feel a little guilty, but now is not the time to bring her mood down. She doesn't need that, not after everything she and Jake have been through. She needs the distraction of Anthony and the mental assurance that Jake's just off playing music. As I stuff my phone in my pocket, the ongoing flirtation in front of me comes back in full force.

"Oh, hey, guys, meet my roommate, Matt. Matt, this is Meg and Ella," Anthony says.

I'm still looking down as the words hit my consciousness. He says the name so casually, obviously unaware of what it means to me. *Matt.* I know it's not him, it can't be, but every time I hear *that name* my heart stops and I'm gone. It's as if my mind can't process what would happen if he were to come back, so instead of reacting, it gives up, checks out, and leaves town. Just like Matt did. But I know it can't be him. It never is, and it never will be.

And then Meg gasps.

And her hand shoots down and I feel her fingers lace through mine.

And then my heart wakes up and it drums, pounds, shows that it's alive and that I, too, am alive and should look up.

So I do, and when our eyes meet, I swear I stop breathing.

Because it is him. Here. Standing in front of me. Looking like he never left. Looking like this is any other night and he's just stopping by to say hi.

And I don't know what to say because my heart is in my throat and I don't know if I want to throw up or cry or scream or smile.

So I just stare, unable to blink, and watch as a word comes out of his mouth.

"Hey . . ."

CHAPTER 2

THEN
ONE YEAR EARLIER
8:00 P.M.

"El, turn it up!"

I ran across Meg's bedroom to her laptop and adjusted the volume. Music poured through the room, covering everything with a blanket of melodies and lyrics. Smiling, I danced my way back into the bathroom, where we were getting ready.

"I love this song. It's perfect getting-ready music," Meg said as I sang along to the lyrics. We were primping and plucking for the first party of the summer. We'd started this routine last year, when we realized our pre-party was oftentimes better than the actual event.

"What time does it start again?" I asked, handing Meg her lipstick back. She took it, gave me a quick look, and grabbed a tissue.

"Blot," she said, holding the tissue out to me. I did as she said because in areas of fashion and makeup, Meg definitely knew best. "Jake said the first band goes on at eight thirty," she continued, "so I'm assuming his band isn't on until nine thirtyish. So, we should get there around nine. Not too early, but early enough to chat with the guys before they play."

"And you're sure you'll be okay?" I'd asked at least five times already, and I wasn't afraid to go for six. Each time she'd responded with a halfhearted "yeah" or "sure," which didn't really answer anything. Meg had a tendency to bulldoze over questions she didn't want to answer, so over time I'd learned the repetition technique. And in this case, I really needed her to answer truthfully because I didn't want to see her hurt. Again. I knew she bounced back easily—most of the time—but I worried about her.

"For the seventeenth time, yes. I'm fine. We're talking and all. I mean, it's Jake. Even though we broke up, I can't just . . . you know . . . stop." She stared at the mirror, darkening her lips until they were a completely different shade, transforming herself as she often did when she wanted to feel like someone else. I didn't have the skill to do that; I wasn't able to simply morph and pretend things were okay when they weren't.

"I just worry," I admitted, packing my makeup back

into my bag so as not to meet her eyes. Earlier that year, Meg had ended her relationship with Jake, the lead singer and guitar player in the Pepperpots, a three-person pop punk band that we were good friends with. Their relationship was pretty much doomed from the start, so no one was surprised, including myself. They were volatile, passionate to a fault. Both had fiery personalities, which were nearly explosive when ignited. I didn't think it would last past their first blowup, when Meg literally pushed Jake into a Dumpster. They made up—and made out—right after, but still. Even though I cheered them on—I had to, I was Meg's best friend—I was also skeptical. Clearly with reason.

"I'm fine," she said again. "Like I've said before, if he'd rather flirt with girls after a show because he thinks he's some sort of a rock god and needs to act like the hot, single lead singer, go for it. I just can't be around to watch." She breathed in deep, shaking her head and grabbing gel off the counter. "I loved him, but it wasn't worth it."

"At least he's stopped trying to get back together with you," I said, not adding "for the time being."

"Yeah, but it was kind of cool having two songs written about me," she said with a fake laugh. "Not every girl has that."

"Not every girl dates a self-proclaimed rock god," I joked, brushing my dark brown hair.

"Very true," she said. "At least all the breakup drama is over, and we can move on."

"Yes, please, no more drama for a while." We were all great friends for so long—me, Meg, Jake, and Barker, the drummer—but the breakup put up a wall, with me and Meg on one side and the band on the other. I straddled the line at times, playing messenger for each side. I missed the guys; they were my friends, too.

Of all things, it took a school field trip to break down the barrier. One trip to see a poorly performed Shakespeare play and we were talking again, comparing notes on which actor was worst. It was as if nothing had happened. I loved being back with them again—they were my family. I felt complete.

"Besides," Meg said, dabbing her lips with a tissue, "you're the one we should be worried about."

I sighed. "Whatever." Worrying about Meg allowed me to be distracted from my own breakup, which was far more recent . . . and far more questionable.

When Nick broke up with me, it wasn't the typical "it's not you, it's me." It was so far from typical that it took me a while to really process. I met him at his car after school. As I approached, he was sitting on the hood, guitar in hand.

"Hey," I said, leaning over the guitar to give him a kiss. But he didn't look up; he kept his eyes focused on his guitar. I leaned back, confused. "Is something wrong?"

"Ella, listen." Hearing my full first name coupled with the word "listen" made my stomach clench and I knew at that moment we were breaking up. "The band's going to start touring soon." (Lie. His band, No Signal, wasn't touring for another two months, and it was only touring around Orlando, where we lived.) "And we're getting pretty big." (Lie. No one knew who they were.) "And I just don't think I can have a girlfriend right now." (Lie. He started dating someone else not long after me.) "So, how about . . . a high five for friendship?"

After I picked my jaw up off the ground, I just turned around and walked away. I mean, how do you even respond to "high five for friendship"? And that was it.

"Are *you* sure you're going to be okay tonight?" she asked, using my question against me.

"About being high fived? I don't think I'll ever feel okay being high fived. He has forever ruined high fiving for me," I said, shaking my head.

"Should we ban high fiving from our friendship, then?" she asked with a giggle, and I rolled my eyes.

"A few days ago, Nick and his new whatever walked by just as Jake high fived me over the vending machine having Snickers. I don't think Nick saw the humor in it as much as we did."

"I'm glad you have a sense of humor about it, but if he—okay, we—ever get annoying, let me know," she said seriously, and I appreciated the sentiment. Because though I didn't mind joking about the high fiving, the breakup was still fresh, a wound exposed. "Because, seriously, after finding out that he cheated on you? I wanted to murder him."

"For some reason, I don't doubt you actually would follow through with that threat," I joked. "Then again, I wanted to, too."

The breakup was hard enough, but learning about the cheating made everything worse. I hated feeling so . . . rejected. Because honestly—it sucked. The entire thing sucked. But as long as I didn't let myself remember that, as long as I didn't remind myself every moment that not only was I dumped, but cheated on as well, I was okay. I was able to believe that one day I'd find a guy who would never break up with me using a high five. I was able to believe that maybe the next guy would be better. I *had* to believe that, because after living through the Nick situation, and seeing what Meg went through with Jake, I was losing hope. I wasn't in love with Nick or anything, but he was my first boyfriend, after all.

"He is going to be there tonight, right?" Meg asked. "Because I can, you know, murder him," she added, giving me an evil glare. I laughed at her offer.

"No need to break out the weapons. And I don't know—I'm assuming so," I said, feeling my nerves acting up. "But . . . yeah . . . tonight should be fun. And you don't have to worry about me. I'm over it. I just . . . I honestly don't care anymore." I made my point by emphatically zipping up my makeup bag. Nick might have been around, but he wasn't part of my plan for the night. I was going to go out. I was going to have fun. I was ready to avoid all distractions of the male variety. I wanted excitement, not drama, and Meg was usually good at leading me to both.

"Good. You'll finally get to meet Matt, too."

"The Pepperpots' new bassist? It sucks that they lost their old one."

"Yeah, but apparently Matt's much better. Jake met him at a show and said he was phenomenal. Plus, he's hot."

"Jake said he was hot?" I asked jokingly.

"Ha. Ha. I think you'll like him. He has black-rimmed glasses."

"That *is* a requirement," I said with a smile. It wasn't, but she knew I had a thing for the dorky look. Nick did not embody that look, so I really should have known it was doomed from the start. Nick was more of a Jake, with that leading-man rock-star look. It might have worked for Meg, but not me.

"That reminds me." Meg dropped her hairbrush and ran back to her bedroom. She returned with a jewel-toned purple bag, with silver tissue paper piled on top. "Open."

"What's this?" I asked, tentatively taking the bag.

"It's a surprise," Meg said, wiggling her eyebrows.

"Should I be worried? I mean, remember the goldfish?"

"I'm never living that down, am I?" she groaned, and I grinned, remembering the present she got me after my dog died. Not the best present, seeing as how the goldfish died three days later, but incredibly thoughtful nonetheless. "Okay, what's the best way to get revenge on an ex?" she asked, waiting for my reaction.

I shrugged, playing with the tissue paper and wondering what her almighty plan was. "Firing squad? Negative rumor spread throughout school? Millions of spam texts?"

She sighed in response. "Look *amazing*."

"Right." I clearly hadn't learned all Meg had to teach in the fashion department yet. It was my favorite class—there was never any homework and the subject matter was actually interesting. And, sometimes, there were gifts involved.

I tilted my head and smiled, digging my hand into the bag. Inside, I felt a soft, slippery fabric. I pulled out a stunning deep green top that matched my eyes.

"Meg!" I grabbed her, hugging her close. She knew me better than I knew myself sometimes. I never would have thought to get something like that, but seeing it, just holding it, made me feel braver and more ready to face the night.

Through everything, we'd been there for each other. She went through every awkward phase of mine, and I hers. She knew I hated being the center of attention, and would often shy away from making decisions. I knew that if I took down the Clash poster on her bedroom wall, I'd find the Jack Skellington one from her goth phase at fifteen, and then a Barbie one from her pink phase at six. Meg was always really good at that—covering her past with another layer. Sometimes I didn't know which layer would stick, and sometimes I didn't know which layer was showing, but it didn't matter. I always figured it out eventually.

"To tonight!" she said, lifting her pinkie up.

"Tonight," I said, shaking my head and locking pinkies with her—a gesture we started long ago—her snow-white skin atop my olive. We always did it to remind each other that we were there, that we'd never let go no matter the problem or hurdle.

"But what are *you* going to wear?" I asked, staring once again at my new shirt. It was beautiful.

"Um, did you not see the other bag in my bedroom?" I looked out to see a matching bag laying on her bed. Our night was packed away inside it, waiting to get out.

◇◇◇◇

Meg's parents let us borrow their silver Volkswagen Passat for the night. As Meg turned the key, I flipped through her iPod, finding the best songs to soundtrack our night. Most of them were older punk songs from the '90s, ones Jake downloaded for her; she never got rid of them. He could break her heart, but he couldn't take away her music. The first song I chose was fast, upbeat, and one we knew by heart. One that didn't have a connection to Jake or Nick, so we were able to scream out the lyrics and let the night steal our voices without thinking of anything but what lay ahead. Our giggles echoed through the streets, informing each house that we were still awake and ready to take on anything. It was easy singing along with Meg—neither of us had the best voice, but that never stopped us from being rock stars in the comfort (and secrecy) of the car. I loved it.

After a few songs like that, I slowed it down so we still had voices left for the party.

"I'm excited to see the band play tonight, after their gigless stint without a bassist," I admitted.

"Me too, actually." Meg stared straight ahead and slowly approached a red light. "He's got a new girl, you know."

"Who?" I turned and faced her, and I could have sworn her eyes were glassy with tears. "Jake? Really?"

"Some girl he met at a club. Of course." Her eyebrows took a quick decline, searching for answers she wouldn't find. Within a second, as if the mood had never crossed her face, her steady gaze was back. She was such a master of disguise, I often had to dig through her layers to prod out the one that needed comforting.

"Whatever. She's not you, that's for sure," I said, ready to reassure her again.

"Heh, yeah. I just don't . . . want to see them together. You know? It's like you and Nick. It's okay that there's another girl. Just . . . don't rub it in our faces."

"I honestly don't think Jake's like that," I answered, talking over the music. As if on cue, a new song came on, a slow instrumental piece from a movie soundtrack. Perfect. "He's an ass, but he's not showy like that. The breakup hurt him, too."

"Yeah, I guess. Nick, on the other hand—"

"Is just an ass. So, we have that to look forward to," I

pointed out, trying to ignore the uneasy feeling coming over me.

"I'm sorry."

"Eh, it was my fault. I trusted him."

"You know, it never felt like the right time to tell you. But we all kind of hated him."

"You did?" I asked, whipping my head toward her. "I knew you guys didn't *love* him, but I didn't know it was that bad."

"He was just . . . awful. I mean, he was nice to you sometimes, but he didn't really *care*. He was all show, no substance."

"Why didn't you ever tell me?" I asked, a bit offended and hurt. "I thought we told each other everything."

"I know, but you were just so . . . happy." She looked over at me. "I was going to after the breakup, but then you found out about the other girl and . . . I don't know. I just didn't want to bring it up. You were . . . you again. And I knew it would hurt you if I told you."

"So why tell me now?" I asked, still taken aback and feeling slightly betrayed.

"Because I know it's over. I know there isn't a part of you still thinking about him." She paused. "And if I hate your next guy, I promise you'll be the first to know."

"I better be," I said, remembering back to how my friends didn't hang out with Nick really, they didn't involve him. Maybe I should have known they hated him. Then again, maybe I should have known about him, too. "I mean, you're right, I don't want him back or anything, but I wish you'd told me earlier, I guess."

"If I did, would it have changed anything?"

"Maybe . . . I don't know." I was used to her always revealing her position. Not knowing something she thought made me feel kind of alone. "I like your opinions."

"And I like you being happy," she explained. "I didn't want to kill that, you know?"

"Yeah, okay." I relented because even if she had told me, I'm not sure if I would have listened. "Next time?" I asked anyway, pressing on.

"Next time." She nodded. We didn't apologize really, not like normal people. We just kept going. It was more natural that way. We drove the rest of the way letting the music do the talking. For us, words weren't always necessary.

The party was at our friend Ross's house, which was large, had two floors, and was in a secluded part of town. Because of the location, he could have bands play without the neighbors complaining. Cars lined the sidewalks, parked crookedly all the way down the street. While we drove through the neighborhood, nobody was out—the streets were still and asleep. But at the house, it was as if everyone in town was already there, waiting for us.

"All good?" Meg asked, standing beside her car. Any trace of emotion from earlier had been wiped from her face.

I gave her the once-over and nodded. We were ready. It was my favorite part of the night—when the evening's events were still unknown and unpredictable. It was the sense of possibility that I loved, the idea that anything could happen next.

We walked to the front door, only to find a wall of people blocking it. Meg gave her signature half smile—the one that says she's better than this—and pushed through, owning the party with a single look. I followed behind, feeling taller than I had earlier. Meg had the power to transmit her self-esteem onto me sometimes, and I liked it. People were everywhere, broken into groups small and large, all talking over one another.

"Okay, what now?" Meg asked as we stood in the entranceway.

"Kitchen?" I suggested, grabbing her hand and pulling her along. I'd been to Ross's house before and knew the ins and outs. The kitchen was brighter than the rest of the house, and still full of people. There must have been at least twenty in the small space. Most were gathered around the keg in the corner, pumping out foamy beer. I could hear the band in the other room, performing a cover of some pop song I kind of recognized, really screaming out the lyrics. Not great, but not bad either. At least we weren't late.

Meg grabbed two cups and went to get us drinks.

"Hey!" A shout came from across the room. I knew that voice. I turned around and saw Barker pushing his way into the room. He was wearing an Oingo Boingo thrift store T-shirt and brown corduroy pants. He was half indie, half professor, and it somehow worked on him.

"Hey Barker," I said, waving. "We're not too late, right?"

"Nope, these guys just started, so there's time before we go on. Hey, I want you to meet Matt, the new bassist."

Barker turned around and grabbed the guy behind him. I self-consciously looked down to check my shirt, and as I adjusted it, I saw his red Converse sneakers. They were similar to ones I owned, which I found funny. He had on dark blue jeans that looked worn, but not in that purposeful way that was sold in stores, but more in the way that meant he actually wore them a lot. His black T-shirt was a bit tight and featured a band I'd never heard of before. And then I saw his face, with his dark brown messy hair and black-rimmed glasses. He was tall, taller than me, and his face lit up when our eyes met. Okay, Meg was right, he was cute.

"Matt, this is Ella. El, Matt."

"Hey," he said, smiling. It was a cute smile, crooked and shy.

"Hi," I said back, officially excited to start the night.

CHAPTER 3

NOW
8:30 P.M.

"Hi," I manage to respond, still staring; because never in a million years would I have thought Matt would be here, at Evan's party. Never would I have thought he'd come back. When he left, he took away everything, and every day since then I feel that gaping hole, every day I remember what's missing. I can feel it now, growing larger as my heart races and my hands shake.

"Hey? That's it? That's all you have to say?" Meg says, eyeing him.

"You guys know each other?" Anthony asks, face darting from mine to Meg's to Matt's and then back around again.

"Hey Meg," Matt says, running his hand through his

hair, avoiding her glare. "How're you? How's Jake? Is he . . . here?"

"No, he's not here. And you'd know how he was if you ever called him. Or her," she says, nodding toward me and squeezing my hand at the same time. Her words, though true, are piercing me, digging deep into my body. I don't know what to say, so instead I put my free arm around my torso, trying to keep myself together in case I really do rip apart at the seams and fall to the ground, where Matt can proceed to step on me and finish what he started.

"I think I missed something," Anthony interjects, still bopping his head, trying to keep up. The hopeful look washes away as he realizes his plans for Meg may not materialize after all. And I stay quiet in the middle of it all because I might just vomit.

"I think *he* missed something," Meg answers, pointing to Matt. "Like, half a year of somethings. How could you just leave like that?" she continues, spite in her voice.

"Meg, please," I whisper, squeezing her hand. And as quickly as she got fired up, she calms down and shakes her head. It's my fight, not hers. "You know what, forget it. Come on, Anthony, let's get out of here." As her hand slips out of mine, my heart races faster, louder. She doesn't have to fight my fights, but she also doesn't need to leave me out here alone. I don't know if I can do this. "You need to talk to her," she says back to Matt. "She deserves answers. And Jake does, too."

I watch as she leaves in a huff with Anthony, his arm slowly trying to drape over her shoulders. She shrugs him off; he should know by her look that she doesn't want to be touched. Never touch lit dynamite.

I turn back to Matt, scared. I'm not ready to do this, to simply talk to him after six months apart. He's staring at his untied laces, not meeting my eyes. His shoelaces were always untied, and the memory hits me with a force I wasn't expecting. Him always sighing when I pointed it out. Me always laughing at the repeated act, and loving him even more for the simple imperfection.

He drops down to tie them, taking his time, and brushing them off when he's done. And inside I want to cry because *he's here*. And him being here proves it all happened. I want to touch him and make sure this is all real and tangible. I close my eyes and feel every emotion I tried to hide when I was being braver, stronger, moving on. The pain. The loneliness. The shame.

"Um. How're you?" he asks, standing back up.

How am I? I almost laugh at the question, because I'm a complete wreck. My heart isn't sure if it should soar or crash and my body is both pushing me closer to him and pulling me away. And I don't know what's right, and I need Meg here to tell me. But I can't say all that, so instead I open my eyes and say, "Fine, you?"

"Okay," he answers, putting his hands in his pockets and he's still so cute. It kills me seeing him there, so nonchalantly.

So *there*. He doesn't move from where he is, staying a few feet away, still behind the bar where Anthony was. "This is incredibly awkward, isn't it?"

My body loosens and a brief calm washes over me. I smile slightly, agreeing. He's always had a way of pointing out the obvious when it needs to be said. I take a moment to look at him. He's different, but not really. His glasses are new; thin frames instead of his black-rimmed plastic ones. They make him look older, more mature. But behind them, his eyes are still the same. They're the eyes I fell for. Green with hazel flecks. It's dark, but I can still see them flash in the tiki lights. The familiarity pushes me to ask him the first thing I can think of.

"What are you doing here?"

"I go here now. To UCF. I just moved back," he says, finally meeting my eyes. It's as if he wants his look to convey an inner meaning his words won't allow. And when my heart flips, stupidly I want his look to say *I'm back for you, this whole year was a mess, let's run away together and never look back*. But I can't want that. I can't allow myself to get hopeful again, not after what he did. I hated him once—I have to remember that, and not the way his lips felt on mine.

"Oh," I answer, because it's all I can say.

Sensing my discomfort—as if it's hard to—he walks toward me, closing the gap that has stood between us ever since he left.

As he comes close, my stomach clenches and instinctively

I put my hand up. An image of the letter he sent me—the one I promptly ripped up and burned—flashes in my mind and I can't go back to that moment. I can't be the Ella that was innocent and vulnerable and easily fell for him after a crazy night. That Ella is gone.

"It was nice seeing you," I say, quickly, eyes searching for an out.

"Oh," he says, head down again. "Yeah, okay, you too."

"I'll see you around," I add, but my words hold no real meaning, and he probably knows that.

"Yeah? Okay, cool," he says, nodding, and still not looking at me.

"Bye," I mumble as I turn to leave. I know he's still behind me, I can feel him there, staring at me. But I have no clue what it all means. I have no clue why he's even trying to start a conversation with me after all this time. We are over; we are in the past. We should have stayed there.

I find Meg by the door once I get inside. She's leaning against the counter but she looks *too* comfortable, too posed. She was spying, of course.

"How'd it go?" she asks as soon as I shut the door.

"Uggghhh," I answer, knowing she'll understand the sound better than any assortment of words. I lean back against the wall and close my eyes as I wait for my hands to stop shaking and the lump in my chest to dissipate. I can't erase the memory of him glancing down, looking almost pained. I won't cry. Not here, not now.

"That good?"

"Why is he here?" I whine, frustrated with him, myself, everything.

"Did you ask him?"

"Yeah. He's going to UCF now. Like, he's back. For good."

"Seriously?"

"Seriously." I open my eyes.

"You'd think he would've let one of us know," Meg answers, going back into her angry self. I know she's thinking of me, but I know she's also thinking of Jake, and the friendship he lost when Matt left. "I mean, coming to my brother's party like this? What the hell? He had to have known we'd be here. It's ridiculous, and it pisses me off that he thinks he can just worm his way back in."

"Right?" I continue where she left off, feeling myself getting heated up. "And what does he want, anyway? Him here, acting all shy? Does he want to be friends again or something? Because, no."

"Where is he now?"

"He's still outside," I answer, joining her by the counter and leaning my head on her shoulder. "Why does this suck so much?"

"Because he sucks," she answers, and I laugh a little. I can always count on her to make me feel better. "And because he's important to you," she sighs.

"Yeah, he was, like, a year ago," I answer, shaking my head, but she eyes me and I stop.

"When you and Nick broke up, how long did it take you to get over him?"

"Like, a day." Which isn't exactly true, but close enough.

"And after Matt?"

I want to say a day, too, but that's a lie. It took longer, much longer. And seeing him now—I guess the feelings never fully went away. So I don't answer, but Meg is already eyeing me again.

"Exactly," she says. "It sucks that it hurts so much. But it hurts because he's still important to you."

She's right, of course, no matter how much I don't want to admit it.

"I guess," I mumble. I stare across the room at the wall I was previously leaning against. I can't meet her eyes, not yet, because despite myself, I know what I should do, but I'm not ready for it. I know that if I look at Meg, she'll agree with my right and logical conclusion, despite oftentimes not being right or logical about her own life. For the moment, though, I just want to bask in the melancholy of the situation because it's easier than dealing with it. I want the feeling to wash over my body and take me hostage.

"You should go back out."

"Why?" I still won't look at her.

"As much as I hate the fact that he's doing this to you— and as much as I want to kill him right now—you need answers. You spent half a year wondering what happened. This is your chance to find out. It's why I left you out there alone in the first place."

"Yeah, about that." I sigh and shut my eyes. "And Jake?"

"Oh, I've already texted him. There were a lot of expletives in his response."

I laugh, shaking my head. "I can imagine."

"Plus, despite Evan's best efforts, this party kinda sucks."

I finally look at her. She's turned to face me, leaning her right side on the counter. Her perfectly colored lips have a slight smirk, as if she's daring me to go back out. It's always a game with her, and right now I'm not sure whether to love or hate her for making me play.

Especially because she's reminding me of all the little dares Matt and I used to have, ones where we pushed each other to do something different or scary or necessary. How he dared me to submit an article to the school newspaper, despite my fear that it would be rejected. (I did; it wasn't.) How I dared him to play a song he wrote for the rest of the band, despite his conviction that Jake would hate it. (He did; Jake didn't.)

As I hear the song drifting in my mind, the melancholy ebbs, sliding away like a current. It's still there, mucking around and ready to be called back, but the waves are calm, and I want answers. So I dare myself to return to him.

"Fine," I sigh. She grabs me in a hug. "But first I need some air," I say to her, feeling claustrophobic. I give her a look and walk toward the front of the house. The party is still going on, oblivious to the reunion that just happened.

Oblivious to the fact that my world is completely changing, all due to a single "Hey."

I walk outside to the front yard, past people talking and making out, and breathe in and out until my eyes don't feel watery and my mind feels light. The air feels good, soft against my skin, and I find solace in the mere action of walking away. In the grass is a crumpled-up piece of sheet music that I pick up instinctively, and curse myself for doing it. Matt might have left, but our game of collecting found objects, much to my dismay, stayed. Some habits are hard to break. I smooth the paper out to reveal the lyrics.

Deep in December, our hearts should remember

Well, that's annoyingly appropriate. The line seems to cut off abruptly and though I haven't heard the song before, I know there has to be more. I turn the sheet over, but there's nothing.

"What'd you find?"

I spin around at the voice and it's him, of course, standing behind me. My heart leaps again, but this time I'm ready for him. I've had my pep talk, and I no longer have a force field around me, stopping him from getting too close. It's just me. So I hand him the paper and he gets a pained look on his face, like he's almost sad he's passed this habit on to me.

"It's *The Fantasticks*."

"Huh?" I ask, walking next to him so I can look at it, too.

★ ⋆31

"The musical. My mom loves it—she plays the soundtrack a lot."

"How does it end?" I ask, needing to know.

"The musical?"

"No, the song."

He looks over at me, finally meeting my eyes, and I suppress the urge to sigh, because that can't be me. I can be strong. I can do this. I need to know.

"Can we go somewhere and talk?" he answers instead.

"What?"

"It's been a while and . . ." He lowers the paper to his side. ". . . I don't know. I'd just like to talk."

"I don't know," I answer, because talking is one thing, but going somewhere to do it is another.

"Come on. The party is loud and I'd like to, you know, see how you're doing."

I raise an eyebrow in response. He should know. He should *really* know.

"Scratch that last part," he says, looking down as a flush comes to his face. "I have the song in my car. I can play it for you."

"Are you trying to kidnap me?" I ask dryly.

"Only a little." He grins shyly and I can't help but wonder, *Was he just flirting?* "I'm parked over there." He points, and the sight of his car makes me pause. It's exactly as I remember it, parked along the side of the road as if it has been waiting for me this entire year. The right side is still scratched from when the band tried to stuff Barker's drum set in the backseat. Of course it didn't work, but they weren't ones to turn down a challenge.

"I don't know," I say again, weighing the options in my mind. Go with him and get answers. Stay here and avoid everything. I've done a really good job at avoiding lately. Is it even worth it?

He turns around and starts walking backward to his car, still facing me, and in his own way challenging me. The light from the lamppost reflects off his glasses, making his eyes almost look illuminated. He keeps walking until his shoe hits a rock and he stumbles.

"Whoops," he says nervously, and stops walking. He straightens out and runs his fingers through his hair again. With that small imperfection I realize for the first time that he's uncomfortable too. He's just as nervous and unsure as I am. The realization calms me; we're in this weird, awkward situation together.

"I have an idea, but feel free to say no," he says from where he is, across the yard, allowing me space to breathe and decide.

"That good of an idea?" I ask, raising my eyebrow.

"Want to get food? I haven't eaten."

And again he's trying to get me to leave. Again he's making a weird effort. I could easily just say no, go back to the party—or better yet, go home—and call it a night. Not let him get under my skin, even though he's already started slipping in. Not go down the road we've already traveled. Not let it dead-end again.

But even though my mind is saying that it's smart to stay, my heart is racing for me to go. Because last year with him and my friends I felt strong and invincible. I was able to live out fears, wake myself up, and be in the spotlight only Meg previously occupied. And since he left, I've simply been living in a cocoon, afraid to put myself out there again. Afraid to be let down again.

I miss that feeling of being alive.

I look over to him and his eyes hold me. I can never say no to those eyes.

Before I answer, he calls out, "And follow."

"Huh?" I answer, confused.

"The end of the lyric. It's 'and follow.'"

A piece clicks in place as he waves the sheet music in his hand, and without realizing it, I nod. I follow.

"Where to?" I ask.

"Wing King?"

CHAPTER 4

THEN
8:50 P.M.

"So you're the new bassist I've been hearing about?" I yelled to Matt over the noise at the house party.

"It depends, what have you heard?" he asked with a smile.

"That you're going to save the dying Pepperpots."

"I resent that," Barker interjected.

"Heh, they're pretty good. I don't know if they need me to save them. But, yes, I am that superhero." He nodded, striking a Superman pose.

I smiled at him, in awe of how *comfortable* I felt. I never felt this comfortable in front of Nick; I never was able to make jokes or make him laugh. He didn't care about my retorts, something I realized much too late.

"I'm going to grab a drink, do you want one?" he asked. Meg still hadn't returned with my drink, so I shook my head.

"I'm good, thanks."

"Okay, cool," he answered, combing his fingers through his hair, and letting it fall back into place. I watched as he turned away and walked toward the keg.

"Hey," Barker whispered—well, loudly whispered. "She's here."

"Who's here?"

"Jake's new girl. Does Meg know about her?" he asked cautiously, glancing at Meg to make sure she didn't hear.

I looked over at Meg. She was laughing with a girl from her math class, her head tilted far back, full-on reckless. She looked so happy, and it made me scared to think of how quickly Jake and his new girl could sink it all. "Yeah, she mentioned her on the way over. Thus the, er, outfits."

"I noticed that," he said. "I was wondering who it was for."

"Well you know I'd never buy a shirt like this for myself," I said, playing with the sleeve.

"Eh, it suits you. You look nice." Barker and I had only been friends for a few years, but he knew me better than any other guy. We got along well, and there was never an attraction to ruin it. He could call my bluffs; I could call his. Anyway, he was so ridiculously happy with his girlfriend, Gabby, that it didn't matter. They were like a married couple. They cooked dinners together.

"So what do you think of Matt?" Meg asked, sneaking back over and handing me a cup of foamy beer.

"Is this the goal for the night? Hook me up with him?" I asked the question jokingly, but at the same time my heart expectantly flipped. I didn't feel ready for a relationship, I didn't feel ready to be interested in a new guy, but it didn't hurt to meet someone new. I looked over and saw him coming back. My face heated right up.

"Pretty much." Meg nodded.

"Yeah," Barker agreed. I rolled my eyes, smiling at my very persuasive friends.

The kitchen started to fill up more, bodies pressed against bodies. A last chord rang out as the first band ended their set, so we were finally able to properly hear one another.

"I'm gonna go look for Gabby. She should be here by now." Barker turned to go.

"Um, want me to come?" Matt asked, a crease forming on his forehead. He was obviously unsure where to go, considering he didn't know anyone else here. Well, except for Jake, who, if I knew Jake, was probably off with his new girl doing something Matt didn't want to see. I hoped Barker would tell him to stay with us.

"Nah, stick with the girls. In about twenty minutes, meet me by the stage. I'd say earlier, but it might take this band two hours to take down their gear. Let's just say they're not the best." He gave Matt a small salute and walked away.

"I . . . guess you're stuck with me?" Matt asked. I looked back at him, knowing I was okay with that.

"So how do you like Orlando?" I asked. There were tons of things I wanted to know, but it was the first question that popped in my head.

"It's okay. I've only been here for about a month. I don't know much about it yet, really."

"We'll have to take you out, then," I answered, carefully using the plural so it would seem casual.

"That would be cool," he agreed. "You know, I'm really glad Jake offered me the spot. It sounds like fun, playing again."

"Did you play a lot before?"

"A bit. I'm not a pro or anything," he said with a shrug.

"Don't worry, neither are they." I smiled back, still feeling at ease. He had little dimples that popped when he smiled; they were adorable. "So, where did you go to school before you—"

"Mingle?" Meg interrupted, cocking her head to one side. I was slightly irritated by her sudden desire to join us, but it was Meg. As I looked at her, a small part of me questioned—what if he liked her better? She was taller, blonder, prettier . . . why wouldn't he? But as I looked back, he was still gazing at me—not Meg—still waiting for me to finish my question. So I shrugged, silently agreeing and knowing we had a full night of conversation ahead of us. It didn't end there. Matt nodded in response as well. I put my cup on the table, trading my drink for Meg's hand, grabbing hold so I didn't lose her in the crowd. It looked like our entire high school and the neighboring high school were there. Rivals in football, best friends in parties. Some were there for the bands, still surrounding the stage and pumping their fists; some for the beer, chugging drinks faster than the drummer hit his drums; and some for the company. I was there for friends.

We pushed past a few people I vaguely recognized, to whom I offered a nod or wave. I looked back, hoping to make eye contact with Matt, but realized he hadn't kept up with us. Stuck a couple of people behind, he was vigorously trying to catch up. To help, I reached back through the throng of bodies until I felt a hand grasp mine. A shiver spread through my body.

We made it to the living room, where, as predicted, the band was unsuccessfully packing up their equipment. Wires were crisscrossed, cymbals were tossed about. The bodies milling around in the hot, small space were clammy and packed in close. I held on tight to both Meg and Matt, not wanting to lose them in the crowd.

"Oh god." Meg stopped dead in her tracks, forcing me to halt behind her. Matt, unaware of our pause, crashed into me.

"Oh, sorry, I didn't—"

But I ignored him because through the mess of people I saw what had caused Meg to stop. And my heart dropped. Jake had his back to us, but we knew it was him. The black

T-shirt was his staple. His dyed-orange hair, curly and usually gelled, was disheveled. And that was because two hands were raking through it, pulling his face toward hers. While I couldn't see who was currently ruining Meg's life, I assumed it was Jake's new girl. I hated her instantly.

"I . . ." Meg started, turning back to me. Her normally composed face was ashen, her eyes huge.

"Drink? Kitchen?" I asked, looking for something to distract her. I knew drowning her sorrows in alcohol wasn't the best idea, but it was the only thing I had.

"What's the matter?" Matt asked, but before I could answer, there was a stampede of people yelling, running, charging directly at us. It was a domino effect starting at the front of the house.

"Oh, what now!" Meg yelled. Shouts informed us that those outside groups who'd been talking, smoking, or puking were the first to see the cops pull up.

I didn't even have the chance to panic. Cups were flying everywhere as people grabbed their belongings and tried to escape the house before they were caught. Like a herd of animals, everyone ran toward the back door. Bodies pushed against bodies, yells and screams bounced throughout the room. I tried to see what was going on but every time I looked up, someone else rammed into me, knocking me to the side. One guy, easily twice my size, tried running through me as if I wasn't there, my body just an obstacle in his way. He hit my side hard, and I dropped Matt's hand. In the current of people, I lost my balance and started to fall. But before I was trampled, I felt an arm slide under my shoulders.

"You okay?" Matt yelled.

I nodded, in shock from the moment and how quickly it passed. Matt's face was close, his body protecting me from the pandemonium. I felt my heart skip a beat as my face flushed. His eyes were fierce, determined.

With my left arm draped over his shoulder, I held on tight as we steadied ourselves. Meg still held my other hand, unaware of my near fall. Her phone was out, and she was reading a text.

"Upstairs," she yelled.

Matt let his arm drop, moving in front of us to block our little group from those running past. His arms spread around us, creating a circle of protection. A tossed cup hit me in the head, and it took me a second to realize that beer was now dripping through my hair in streams. I was frozen in place. Thankfully, Meg jolted me back.

"Go upstairs," she said again. Holding my hand tight, she pushed her way to the stairs. I grabbed Matt's hand instinctively, and he squeezed it back.

"But what's upstairs?" he shouted. I shook my head, wondering the same thing.

"Meg, what's upstairs?" I repeated, the situation starting to scare me.

She continued to run, ignoring our questions. Just as we touched the stairs, light beams passed over us. The cops were inside the house. Not one person was twenty-one, and there was a lot of alcohol. Someone was definitely going to be in trouble. I thought of Barker and Jake, and pulled on Meg's hand. Despite not liking the latter too much at the moment, we couldn't just leave him behind.

"Meg, the guys," I yelled as we climbed the stairs. We were the only ones going in a different direction. While the reprieve from the crowd was nice, I was worried about being alone. I trusted her, but what good could come from going upstairs? Were we supposed to hide under a bed?

"Don't worry," she answered, glancing at me in a way that said *they're fine*. Upstairs, it was empty. We followed her into Ross's bedroom. It was a typical guy's room, full of video games and leftovers. It was then that I heard the foot-steps behind us, and my heart picked up the pace in fear.

"There you are. Thanks for the text." It was Jake, sans lady friend. Relief hit me fast. We weren't caught. He was okay. "Barker's already gone; let's go."

I stayed back with Matt as Jake followed Meg to the window.

"I hate to point this out, but we can't fly," Matt said. Lines deepened on his forehead as he raised his eyebrows. Great introduction to our social scene, I thought.

"There's a ladder," Meg pointed out, as if it were the most obvious thing in the world. I glanced at Matt and we ran over. We were still holding hands.

Jake opened the window and voices flew in, a cluster of

screams, cheers, and cries. I looked out and finally understood. There was a long metal ladder that stretched down the side of the house, away from the back door, the cops, and the mass of people. It was secluded, a side of the house no one even thought to visit. Clearly, Ross snuck out quite often.

"Ladies first," Jake said. Meg glared at him, but started her descent. I followed after.

"This is not how I expected tonight to go," I whispered to Meg as we climbed down. She landed first, quietly, and then grabbed my arm, pulling me down beside her. The grass was wet from a recent downpour and squished where I landed.

"Keep moving," Meg demanded. Pieces of hair were in her mouth from the wind that was still shaking the trees. I looked back and saw that Matt and Jake were down from the ladder and right behind us. We ran across the yard, keeping to the shadows, not wanting to attract attention. Thankfully, the yard was only a few feet long, so we made it to the fence in about two breaths.

"I'll go first," Jake whispered, taking the lead as usual. His hair was still disheveled, and even in the dark, I noticed the purple hickey mark on his neck. I wanted to slap him.

Jake easily reached the top of the wooden fence and hoisted himself over, landing with a rough thud.

"You guys next," Matt whispered, meaning Meg and me. The fence was a little taller than I could reach, so he grabbed my waist and, with a quick lift, helped me reach the top. The wood was wet under my grasp. I flung my legs over so Jake could grab me and support my landing.

"Gotcha," Jake said, holding tightly so I wouldn't fall.

I moved over for Meg, who landed next, and then Matt, who came down in one swift movement. We paused for a second, waiting to hear if we were caught, or lucky escapees. When no one came, I let out a deep breath and closed my eyes in relief.

"Hey, man," Jake said, slapping Matt on the back. "Glad you came."

"Hey, yeah, thanks," Matt replied, pushing his hair out of his face. He then turned to me. "Okay?" he whispered, touching my back. His hand was still damp from the fence and tickled my skin. I nodded, looking at him and adjusting my clothes, my hair. We were behind the house, standing on a sidewalk that snaked around the neighborhood. With the fence in front of us and forest behind us, our only options were walking to the left or right.

"What now?" I asked, heart still racing.

"This way, it'll lead to the street," Meg announced, and started walking to the left.

"And how do you know this?" Jake asked, shoving his hands in his pockets. Meg simply eyed him, obviously trying to lead him on. I knew the truth, though; all last semester she visited Ross once a week to tutor him in geometry. I assumed at one point during their sessions she'd learned about the ladder.

"What about your cars?" Matt asked.

"We'll come back once everything dies down," I reassured him, adrenaline still coursing through my body. "There are cars parked all up and down the street. They can't, like, assume all of them are there for the one party. And by the way, welcome to a Jefferson High party. They're not all this exciting, unfortunately."

"I don't know. I think we hit my quota on near-police-bust-ups for the year," he said nervously. He, too, looked like he wasn't used to this much action at a party. His breathing was heavy, and he kept looking back; I assumed to make sure we weren't being followed.

We stayed a few steps behind Meg and Jake, who were clearly being cordial only for our benefit. Like two parents fearful of telling their children they're getting a divorce. We walked silently, too scared to talk, afraid it might bring on more trouble. We let the night air talk for us. The crickets chirped in unison, while the wind answered with a breeze. The forest to our right was dark, full of unknowns, much like our night ahead. I braced myself for what might be next.

"Finally," Jake said when a streetlight emerged on the path, signifying a street.

"I told you," Meg answered. "Where now? What's within walking distance?"

"Wing King?" Jake asked with a smirk.

CHAPTER 5

NOW
9:00 P.M.

"Um, I kind of lied," Matt says as he pulls onto Alafaya Trail, a block away from Evan's house. My head jerks up because this is not what I want to hear after leaving a party with him.

"About?"

"The song? I don't have it in the car. I thought I did . . ." he says, then continues. "Okay, I knew I didn't, but I just thought . . ."

"So you *are* trying to kidnap me," I answer, because as much as I want to slap him for lying, I kind of get it. It was his way of pleading for me to come with him. But, honestly, I probably would have gone anyway, because I think I need to be here.

He laughs a little, but still looks worried; there are lines plaguing his forehead. Despite myself, I wonder what happened to him while he was away. If it was as bad as it was for me. If maybe it's more than just being here that's caused the worry lines.

"Only a little," he says, and I nod.

"Well, just know I have backup ready and waiting," I say.

"I'm sure you do," he answers, and after a few seconds of silence adds, "So you're still picking up objects?"

"Not often," I lie. It's still great writing inspiration, but mostly it reminds me of him. I might have gotten rid of every other reminder, but the physical act of picking up a piece of paper or picture off the floor keeps me thinking of him, despite not wanting to. It's like I'm trying to find him in these objects. "Just when they're good."

"Like song lyrics." He nods toward the sheet music still in my hand.

"Well, you never know when a guy will have the song in his car," I answer, and he smiles slightly.

We stay quiet for the rest of the ride. He lowers the windows and lets the wind come in and surround us. We need the silence to acclimate us to each other again, to our sounds, smells, looks. It's easier this way.

Wing King is all dark wood and bright lights. Booths and picnic tables give the place a southern backyard barbecue feel. Old tin signs hang on the walls, advertising oil, milk, and pig feed. It's not the nicest of places, but at one time it was ours.

"Two, please," he says to the hostess.

It was presumptuous of him to bring me here since the place holds so many memories for us; I can practically breathe them in. The waiters and waitresses saw every phase of our relationship, from early flirtations to final conversations. I pick at my nails as I follow him to a table—to *our* table, the secluded booth in the corner where we used to plan epic nights full of adventure and excitement. Just as he's about to sit down, he stalls, fidgeting in contemplation.

"Um." He pauses. "Is this okay?" He looks over at me, just barely meeting my eyes.

"Yeah, sure," I answer, sitting down. It's too late to go back now. Since leaving the party, my heart has calmed down, but the *weirdness* of the situation hasn't dissolved. I'm still jittery, still trying to figure out how I feel about everything.

"I've missed this place," he says, and I wonder what it means.

"I'm sure it missed you, too," I say offhand, pulling on my bracelet. I look up quickly, realizing what I said, realizing what he might think it means.

"It's been a while," he adds, looking away.

"Yeah, it has," I answer softly, but what I don't add is the exact amount of time it's been. That it's been six months since he's lived in the state. That it's been a year since I first met him. I wonder if he remembers that, of all the times to show up, this night would have marked our one-year anniversary. I wonder if he knows.

He looks down at his wrist, twisting his watch around and around like he always does when he's nervous. I observe, cautiously, unsure of what to say next, but also kind of enjoying seeing him squirm. "Your hair," he says, clearly grasping at straws himself. "Is it darker?"

I subconsciously grab a piece and twirl it around my finger. It's been so long, I almost forgot Meg and I dyed it black earlier this year. It was yet another one of her attempts to help me move on. Change my hair, change into a new person, I suppose.

"Oh, yeah," I answer. There's so much to say but so little I feel comfortable revealing just yet. I look over and feel his eyes staring at me—no, not me, my hair. As if he's trying to un-dye it with his mind, and bring it back to something more familiar.

I tap my fingers impatiently and breathe out. This is annoying because I want us to talk, but we can't seem to find the rhythm we once had, the ability to talk for hours—in person and on the phone—without any bit of silence or discomfort. The ability to know what the other wanted to hear with just a look, a sound, or a nod. He knew I was hungry when I started sounding tense. I knew he was tired when his s's started to lisp. That knowledge, though still so familiar, can't be tapped into anymore. It's another reminder of the barrier between us, separating the Us of now from the Us of then.

"What will you guys have?" a waitress asks, wearing the required uniform: a tight, low-cut red top, black short shorts, and a tiny red-and-white-striped apron. It looks ridiculous, but guys love it.

"Oh, um, Coke?" Matt says, more of a question than an answer.

"Same," I say, and watch the waitress walk away.

"I forgot we actually had to order," Matt says with a nervous glance.

"It's usually what you do at restaurants," I say dryly. I look down and see the engraving on the table that we used to always joke about. The misspelled insult, which is more ridiculous than insulting (who misspells an insult?), and the *PG hearts TA*. At one point two people engraved their initials because they, for a split moment, felt love could conquer all and withstand time. But did it? Are they still together? We always wondered what happened to them—if they're still connected at the heart or if they, too, broke up. While I know the probability of them still being together is slim, for some reason I still hope for them. Looking at their hastily scratched initials, I find courage to continue the conversation. I can tell Matt's bursting to talk but having a hard time, so I give him the chance. Put him out of his misery. "So, you're back."

"Yeah," he says, a bit more animated. "It feels good to,

you know, put my roots down somewhere, I guess, after moving around so much." Matt's dad works for the air force, fixing computers and other technological machines, so whenever one job is done, the family is off to a new city, state, or even, sometimes, country. He said the benefit of moving around so often was seeing the world and learning other languages. The downside was never really having a home.

"So you'll be here for all four years?" I ask, not allowing myself to contemplate what that means.

"That's the plan. Unless I do something completely stupid. Which, as it happens, I have a tendency to do," he says, looking right at me, and this time *I know* he's trying to tell me something. So I go along to see how far it'll go.

"You *do* have a tendency to be stupid."

"I know." He pauses.

"So why here, out of all the schools?" I ask, starting my line of questioning. I'll go in slow, hoping he'll pick up. Hoping he'll answer some without me even asking.

"Um, I don't know," he says, looking around and trying to find an acceptable reason. "Even though I wasn't here long, this place felt . . . most like home to me. Which, as you know, doesn't happen often."

"Right," I say, wondering what he means by "home."

"What about you? What are you doing?"

I pause before answering. He doesn't know I'm leaving. Do I tell him now? "Still going to major in writing," I say instead, something comfortable, something easy to talk about. I don't need to tell him that I want to get away and start over because I'm tired of here, and everything that's happened. Not yet, at least.

"You were always really good at it," he says, and I smile.

"Thanks. It took my parents some convincing that pre-law wasn't for me. But they're okay now."

"I can't see you as a lawyer."

"Right? I'd be awful." I chuckle, and I miss how *easy* it used to be. "And you? Still want to open a recording studio?"

"I'd like to, yeah. I'm majoring in business and minoring in music. So, hopefully I'll get experience in both fields."

"How do you minor in music? Are the requirements playing 'Mary Had a Little Lamb'?" I ask.

"Harder. 'Hot Cross Buns.'" We laugh again, and this time we look at each other. The tension is still there, but . . . less so.

The waitress brings us our drinks and waits for our orders.

"An order of honey barbecue wings? To share?" This time he asks me, not her. It's our usual order. I nod in agreement. "So . . . how's Meg doing?"

The question makes it awkward again. Like Meg said, he'd know if he kept in touch. He shouldn't have to ask how his friends are. But still, I reply. "She's good; you know, as good as Meg ever is."

"That sounds about right. Still crazy?" He smiles.

"Delightfully so." I tentatively smile back.

"And . . . Jake?"

I knew this was coming. Jake didn't take it well when Matt left. How could he; they were best friends. And he got no more of an explanation than I did. Jake wanted to kill him half the time, stalk him down the other half. Until he did actually track him down. He played like he didn't care, but I could tell. We all could.

"He's recording right now with Barker and . . . the new bassist," I say, knowing it will sting. But he should know that after he left, they still had gigs lined up, so they had to grab a random guy to fill in. He's nowhere near as good as Matt, but they keep getting more shows, so he's kind of stayed around.

"Oh, yeah, I forgot. I mean, of course they replaced me. I just . . . didn't know. I'm glad they're still going strong, though. God, Jake is so talented."

"Yeah, it's a major asset and major downfall."

"How so?"

"He's so talented, and he has so many great ideas, but practically no follow-through. It's gotten worse this year."

"I remember that about him."

"They're recording because Barker set it up. But Barker's moving to Chicago at the end of the summer."

"He is?"

"Yeah, college. He's really excited, and I think it'll be good for him."

"Gabby?"

"She's going, too."

"Not surprised. I half expected them to be married with seven kids by now."

"Right? So, yeah, with Barker gone, Jake won't have anyone to push him. The new bassist is kind of useless, and I think he's leaving as well. Jake's staying here, of course. But you can't really get big in Central Florida."

"Unless you're a boy band," Matt points out. "What about Meg?"

"She's staying too."

"And they're . . . ?" he asks.

"It's a long story," I say, thinking of their on-again, off-again relationship, and how I could never have that. I could never know that a relationship might just be temporary. I still don't know how she holds it together. Had I known Matt would only be here for a handful of months, and not at least a year, I think our story would have been much different. Then again, maybe not.

"I've missed them. You know, I haven't played bass since I left, really," he admits, his eyes wandering.

"You missed them?" I ask, tilting my head, and feeling my face start to heat up. "You could have kept in touch, you know. With them." With me.

"I know." He lowers his head, clearly unhappy with the turn of the conversation. And it had been going so well. "It was . . . complicated."

"Too complicated to make a phone call?" I start,

readying myself for his answer. And as if on cue, my phone rings. It's Meg. Matt sees, too.

"You should—"

I grab my phone, get up, and walk outside. "Hey Meg," I answer.

"Where are you?" she demands.

"Wing King. With Matt."

"*What*? What are you doing there?" she practically yells. In the background I can still hear the party going on without me and my drama.

"He suggested we get away to talk. You said I should get answers," I remind her.

"Yeah, but I didn't want you to *leave*. What if something happens?"

"What's going to happen? He's going to get upset and sigh loudly? This is Matt we're talking about. He's not exactly dangerous."

"God, I'm not talking about *that*," she says, and I can almost feel her nudge me until I get what she's saying.

"We're not going to make out."

"Good. Because I'll sooner punch you than let you do that."

"Gee, thanks," I say. I turn around and look into the restaurant's window and can just spot Matt in the corner. He's glancing at his phone, too, and I wonder what he's looking at.

"Just be careful. And keep in touch, 'kay?"

"I will," I promise her, still looking at Matt. "How's Jake?"

"He'll probably be calling you soon," she warns.

"Not surprised. Anyway, I should go."

"Yeah," she sighs. "Just . . . get answers and come back."

"I will," I say, and hang up after saying good-bye. I take another look at Matt and my heart leaps like it used to when he was around. I *will* be careful.

I walk inside and back to our table. He looks up when I'm near, and his mouth twitches.

"Meg making sure I haven't hurt you?" Matt asks, trying to make light of the situation. I smile in response.

"Something like that," I respond, sitting down.

"Your wings," the waitress says, setting them down and pushing away our previous conversation. There's no going back now.

We split up the food and start eating in silence, my last question, prior to the phone call, still echoing in my mind.

"I'm glad you're here. With me, that is," Matt says, finally, looking up at me. I catch his eyes and once again I'm not sure if I want to slap him or kiss him. Because I'm happy we're here together, too, and I hate him for making me think that. So I simply nod and sadly smile, and look back down.

"I know I don't deserve it," he admits, and I look back up. It's the first time he's mentioned that he was wrong, first time that he verified that I was right. I open my mouth to speak, but first notice barbecue sauce on his nose and smile at the sight. "What?"

"Your nose," I say, pointing at his face. Confused, he touches his nose and accidentally gets more barbecue sauce on it. He's now covered in orange-brown goo, and I can't help but laugh.

"Oh, you think that's funny?" he asks, smiling. He reaches over and taps a glob of sauce on the tip of my nose.

"Hey!" I yell, ready to fire back.

"Oh, don't you dare. I've got ranch dressing just waiting to be spilled," he threatens. But I dare, leaning toward him and wiping my fingers on his cheek. "That's it!" He grabs my wrist and I struggle, trying to get free while he tries to further drench me. His hand grazes my cheek, but I grab it with my other hand to stop more sauce from getting on me. In the pushing and pulling and laughing, my hand, still restrained, reaches his face. My thumb presses against his lips.

I jump, electrified by the contact. He lets go, pushing himself as far back as possible on his side of the table. His face is blank, unreadable. I look around and notice most of the other patrons are looking at us.

"Sorry about that," Matt says, his voice low.

"Yeah," I respond, grabbing my napkin and wiping the mess from my face. Erase the past. How did we get so far so soon?

We eat in silence, concentrating way too hard on our food. All words flew away with our touch. A simple act I took for granted a year ago now feels illegal, almost unmentionable. And despite everything, I want to feel the spark again—see what it means.

After what feels like two hours, the bill finally comes. "I've got it," he says, picking up the check before I can protest. He used to always pay; it seems so wrong now. "Oh crap," he says, his face going ashen.

"What's wrong?"

"I think I left my wallet at home," he admits.

"Oh, it's okay, I've got it." I wave him off and grab the bill from him.

"No, I mean, that's not—"

"Matt, it's okay. I can do it," I say, putting some cash on the table. I look over at him and his head is in his hands. He's . . . hurt. From this. Because this, I realize, was his plan all along. He wanted to take me out. Maybe he was flirting, after all.

"Thanks," he murmurs.

As I get up, I hear a whisper of a phrase, about not deserving it. I turn back to him and question it. "Did you just say something?"

He lowers his hands and shakes his head. He looks so sad, so helpless. What happened to his fearlessness, his charm? When we get to his car, I open my mouth to speak, but he pipes in first.

"I know . . . things are awkward between us right now. But I'd like to change that. Do you . . . by any chance . . . do you want to keep hanging out tonight?"

The remorse in his face is unbearable. His eyes squinting, hair a mess. He's clawing for anything, and I can't help but give in. Because one thing is clear—I don't want the night to end yet.

"I'd like that," I admit, entranced by his sudden smile. "What do you want to do?"

"How about . . . a night of saying yes." He says it as a statement, with a period, not as a question. There's no room for debate. I nod, knowing exactly what he means. Knowing exactly where we're going next.

CHAPTER 6

THEN
9:20 P.M.

Inside was bright. It took a minute for my eyes to fully adjust, as they were used to the subdued streetlights from outside. The restaurant, much like the party we'd just fled, was crowded and loud; everyone talking, but no one listening. Waitresses in the skimpiest uniforms I'd ever seen roamed around taking orders that were spoken not so much to their faces but to their chests. The smell of grease from fried everything filled the air, and I could almost feel it coat my skin.

"What *is* this place," I whispered, crinkling my nose at Meg.

She rolled her eyes. "Jake's favorite restaurant. Obviously." Jake watched the waitresses with the intensity of someone watching a sporting match. Eyes bopping back and forth, afraid to blink in case he'd miss anything. Matt stood next to me, shifting his weight from foot to foot.

"Back?" Jake asked. We nodded and followed him to a secluded booth in the back corner. It was hard, dark wood, with scratches littering the top. Jake sat down first, sliding to the right. We paused, unsure of who should sit where. Matt took a seat next to Jake, clearly comfortable being next to the only person he'd met more than once. Meg sat across from Jake, me across from Matt. He fidgeted with his watch, spinning it over and over again on his wrist.

"So that was fun," Jake said, leaning back against the booth. He looked relaxed, like he hadn't just run from the police. But that was Jake. He was the kind of guy who wore sunglasses at night and somehow pulled it off. He was tall and built, and obviously hot, with never-ending dimples. His blue eyes lured you in, his words held you captive. Like the time he had three sorority girls clinging to him after he simply recited lyrics from a song he wrote. Granted, the magic ended after he suggested skinny-dipping, but despite his often idiotic demeanor, he was never honestly arrogant; he had this engaging personality that made everyone comfortable instantly, and some—Meg specifically—a little too comfortable.

"Real fun. Escape a lot of parties nowadays?" Meg asked.

"Only the exciting ones," Jake responded with a wide grin and a wink.

"Hey, where did your girlfriend go?" Matt asked, clearly unaware of the implication of his question. I shot Meg a look and held my breath.

"Who? Oh, whatever," Jake answered, looking anywhere but at Meg.

"She looked . . . smart," Meg added, letting him know she'd seen them together.

"You don't have to be smart to be fun," Jake responded, this time at her.

"So, it says here that PG hearts TA," I said, pointing to an inscription on the table. My observation was greeted with silence; everyone was aware of my obvious topic change and no one was going with it.

"Well, it says over here that U. R. stoopid, spelled incorrectly. It's funny that the writer would call someone else stupid when they can't spell the word themselves," Matt offered, tracing the table with his finger. I gave him a smile, appreciating that he was helping me out.

"Oh god, let's not make this any more awkward," Meg said after a pause. "Jake and I used to date. It ended. A bit ago." She looked at Matt. "Thus Ella's fantastic subject changes."

"Okay . . ." Matt said, looking uncomfortable. "Um." He paused. I bit my lip, wanting to chime in, help him out of the situation, but I couldn't think of anything. At all. "I dated a girl who talked to her cat."

"So? A lot of people do that," Meg said. I nudged her,

hoping she'd get the hint and stop directing her attitude at us. Matt was trying, after all.

"Well, yeah, but she said the cat responded to her. Like, she'd have full-on conversations with the cat, as if it was actually replying. As if the cat had opinions about her wardrobe and, as it turned out, guy choices," he explained, talking with his hands.

"Was she hot?" Jake asked. I didn't want to know the answer, so I interrupted.

"What happened?"

"Her cat didn't like me. He told her to break up with me."

"What?" Meg yelled.

"Yep. I mean, I was going to break up with her—she was clearly crazy—but, she got to it first. Or, I guess the cat got to it first." I laughed at the ridiculousness of his story and he caught my eye. It was in that moment that I knew he'd be one of us. "That's almost as good as El's last breakup," Jake added, and I turned to him with wide eyes. Maybe I didn't want Matt to know about my pathetic first relationship just yet. I felt the blood rush from my face as I looked at Jake, panicked.

"What?" Jake said, clearly unaware.

"Smooth move," Meg said.

"What happened?" Matt asked, concerned.

"Err," I started. "Well…" Oh god, I had to tell him. "This guy broke up with me." I looked down, then back at Matt.

His face looked . . . *nice*. Like whatever I said wouldn't bother him. So I continued. "He, um, he asked if we could high five for friendship." I left out the cheating part. He didn't need to know that just yet. I hated reflecting on that part.

"What?" Matt spit out, then started laughing. But not in that embarrassing way that would make me blush and cry. In the way that said *that guy sucks*.

"Please tell me you didn't high five him," he added.

"No, I kind of just walked away. Because, really, what do you do in that situation?"

"Punch him?" Meg answered.

"That's what you'd do," Jake added.

"Needless to say, these guys have not let me live it down."

"Jake! Welcome back!" I looked over to see an exuberant waitress about our age in front of our table. She had a wide smile and black hair piled on the top of her head in an intricate knot. Bangles lined her tiny wrists, and I wondered how she was able to hold trays. I gave Meg a glance and caught her rolling her eyes.

"Hey Elise," Jake responded, grinning hungrily at her.

"What'll y'all be having?" she asked in a thick southern accent.

I still had the stale taste of beer in my mouth, so I opted for water. As did the others. Jake asked for the usual. With a bounce, Elise walked away, on to the next table.

"The usual?" Meg asked.

"This is my home," Jake said. "So Matt—do you like it

here so far?" he added, changing the subject.

"It's fine, yeah."

"Where did you move from?" I asked.

"Italy."

"Italy? Why'd you leave?" I asked, visualizing the amazing sights and mentally tasting the delicious pasta. He was so worldly, compared to me.

"My dad works for the military, so we move a lot. I'm usually not in one place for more than a year." I frowned, noting that his time here might be short. "But, you never know. I always hope the job is prolonged so I can at least get permanent furniture for my room."

"That sucks," Meg said.

"Yeah, it's hard, but I don't know. I like seeing different places," he said in a way that sounded like he was trying to convince himself, not so much us.

"I think it would be sweet. Starting over every year, and all," Jake said, tapping his fingers on the table as if they were drumsticks.

"Sometimes. But it's also hard to really meet people. Not to sound lame, but it's why I started playing bass. I figured I might meet people that way. Every band needs a bassist, right?" He shrugged and it was adorable. I couldn't imagine moving around so much like him. I'd lived in Orlando my entire life. My friends were here, people I'd known since elementary school. How could I leave them all behind?

"Not the White Stripes," Jake pointed out. Matt opened

his mouth to respond, but quickly closed it. I glared at Jake in response. "What? They don't need a bassist," he continued.

"Well, we're glad you're here," I tried to reassure him.

"Hell yeah," Jake pitched in, as if he hadn't just insulted Matt. "And that you like good music." He turned to Meg and me. "This guy kills on the bass. I mean, he's so much better than the last guy."

"That bad?" Matt asked.

"He didn't suck, but he didn't rock," Jake said.

"Right," Matt said, smiling.

Our drinks came with another bounce and wink. Jake's usual ended up being a Coke, which was far less interesting than we had imagined. When the waitress asked what we wanted, we all balked. We hadn't looked at the menu yet.

"Wings?" Jake asked.

"No way. You'll eat them all," Meg responded.

"Still the champion, right, Elise? Seventy in one sitting."

"That's disgusting," Meg said.

"Oh, you loved it. You cheered me on the whole time." It was the first time Jake had referenced their relationship in a while. Meg tried to come up with a comeback—I could see the gears in her mind turning—but she let it go. Maybe she wanted to keep the memory unsoiled.

"Wings for everyone," Jake said. "I'll be good." I silently thanked him for helping to keep the peace now, even if he had nearly started a war a minute ago. He loved egging Meg on, and it only made their *situation* more awkward.

And while I oftentimes played referee, it wasn't my favorite pastime.

"Where's Barker, by the way?" I asked, once the waitress left.

"He was outside with Gabby when the cops came," Jake said. "He called me, then I texted Meg."

"And I told him to meet us upstairs," Meg continued, and I eyed her, understanding how Jake knew to find us up in Ross's room. Jake could have left, run off with his new girl, but instead he came back for us. Meg bit her lip and avoided my glance.

"I'll check in on him," I said, tearing my eyes away.

All OK?

A second later he responded.

Yep. At G's. Stupid cops.

"Barker's fine, at Gabby's," I said to the group.

"Gabby's his . . . ?" Matt asked.

"Girlfriend," I answered.

"Is Barker his first or last name? I never asked."

"Last. He's just always gone by Barker." I added, "It sucks you guys didn't get to play."

"Yeah, considering it's my first show and all," Matt said.

"There'll be other gigs. Believe me," Jake said, smiling.

"Got one lined up?" I asked.

"Come on, it's us. We'll have another one lined up in no time."

"Says the guy who only just got a bassist," Meg teased.

A few minutes later, our food came out. After eating, we sat back, full and energized.

"So, where to next?" Jake asked, rubbing his stomach. He had a trace of barbecue sauce on his lip, which was slightly endearing. Jake could be careless with all of us, but when he decided he wanted to be, or perhaps just when he saw it would benefit him, he could pull off his Mr. Perfect routine so well that, at times, he needed imperfections to remind us he was human.

"We can't end it as the night we ran from a party. Let's make it the night we . . ." I started, waiting for someone to chime in.

"Go to a bar?" Jake asked.

"Riddle me this, how would we all get in?" Meg asked.

"Touché," he answered.

"Go bowling?" I added, knowing no one would agree.

"You always suggest bowling." Jake rolled his eyes.

"I like bowling!"

"Skinny-dipping?" Jake offered instead.

"Anyone notice how Jake's ideas are always appealing only to Jake?" Meg asked.

"You suggest something, then," Jake challenged Meg.

"Oh, hey, how about this," Matt interrupted. "One night

at my last school in Italy we said yes to everything. Like, we made suggestions and, within reason, we said yes to them. It's kind of . . . liberating."

We paused for a second, taking his proposal in, and I gave a pointed look to Meg. I wasn't a daredevil, but for some reason, the idea seemed to excite me. A crazy night was just what I needed after Nick and everything.

"The night we say yes," Jake said. "Brilliant. Now, let's go skinny-dipping."

CHAPTER 7

NOW
9:40 P.M.

From Wing King, Matt and I end up at the Shop & Shop, the hilariously named side-of-the-road store where the owners clearly gave up on a title halfway through the naming process. The parking lot is empty, except for his car. We would have gone to the supermarket instead had we wanted to run into people we knew, but when you're buying alcohol underage, it's best to go where IDs aren't analyzed. Or required.

"Good thing this was in my car, and not my wallet," Matt says, handing me his fake ID.

"You look more like Chris now," I say, holding his older brother's old driver's license. At a quick glance their faces are the same, so much more so than a year ago, but upon further inspection, I can see they're still so different. They have the same light eyes and dark hair, but where his brother's face is smooth, the Matt in front of me has worry lines etched in. I've never met his brother, since he was already away at college by the time Matt moved here, but I know they're close. I wonder if he knows about me.

"I guess," Matt answers, taking the ID back and stuffing it in his pocket. He looks distracted for a second, then morphs back to normal, as if erasing the thought.

"You okay?" I ask, wondering why my comment might have affected him. He's always liked to talk about his brother.

"Fine," he answers quickly. "Are you still Bertha?" he asks, referring to the fake ID Jake got for me right after we realized Matt and I were the only ones who couldn't get into clubs. Matt had his older brother, and I had Bertha, some unknown girl who was about six inches taller and one hundred pounds heavier than me. But Bertha always worked.

I smiled. "Sadly, no. I retired her when my cousin gave me her ID. I look a lot more like her than our girl Bertha."

"It's probably for the best." Matt sighs, looking down at his steering wheel. "As long as the ID's inaugural run was here."

After Matt and I both got our IDs, we tried them out at the Shop & Shop, where they worked perfectly. I couldn't go in there anymore once he left. So when I got my new ID, Meg took me to Kiki's, a relatively new karaoke bar with lenient ID policies. It worked there. But I can't confess I've been steering clear of this store all year on account of him. So instead I say, "Of course."

"Well, good," he says, pleased, then adds, "I'll go in." He nods toward the store. "Anything you want?"

"Surprise me," I answer. It comes off smoother than I intended. I really only say it because I don't know *what* I want. Whenever I drink, it's at a party where the only option is usually beer.

With a raise of his eyebrows, he gets out of the car and walks into the store. I stay behind, scrolling through the music on his iPhone. I did it earlier while he was driving so I know he doesn't mind. I recognize most of his music, except for a few songs here or there, which, although ridiculous, feels weird, feels like he's musically cheating on me. I used to know everything he listened to, every song and every artist, so each time I pass something new, it's another reminder that so much time has gone by. That he can like new bands. That he's moved on.

It was awkward again, driving here from Wing King. And while the drive wasn't as silent as it was before, it still didn't reveal anything new, anything important. It seemed like we didn't work when we were in motion. But when we were seated face-to-face, it was like we could see at least a little bit of our old selves in each other.

I keep flipping through the iPhone until I come to the photo folder. My finger pauses right above the icon. Should

I open it, or is that a complete invasion of privacy? Seeing as I'm already going through his music, I suppose he wouldn't mind if I went through his photos, too. Right?

I press the button and immediately gasp because it's my face I see. Not my face now, but mine from a year ago when it was still happy, still unscarred. I'm laughing and Matt's giving me that *oh you* face he used to make when I was acting silly. I remember the afternoon—we were at the springs, splashing in the water. Meg was on the edge, her feet just dangling in the water, when she took the picture. Moments later Jake pushed her in and I can almost still feel the water hitting my face, and Matt's arms wrapped around my waist. I can't help but smile.

The next photo is of him and his brother. I don't recognize it, but from Matt's glasses I can tell it was taken more recently. They're waving to the camera, and I can only imagine what the story behind the photo is, because I wasn't part of his life at that time to actually know.

The next photo is one I also remember. We were at Meg's house, where Evan was having a bonfire in the backyard. It was soon after Matt and I met, soon after we started dating, so everything was new and exciting. The touch of his hand still shot tingles up my body. Meg pulled me away quickly to giggle about everything and he took a picture of us just barely illuminated by the fire. Meg's blurred, but I'm in focus, shaded in orange and glowing.

The last photo is of the Pepperpots performing. They're

midsong and I can hear Jake's voice in my head. His mouth is open and the lyrics are just screaming out of him. Matt is absorbed in the music, plucking the bass, trying to get his feelings into song. It was one of their last performances before Matt left. I know because I took the photo.

I can't believe he still has them all on his phone. I can't believe he never deleted them. And I'm not entirely sure what that means.

My phone buzzing in my purse jerks me back. I pull it out to see the ever-expected call from Jake.

"Hey Jake," I answer.

"So Meg says he's back," he starts, straight to the point as usual.

"Yep. I'm out with him now." I pause, then say, "I mean, I'm out with him, but he's inside right now; I'm waiting. So I can talk."

"Where are you?"

I pause before answering, because he'll know. Of course he'll know. "Shop & Shop."

"You're kidding."

"I think he has a plan," I admit, looking up to see him wandering around the store. He looks unsure and nervous, scratching his head at each turn. He's looked unsure and nervous all night.

"Screw his plan. Why are you even with him right now?" Jake says stubbornly. And though he asks it, I *know* he already knows the answer.

"I'm . . . hearing him out," I say, keeping it light. "You would have, too, if he found you first."

"Hell no. He left, end of story. He doesn't deserve it."

"Maybe not, but I want to know why he left the way he did. And why he's back."

"Who cares why he's back! Ella, come on. After what he did to you?" He doesn't add the unspoken "and me," but I know he means it.

"Jake, you were the one who was going to drive to Texas to get answers. You were the one who was just as pissed as I was. Let me at least find out what really happened."

"And then what?"

"Then . . . maybe we can stop guessing," I say.

He sighs, struggling with himself. Matt is another person on Jake's long list of people he trusted that have let him down. He has a different reason than me to be upset, but his reason is still important.

"Jake." I close my eyes, because I don't want to explain myself.

"Fine, just . . . whatever." He gives up and I know there's so much more he wants to say, feels like he needs to say, but can't or won't. That's not him. "He was a dick to you; I'd hate to see him do it again."

"I know," I say, touched by his compassion. "I'll keep you posted."

"Uh-huh."

"How's recording?" I change the subject.

"Awesome, as always," he says, and I smile because I know he's compensating.

"I'll talk to you later. Tell Barker I say hi."

"Will do," he says, then, "You know I'll still kick his ass if I need to."

"I know," I say before hanging up. Just like Meg and I don't do apologies, Jake and I don't do good-byes.

I glance back up and Matt is still walking through the aisles. My heart leaps and I've almost gotten used to it. I close my eyes and think of what Jake said and didn't say. He would be here too, despite his denial. He'd want to know. I'm not just doing this—hanging out with him to see what happened and what might happen next—for myself. I'm doing it for all of us. For the nights Matt helped Jake out of trouble when he challenged guys to drink-offs. For the nights Matt sat and just listened when Jake just needed to vent about Meg, and clearly couldn't come to me. For the assurance he gave Jake that the band could get even better, and how, in time, it did.

I realize I'm still holding Matt's phone, so I put it down in the cup holder, where I find a piece of paper with writing that isn't his. It's another found object, just like the sheet music I discovered earlier. We used to pick these up all the time together, after he told me about his habit. I guess he didn't stop doing it, either, and I'm not sure if it makes me comforted or sad.

My phone buzzes again. It's a message from Barker.

Matt's in town? Weird. Call if you need.

I smile, thinking of Jake, flustered, reciting the development. And of Barker, stopping their recording session to send me this. I think Barker really took it to heart after Matt left, since he was the one who introduced us, so he's always checking up on me. It's cute in that really-I'm-fine kind of way.

A few minutes later, Matt materializes in front of the car. I want to tell him everything that's happened—how I saw the photos, how I spoke to Jake—but the words aren't forming. Maybe it's not the time to start opening up again.

"Hey," I say instead as he sits down inside. "All okay?"

"Yeah," he answers, stuffing a brown paper bag in the backseat. "No problem at all. Didn't even look at my ID."

"What did you get?"

"The penguin wine." He smiles. Instinctively, I smile back. Of course he remembers. It was what we drank before he left, on our six-month anniversary. I picked it out because I thought the penguin was cute.

I shake away the memory and run my finger over my bracelet's pattern.

"So are we really going to Jefferson?" I ask, breaking the silence.

"If you want to," he answers. "I mean, yes. Yes we are. It's a night of saying yes, after all."

"This feels so . . . one year ago."

"I know." He hesitates. "Kind of the idea."

It's not until we're a few minutes down the road that I realize he's had this night planned for longer than I thought.

CHAPTER 8

THEN
9:50 P.M.

After eating at Wing King, we walked back to Ross's house to pick up our cars. We took the main roads; they were easier to navigate than the sidewalks behind the houses we had previously crept along. Some cars passed by, but for the most part we were alone. Along the way, we made our first plan for the night.

"So, for a night of saying yes, we need drinks first," Jake said, walking with his hands in his pockets.

"How do you expect us all to get them?" Meg asked, walking in step with him. Despite their fighting, they were still magnets, always drawn to each other. An attraction that couldn't be broken, no matter the amount of pushing and pulling.

"I've got an ID. Let's grab our cars and head to Shop & Shop," Jake answered.

"Where to after that?" I asked.

"We'll decide then," Jake responded, winking at Meg. She shook her head and I could see the crack of a smile. I looked over at Matt, but he wasn't next to me anymore. I stopped and noticed him a few feet behind, picking something up off the ground. I walked back over to him.

"What's up?"

"Oh, sorry, nothing," he said, straightening up quickly with something in his hand.

"Drop something?"

"No, um, it's stupid," he said, putting whatever he had picked up into his pocket. He started walking again, so I continued behind him. I didn't want to pry, but I was curious.

"What's stupid?"

He was quiet for a moment, and then spoke. "I pick up things whenever I find them. Not, like, trash or anything, but notes and photos. Glimpses into people's lives and stuff."

"So, like, found objects?" I asked, feeling him out.

"Yeah, exactly. It started in Italy. I was walking around this little market in Florence and found a photo of three people laughing, a guy and two girls. They looked so in the moment, like the photo almost felt private. But I couldn't put it down. What were they laughing about, you know? How did they know each other? So, I kept the photo, and

since then, I haven't really stopped picking these things up."
He paused, glancing at me. "It's weird, I know."

"Not weird," I said. "Just interesting."

"Interesting in a creepy way?" he asked in a self-deprecating manner.

"Totally creepy. I'm afraid you're going to read my diary now, or something," I joked. "No, I think it's cool. I like the idea of seeing people's private moments. You can learn a lot about them." I think about my writing, and how I do something similar when creating characters. Finding stories on the ground could be good inspiration for me.

"Exactly!" he said, as if I was the first person to understand, and I wondered if, perhaps, I was. "I mean, I move around so much that I *don't* have these things—you know, photos with friends, and notes and stuff. So, I guess it's nice seeing that other people do."

"That's really sad," I sympathized.

"Oh god, I'm the pathetic, sad, creepy guy now, aren't I?"

"No! It's just . . ." I paused, and thought about all of the photos I had hanging on my walls, all of the notes Meg and I passed, and all of the memories I had wrapped up in my group of friends. He didn't have any of that. He was layered with life experiences, but none of them were personal. "It's sad your life is so temporary, you know? That you don't have a chance to have any of that stuff."

"Yeah," he said. "But, I don't know, these things don't make me depressed or anything. They're kind of comforting,

I guess." With a quick shrug he stuffed his hands into his pockets.

"What are some of the best things you've found?" I asked, intending to lighten the mood. I hoped I hadn't made him feel uncomfortable.

"Um, I pick up photos, mostly. Notes are pretty personal, but also interesting. Oh, I found wedding vows once."

"Really?"

"Yeah. Kind of wondered *why* they'd be on the side of the road. It's sad if you think about it."

"Definitely." I wondered what type of person would throw away their wedding vows . . . and also what type of person would pick them up.

"It's pretty addictive. You'll start noticing things now, too."

"I bet," I said, pondering if him picking up other people's found items was really his way of living other lives, since his was always in transition. I wanted to let him know that I wanted to make memories with him, even if they were just from one night. Memories that wouldn't be tossed away and found by someone else searching for paper on the floor.

So I reached out and held my wrist in front of his face. It was decorated with eight small, tightly knotted friendship bracelets, each of varying colors. It was something Meg and I did when we were kids, to remind ourselves we were friends. Then, last year, we brought it back on a whim. But instead of reminding us that we were friends—because, come on, we already knew that—each bracelet was made with a different purpose in mind. "This is my weird habit. Whenever Meg and I have a big night, we make a bracelet to remember the moment. So, each one represents a different experience. It's silly, but kind of our thing, I guess."

"Really?" he asked, taking my wrist in his hand. "That's cool. What do all of these mean?"

"It's a secret," I whispered with a smile, taking my wrist back.

"I see." He smiled. "Maybe one day I'll make your wrist?"

I'm not sure what came over me. Maybe it was the darkness of the night, maybe it was my newfound braveness, maybe it was the strength I got from knowing Meg was always with me in my bracelets, or maybe it was the warmth in his eyes. I reached down, grabbed his hand, and squeezed it. He jumped a little and looked me right in the eyes.

"This night may be memorable enough for that," I responded, and as I let go, he grabbed my hand and squeezed it back.

We spent the rest of the walk not touching, but I was completely aware of the space between our hands.

◇◇◇◇

"I guess the party is officially over," Matt said as we walked up toward the house we were at earlier. It was quiet, dark except for a few lights on downstairs. A lot of the cars were still there, but that was probably because most people ran away, like us.

Matt had driven with Jake to the party, so they took one car, and I jumped in with Meg. We forced Matt to drive, since Jake had been drinking at the party for a while.

Inside the car, I scrolled through Meg's iPod just to give my hands something to do as I kept flashing back to the conversation about memories and to our touch. My hand still felt warm from where he grabbed it, as if the moment was imprinted on my skin.

"You looked like you were getting friendly with Matt," Meg said, starting the car.

"He's nice," was all I could respond.

"Uh-huh. And you, my dear, need nice right now."

"It won't work. I mean, he moves around so often. I can't date someone and know it'll only be temporary."

"Why not? Did you think Nick would be forever?" When I first learned Nick liked me, Meg was up to boyfriend number four and I was still at a staggering zero. I was always happy for her, but my constant lack of a significant other started getting to me—I felt rejected, lonely. I was always the third wheel, and while Meg didn't mind, I did. So when Nick asked me out, I had to say yes. As it turned out, saying yes wasn't *always* the best solution. "Because, let's be honest. He was clearly temporary."

"I know, but—"

"Plus, you'll be graduating in a year. Think of that. Do you really want to go off to college with a boyfriend?"

"I don't know, I just think—"

"Stop thinking, and just do. Isn't that what tonight's all about? You need to have fun. You need to get over Nick. And you need to stop stressing about the future. Just enjoy the moment." I nodded, knowing she was right. I was always wrapped up in the future, planning what would happen next. I didn't like surprises. "It's like when you didn't cut your hair this year, because you were afraid it would be too short for homecoming. Just . . . cut your hair!"

"Okay!" I said, exasperated from her urging, and wondering if it was that easy to simply change. "Okay."

"Good." She smirked.

"Good," I responded. "And what about you and Jake?"

"What about us?"

"Is everything okay? I mean, you were ready for a fight most of the night."

"I have to be when it comes to him. If I let my guard down, he'll just swoop right back in. Believe me."

"Do you want that?" I asked tentatively.

"Of course not," she said with a toss of her hair, but I could see the hesitance cross her face. I reached for her hand and grabbed the yellow-and-red string bracelet that was about a year old.

"You're still wearing this." I eyed her.

"It was a big night," she said. "I mean, aside from me and Jake making up for the thousandth time. We both passed that chem quiz we were worried about. . . ."

"Uh-huh." I smiled, knowing the reason she hadn't cut

it off had nothing to do with chemistry. Or perhaps it did. "You and Jake do have a lot of chemistry."

"Oh shut up." She stifled a laugh.

"And physics," I added, and she shook her head at me.

"You're ridiculous."

We drove up behind Shop & Shop and parked next to a loud radiator and a row of trash cans. A black cat was perched atop one of the bins, eyeing the car as it pulled up. It didn't run away, or even flinch when the lights beamed onto it.

Matt pulled Jake's truck up beside Meg's car. We'd agreed earlier to park in the back so the store clerk didn't see Jake buying alcohol for four people, all of whom were underage. I never would have thought of that, as it was my first booze run.

"What will we have?" Jake asked, getting out of the truck.

"I'll come with you," Meg said, opening her door. I jerked my head in her direction. How did she expect to get away with it? "I have an ID, too," she said to me, lowering her eyes.

"Since when? You never told me."

"Since Jake." She sighed. "We'll be back."

They walked around the building together. I watched until I couldn't see them anymore. This was not a good idea.

A knock at my window jumped me out of my thoughts. I turned and found Matt smiling, with his head tilted to the side. "Truck bed?" he asked, nodding toward the back of the truck. The word "bed" made me blush, but I nodded and unbuckled my seat belt as he opened my door. "I thought it would be more comfortable than sitting in the truck. Do you realize how bad it smells in there?"

"Why do you think I drive with Meg?" I said. "I once found a black French fry in there. How a French fry turned black, I have no idea."

"Gross," Matt said.

I followed him to the back of the truck, and we sat down, letting our legs hang over the side. My hand gripped the edge of the truck, and I noticed Matt's hand was inches away from mine. I wanted to grab it, feel his touch again. His pinkie twitched and I wondered if he was thinking the same thing. When I looked up, I caught him staring at our not-quite-touching hands, too.

"So, excited for the night?" Matt asked, turning his face toward the blackness in front of us. The parking lot was empty, save for the trash cans. The smell out there wasn't much better than inside Jake's truck. The cat, I noticed, was still there, only now it was distracting itself with a paper bag. Behind the lot was a line of trees, which hid us from the main road. We looked at them and I wondered what was going on behind them. Perhaps the cops had broken up another high school party over there.

"Yeah, it's nice to go out once in a while."

"Do you go out often?"

"Not really. I mean, on the weekends, but my weekdays

are pretty much at home, or at Meg's house."

"How well do you know the band?" he asked, finally looking at me.

"Pretty well. Barker's a good friend . . . he's awesome. Their old bassist was fine; I didn't know him that well, but we got along. And then there's Jake, who's . . . Jake."

"That's a good way of describing him," he said with a chuckle. I liked when he laughed; his whole face lit up.

"He's a good guy, despite everything. He really is," I explained. I found myself justifying his behavior more often than I should have. Meg was rubbing off on me. "The situation with Meg was just . . . weird."

"They seem to get along fine now."

"On and off. Today's a good day," I pointed out, not quite condoning their relationship. Because I love them, and love them together, but can't imagine being in a relationship like that, especially after Nick. Our feet were swinging over the side of the truck, his almost touching the ground, while mine flew freely. I felt like a kid on a swing set.

"And high-five guy? He's not part of the group?"

"Oh god, no. He's in a band, but not one as good as the Pepperpots. I met him at a club—clearly a bad idea. The others hated him, apparently." What I didn't say is that he reminded me of Jake, in a way, and that I wanted to see if I, like Meg, could be the girlfriend of a lead singer and guitarist and handle that. Because, at the time, it worked for her. But as it turned out . . . it wasn't so much for me. "He's the lead singer, and I couldn't handle his constant flirting with other girls, you know?"

"I guess it's good he's gone, then," he said with a smirk. Was he flirting? Or was he always like that? He didn't talk to Meg that way, just me. "What he did was pretty ridiculous."

"Well . . . it wasn't just that. He cheated on me, too," I admitted. I didn't know what came over me, but I felt like he had to know. We could joke about my breakup all we wanted, but there was one part that was still sore.

"Seriously?" he asked, taken aback.

"Yeah, I didn't know at the time, obviously. I heard about it later on. One of our friends—Gabby—saw him at a club with a girl. After we broke up, she told me."

"That sucks," Matt said, looking at me. "Wait, Gabby, Barker's girlfriend?"

"Ahh, yeah, her. You've met her?"

"Briefly, at one of our practices. Why didn't she tell you sooner?" he asked. It was a question I, too, continued to ask myself.

"I don't know. I think she just didn't want me to be upset. That's what Meg says, at least."

"Meg knew too?"

"Oh, no. She found out when I did. If she knew sooner, she probably would have punched Nick. Like, on the spot."

"Can I be honest? I'm kind of scared of her," he joked, and it was cute.

"You're not the only one," I laughed, and paused a

moment to fully take him in. "What about you?" I asked to get the subject firmly off of Nick. "Any girls back in Italy?"

"Well, after cat girl, I gave up on dating for a while."

"Afraid that the next girl would talk to her dog or something?" I joked.

"Or worse. Really, my self-esteem couldn't handle being rejected by another animal."

I laughed, and added, "Perhaps next time it'll be a plant."

"I don't know if I could go on after that," he said, putting his hand on his heart and feigning death. "New rule: no dating girls with pets."

"Or houseplants," I added.

"Or houseplants." He smiled. "My brother is the complete opposite. He has a new girl in every place we end up. I've started referring to the girls by the place names—like Sofia is just Italy to me."

"Please don't tell me he dates them all at the same time," I said, wondering if his brother was like Jake, and if there was a bit of that in Matt, too.

"Oh, no, he has this insurmountable amount of faith, though. Like, whenever we move, he assumes the relationship will continue and tries for weeks until they just, you know, break up because of distance. Then he finds someone else within days."

"At least he waits," I said, contemplating this idea of long-distance relationships not working. Could they? I never really had to think about it. But I thought, maybe, with the right person—who didn't rebound after a few seconds—it just might. "What do you think about that—long-distance relationships?" I asked, pushing him.

"I don't know," he said, scratching his head. "I never had one." Then, "You?"

"Same," I said.

There was an awkward "I should say something, but can't think of actual words" silence. So I tried. "So where's your brother now?"

"Houston. He's two years older than me and in college. It's weird him being there and the rest of us here. Do you have any brothers or sisters?"

"Nope, just me." I looked up at him and we both kind of smiled.

Jake and Meg came back at that very moment.

"What'd you get?" Matt asked, nodding toward the brown paper bag Jake held.

"Liquid courage," he responded, hugging the bag.

"No problems?" I asked Meg, eyeing her carefully. I hoped she understood my double meaning.

"None at all," she answered carefully.

"So, next stop?" Jake asked.

"Bowling's definitely out?" I joked.

"We need to go somewhere where we can actually drink," Jake said.

"Park?" Matt suggested.

"Golf course?" Meg added.

"Jefferson!" Jake shouted.

"You want to go to school?" Meg asked.

"Dude, no—El, the roof."

I knew exactly what he meant.

"We could get in trouble," I murmured, feeling my heart beat faster. It was crazy and dangerous and though I was okay going along with saying yes, this seemed like a bit much. I looked over at Matt and when our eyes met, I also saw that it could be fun, a new memory for him. One he'd hold on to more than a picture of anonymous people.

"But you *have* to say yes," Jake said, egging me on.

"Can someone tell me what all of this is about?" Meg interrupted.

"Apparently it's really easy to jump onto the school's roof by balancing on the second-floor railing," I explained. "Some guys were talking about it in my trig class; they did it as part of hazing for the football team, or something. I told Jake, because I thought it would be funny for them to play a gig up there."

"Funny, or awesome?" Jake said, grinning. "I say we take the booze, break in, and drink on the school's roof," he declared. "We can show Matt the school before he even starts." Pause. "It's been suggested, so we have to say yes."

Meg looked at me and I shrugged. I looked at Matt and he looked pumped. More than pumped; energized as though he'd never done anything illegal before. Other than drinking underage, I suppose. Finally, Meg let out a huge sigh.

"We should have made rules about this 'yes' situation."

"Done, let's meet there," Jake decided.

"Let's park in the neighborhood next to it, so the cars don't look suspicious or anything," I said.

I jumped into Meg's car and watched as the guys pulled away.

"This is going to be a long night," Meg said, but despite her apparent lack of enthusiasm, there was a smile quietly making its way across her face. If she truly didn't want to do this, she would have said so. She was not one to simply go along with plans she didn't agree with, like the time we decided to go to the beach. The weather was perfect, the car was packed with snacks, magazines, and drinks, but midway there, after I got a call from Barker saying he and the guys might be going as well, she decided it was definitely not a beach day. So we turned around and went bowling instead, because, to her, bowling sounded much better than running into an ex-boyfriend. But tonight, instead of complaining or venting or declaring the night over, she started the car and grinned to herself. So I knew there was part of her that was excited.

I looked out the window and thought back to laughing with Matt. I pushed worry out of my head because I had another chance to repeat that moment. And for that, I was excited, too.

CHAPTER 9

NOW
10:15 P.M.

The school is dark and desolate in silhouette against the night sky when Matt and I pull up. A few streetlamps illuminate parts of the campus, leaving long, drawn-out shadows on the lawn. But even without the lights and the moon highlighting our path, we would have known the way.

It is a fairly new school, constructed just before I started. The open campus gives way to the many buildings located around a central courtyard. I haven't returned since the last day of school, just a week prior. My locker in building eight is empty and not technically mine anymore. Every imprint I had on the school is gone. The next group of freshmen won't know me; not that I was important or anything. There will be a new group sitting in the middle of the amphitheater before school starts, instead of our group. We started meeting at that spot during our freshman year and never stopped. Tonight kind of feels like a final good-bye.

Matt parks in the neighborhood bordering the school. I don't know anyone who lives there, but I do know they never call the cops on cars parked there. People do it all the time. Like breaking into the school, hanging out on the roof is kind of a rite of passage.

"Let's go." Matt beckons and hoists himself out of the car. I follow him, my heart thundering in my chest. Everything feels *so familiar*, I'm just not sure if it's in a good way. But still, I follow him because I want to. I need to.

Getting onto campus is easy—there's no border or fence blocking the way. We can simply walk right up to the school as if it's normal to be there at night. Even so, we stay in the shadows as we navigate the abandoned area. We walk over to building six, which is farthest from the road. Late-night walkers can't see us over there.

"It feels weird," I whisper to Matt. "I'm a trespasser now." Touching the cold, white stone building, I hear a loud bang. The noise echoes through the campus, repeating itself.

We freeze. Hearts pounding. Hands sweating. I cover my mouth and look at Matt. His eyes are wide, searching the area. We're both in the shadows, crouched down behind the building. But despite the darkness, we are still out in the open. My breaths grow deeper, heavier, and I'm sure whoever is out there can hear each and every one.

Matt grabs my hand and I jump, not expecting it. He looks at me hard, shooting me courage through his eyes. His skin is warm and his touch strong. We stay quiet, trying to make ourselves as undetectable as possible.

Laughter breaks the silence, but it's not ours. It's from the direction of the bang. An engine roars to life, followed by a few choice swear words. The engine again. It was just a car backfiring.

"Jesus. What's with tonight?" Matt whispers, joining me in my relief. He squeezes my hand and before I have the chance to squeeze back, he lets go.

We get to the stairs easily after that. They're large and concrete, standard school steps that can hold thousands of students pushing at each other between classes. We walk carefully to the top. There are no shadows here, so we are left exposed. My shoes squeak with each step.

At the top, Matt pulls himself up over the metal railing first, steadying himself on the edge. He reaches up for the flat, thick surface of the roof's ledge and presses down to lift his body. I stop myself from watching the muscles in his arms work. Within seconds, he's swinging his legs up.

I balance myself on the railing next, noticing Matt watching me intently the entire time. Instead of grabbing the roof, I grab his outstretched hands.

His grip is tight around my wrists as he pulls, and my arms shake as I hang like a leaf, suspended in midair. I can never get used to this part. My heart beats loudly as I dangle; I put full trust in him and his grip. I feel the roof on my stomach and throw my legs on top. Sitting down, I let out a breath and look over at him. Our laughter echoes around us. With my feet solidly planted, I finally feel safe. Well, as safe as possible while being so high up.

We walk away from the edge onto the center of the roof. For a place that's constantly broken into, it's surprisingly clean. Either the janitors are up here regularly, or everyone is very cautious to leave no traces behind. There's a low wall we lean against, sliding down to the floor, mere inches from each other. We look out toward the town and I can't believe I'm up here, with him.

The view is beautiful. It extends widely, showing a maze of streets, buildings, and trees I grew up within.

"It's weird to think my entire life is laid out down there," I say.

"Kind of cool, too. I mean, everything is a memory that way, isn't it?"

"I guess," I say, looking at the shopping center across the street. "Meg, Jake, Barker, and I used to sneak off campus during lunch and eat at that sandwich shop," I say, pointing down at the red-and-white storefront featuring a giant smiling sandwich. "Then, last year, when we finally were able to leave campus for lunch, we kind of forgot about it. It wasn't as much fun going once the risk was gone."

"I remember you telling me about that," he says, listening

eagerly as I continue my visual trip down memory lane.

"I love the smell of the bakery next door. I feel like if I smell onion bagels anywhere else, it'll always remind me of here," I say wistfully. "Meg and I would go every Friday morning before school to celebrate the last day of the week." Matt nods, as if he remembers, too.

I keep looking and see how familiar every corner, every street is. I know that just out of eyesight is the field that hosts a yearly carnival. Matt took me before he left; we went on rides, ate baby-pink cotton candy, and petted farm animals. It's all there, a map of our past laid out in front of us. It makes everything seem so close, as if I can touch each spot just by reaching out.

"Remember when the ice-cream place named a cone after the Pepperpots?" Matt asks, pointing down to the shop next to the bakery, adding his own memory to the mix.

"Yeah, and you all got to choose a flavor. You chose chocolate—"

"Which you said was really boring," he interrupts.

"It is!" I laugh. "Barker chose cookie dough."

"And Jake topped it off with mint chocolate chip because it matched his hair at the time," Matt concludes, and I smile at the memory. "What color is his hair now?"

"Black." He dyed his hair not long after I did. We never needed to talk about why.

"I love the ice cream there," Matt says.

"It closed about two months ago."

"What? Really?" he asks, almost insulted.

"Yeah. I guess we were its best customers." I watch his eyes wander the surrounding roads, probably wondering what else changed since he's been gone. "We all ordered the Pepperpots cone on the last day. I think Jake ate it in three bites." I smile, remembering the moment. "Barker had just gotten a cowbell, so we went out to celebrate, which was when he heard about the store closing."

Matt looks down, tracing the roof with his finger. I get the bottle out of my purse and hand it over. He opens it with ease, using a corkscrew from his pocket.

"You carry a corkscrew in your pocket? It's as if you knew this would happen," I comment.

"I'm just always prepared," he says, smiling and handing me the bottle first. I take a swig. It's still cold from the store, and it feels good going down. Much better than the drink Evan gave me earlier. It's sweet, almost fruity. I hand it back to Matt and he takes a sip the same way. It's weird sharing a drink with him. It's weird drinking with him to begin with. I'm so conscious of his body next to mine, despite the fact that we're not even touching.

"Your bracelets," he says, pointing to the hand that gave him the bottle. I look down at the single string bracelet on my wrist, still surviving through everything.

"Yeah," I say, not meeting his eyes. "Um, I cut some off."

"Some" is an understatement, and he knows that. I had so many lining my wrist last year, but after he left, I cut them all off and started over. Each bracelet was a physical reminder, and they all burned my wrist.

"What's that one from?" he asks, pointing to the remaining knotted pink-and-purple one.

"My birthday this past year. It was fun," I say, and I know this admission hurts him, since he wasn't here for it, and every other event he was here for I removed. I turn to him and hold his gaze; I want him to see how I've moved on.

"Truth or dare," Matt says, changing the subject. He's bringing the conversation back to something he's familiar with, something he's part of.

"Didn't we play Never Have I Ever?" I ask, remembering that night.

"Yeah, but that's not as much fun with just two people. Plus, we were always good at dares. *Plus*, you have to say yes."

"Ugh." I groan at his rule, as well as the memory. "Okay, dare." There is no way I'm choosing truth. Not yet, at least. I feel a drop fall on me and look up, but there aren't any clouds visible, just the sky.

"I dare you to do a cartwheel. Right now."

"On the roof?" I ask, deadpan.

"On the roof." He smirks, as if the cartwheel will lead to something even crazier.

"You know I'm terrible at these," I protest. "My cartwheels look more like cart-falls."

"They can't be *that* bad," he says, egging me on.

"My legs are never straight, so I look stupid. Also, have

you forgotten that we're on the roof? What if I cartwheel too far and fall off?" I ask him.

"I'll save you," he says, and I feel my cheeks redden a little.

"I can just picture myself falling off the edge to my death as you scream in horror. Or regret."

"Probably regret. Had I known you would die, I might have picked another dare."

"Might have?" I ask.

"I really want to see this terrible cartwheel now. Should I record it? Just in case the news crews need evidence?"

"Imagine the headlines: Ex-boyfriend challenges ex-girlfriend to cartwheel, leading to her demise, tonight at eight." I say it quickly and laugh and when I look at him, I realize he isn't laughing anymore. Perhaps I went too far. So I do what I have to do.

Brushing the dirt off my jeans, I get up and find some empty space that isn't close to the edge. He stands up and turns around to watch me prepare for my flip. I can do this, I really can. I tuck my shirt in, hold my breath, and go.

My hands hit first, crushing against small pebbles and bits of concrete. Then I'm upside down. And then I'm falling, legs first, hitting the ground hard.

"See, no death," Matt calls out, applauding as I straighten up and take a bow. It was far from good, but a noble attempt. I look down at my hands; they're pockmarked from the pebbles.

"Oh, don't you dare think I'm not getting you back. Truth or dare," I call out, walking toward him.

"Dare," he says, with a cheeky grin. He rocks on his feet, waiting for his punishment.

"Okay." I think. "I dare you to do a handstand." An easy dare, truly inconsequential, but I never perform well under pressure. And I can't dare him to do something crazy like streak across the roof. We still have boundaries. I take a sip from the bottle and wait for him to accept.

Without a word, he places his hands on the ground and kicks his legs up. They don't last long in the air, flailing in place before falling down with a thud. He rolls over onto his back and laughs.

"I'm not meant for extreme sports," he says, propping his body up on his elbow and grabbing the bottle from me.

"I don't think handstands are considered extreme," I answer, scooting closer to him.

"Remember when Jake tried to jump out of a moving car?"

"Because he'd watched *The Fast and the Furious* and figured he was meant for racing!" I squeal, laughing at the memory.

"Good thing you were driving close to the side of the road."

"And the side of the road had grass instead of a sidewalk," I add. "Meg and I made green bracelets to commemorate that night and celebrate Jake *not* dying. We were pretty stupid back then, weren't we?" Matt drops his head and sits up. He messes up his hair as he puts the bottle down, not meeting my eyes. "Oh. I mean, that night, not—"

"It's okay. And we were. At least I was," he says, and places his hand on my arm. He's done it so many times in the past; every time I ever felt nervous or excited or overwhelmed, he always placed his hand on my arm to stabilize me. He knew it had some sort of calming effect. But this time, instead of slowing down my heart rate, it only accelerates it. And I don't want that. *I don't want that*, I repeat to myself, willing myself to remember. I look up at him and he blushes, dropping his arm. I look down and feel another raindrop.

"Um, truth or dare," he continues, leading us right back to the game. The present. Right back to where we're sort of comfortable.

"Dare," I answer, of course.

"I dare you to yell as loud as possible."

"That'll definitely *not* get us caught," I say sarcastically.

"Well, you picked dare . . ." he taunts.

"Okay, okay," I relent. I walk cautiously over to the edge and know exactly what I'm going to yell, the exact same thing we yelled just a year ago. "HELLO, ANTARCTICA!" I turn around quickly, cracking up, and run back to him. I grab his arm and pull him behind the structure we were leaning against, so we're almost hidden from the night surrounding us.

"*Of course* you said that," he laughs, and we're so close

I can smell him. He smells like summer. And he's looking at me with eyes so sad and kind I can't help but smile. Suddenly, my phone buzzes in my pocket, breaking our gaze.

I pull it out and, as expected, it's Meg.

Status?

I text her back the one word, knowing she'll understand.

Roof

OF COURSE. No making out.

I look back up at Matt. He's turned away, picking a folded piece of notebook paper up off the ground. "That was Meg," I explain.

"She must be worried."

"She wanted to let you know the knives are sharpened," I joke, and he laughs.

"Ouch. Hey, look at this," he says, handing me the piece of paper.

"What's this?" I ask, reading what it says. "'We claim this roof in the name of Katie, Michelle, Joe, and Sam.'"

"Looks like someone else has been hanging out up here," he says.

"I recognize the names. They're a year younger than us, seniors this year. They're in drama, I think." I pause. "I guess it's their turn to own the roof." I give him back the paper.

"Well, they have to know about the original owners," he says. "Do you have a pen?" I cock my head at him, then nod and walk over to where I left my purse. Finding a pen, I bring it back to him.

"Original explorers, E, J, M, and M, grant you owner-ship," he recites as he writes. "Better to leave our initials rather than names, you know?" I nod and watch as he climbs up a little higher and shakily puts the paper under a rock on the platform.

"Do you still collect them?" I yell up, though he's not more than three feet higher.

He climbs down before answering. "Not really. I mean, every now and then . . . it's a hard habit to break . . . but, I don't know."

"What?" I ask.

"After living here, the desire kind of died," he answers, looking at me.

"Truth or dare," I respond.

"Dare," he says, looking at me with expectant eyes and a slight smile. I feel another drop fall on me, but I ignore it because dares are more important.

The game goes on for a while, with both of us only picking dares. We can't handle truths yet. They'll come out even-tually, but right now we scale rafters, yell to the night, and perform rap songs. We speak in dares, letting each other open up through actions rather than words. We keep going because we don't know what else to do. And we don't want to end the night—not just yet.

The bottle is half empty and I'm buzzed by the time Matt finally says, "Truth."

We're sitting next to each other, leaning against the wall as we were when we first climbed up. We're both out of breath and he's looking at me, his eyes a little droopy. I'm taken aback, unsure if I'm ready to actually talk. I bite my lip and try to think of the perfect question as my heart rages inside my body.

"How was school this year?" I start easy.

"Fine," he answers plainly, looking away, out toward the road we drove up earlier.

"You can't just answer 'fine,'" I say, nudging him with my elbow. "I need details."

"It was school, you know? New school, new life. The house we had was nice—and Texas was fine. Lots of accents. I didn't really fit in."

"What do you mean?"

"I didn't own a cowboy hat." He smiles, looking back at me. "Anyway, isn't it my turn? One question and all."

"Yeah, yeah. Shoot."

"Truth or dare."

"Truth," I answer automatically.

"How was school for you?"

I think before I answer. Honestly, I was miserable after

Matt left, and then nothing really . . . happened. I didn't date anyone else; I was still hung up on him. But I can't tell him that.

"The last year of high school is supposed to be magical and wonderful—at least, that's how it goes in movies. But they don't tell you it's also stressful and scary. I didn't know where I'd end up for most of the year. I didn't know what would happen next."

He nods. "And you love knowing."

"Yeah, exactly. I mean, it wasn't terrible," I continue. I don't want him to think I spent the entire time pining after him. "I had Meg and everyone. And we had some fun times. But I guess I just expected . . . more." I look down and shake my head, not wanting to look at him. After a moment, I say, "Anyway, truth or dare."

"Truth."

"Did you make a lot of friends in Texas?" Specifically female friends with whom you happened to make out. Of course, I don't add that last part.

"Some. None as cool as you guys, though."

I stop myself from adding that he could have kept us as friends. That he didn't have to lose or miss us. That we were always still here, waiting for him. I look over and see our shoulders touching. How we got so close, I don't know, but despite everything I find myself leaning even closer. "Truth or dare."

"Truth."

He pauses and I can tell he's unsure whether he should ask what's coming. "Did you . . . date anyone this year?"

I want to say yes, hundreds of people. That I moved on quickly, and fell in love over and over again, and that he was just a speck of a memory. That he didn't break my heart and leave me lost for the past six months. But I settle on the truth. Because we're opening up and all.

"No." I continue using the game as a buffer. "Truth or dare?"

"Truth," he answers without thinking.

"Did you?" It slips out, really. I want to know if his year mirrored mine. Did he move on, or was he alone? Was he miserable, or did he leave someone new behind?

"I did not," he answers easily, not leaving a second for contemplation. I smile and then catch myself. He can't see how happy that makes me. I notice a flicker of a grin cross his mouth. "How . . . are you?"

And just like that, the game is gone. It's only us now.

"I'm fine," I answer automatically. It's the same response I've been giving this entire year, no need to change it now. I *am* fine; he just doesn't need to know that fine has many definitions.

"You can't just answer 'fine,'" he says, reminding me of my earlier rule.

"I can and I will," I shoot back with a grin. I think about what I want to know next, and finally give myself the courage to ask. "Why UCF? Really this time." It's what I need to know. What I've been waiting to ask. What I've been too scared to ask. *Was it for me?*

"I was offered a scholarship," he says, pushing his hair back and looking away. My heart drops, but I don't take my eyes off him. "Good school and all." He thinks, and then looks at me. My breath catches as our eyes meet. "This was the only place that's ever felt like home. I wanted to come back. I wanted to feel what I did when I lived here. I know you can't return to a time as easily as you can return to a place, but I wanted to try. I like it here." My heart is thumping madly, a tiny drum going off. "I like the people." He pauses again, an awkward silence coming between us. Then he says quietly, "Did you ever think of me?"

"Yes, did you ever think of me?"

"All the time." With each word we grow closer. His breath is heavy as he leans toward me. I feel him again, only this time it's actually him. He's actually touching me, looking right in my eyes and tipping his chin down. My body, my brain try to stop me, but I don't. I feel myself falling again and I don't want to stop. I don't want a safety net or parachute. I want to plummet through this feeling forever. I want to forget everything that happened and start over. I want him.

Just as our lips are about to touch, the drops that were slowly falling culminate to form a torrential downpour.

CHAPTER 10

THEN
10:10 P.M.

As it turned out, the roof, for the four of us, was very hard to get onto.

"So how do we do this?" Meg asked, looking up at the building.

"Climb?" Jake answered, shifting his beer—wielding his backpack on his shoulders.

"Aren't we clever?" she jabbed back.

Jake leaned over to Meg, resting his arm against the wall behind her. "We *are* very clever. And handsome, might I add."

"I don't mean to interrupt, but *will you guys shut up!*" I whisper-yelled, fearing getting caught. We were on the stairs, clearly visible to anyone who walked by. Our voices echoed through the campus and I just knew someone would catch us. "Okay, I guess one person can climb on the railing and then hoist himself up. Then he can help everyone else climb up," I suggested.

"I'll go up first," Matt volunteered.

"You sure?" I asked.

"I'm strong," he said, flexing his skinny arms. You'd think he was bragging to his mom about getting an A; it was adorable. He climbed on the railing and easily touched the ledge. As he lifted up his arms, his shirt rode up and exposed a sliver of skin. I shivered. With a simple press, he hoisted himself onto the roof in one quick motion. He made it look so easy, but I knew I couldn't do it on my own.

"Ella?" he asked. I hopped up on the railing and realized we were much higher than I had thought. "I've got you, don't worry," Matt whispered.

"I should tell you—I don't like heights," I responded before raising my hands. He grabbed my wrists and pulled.

As soon as my legs left the railing my heart raced and I suppressed a scream. I was essentially dangling from the roof and holding on to a guy I barely knew. I mentally kicked myself for my blatant stupidity and cursed that sliver of skin that had enticed me into doing this not moments before. As I felt air brush my skin, I panicked.

"Oh my god, oh my god, oh my god." My hands were turning numb, my legs shaking; I was certain I was about to fall.

"You're fine," Matt reassured, pulling me up. I felt my body climb the building, but I wouldn't open my eyes; I could barely feel his hands. "El, open your eyes," Matt said, and with every ounce of energy, I did. I was waist level with the roof, almost on it. My heart sang. I kicked my left leg up and hooked it, then swung my right leg up to join the other, with Matt still holding on and helping me along. As soon as I was properly up, I practically kissed the roof, holding on as tight as possible. I'd never been so happy to be so high up.

"You're fine, you know," Matt said, letting go of my arms.

"I, er, yeah, sorry." I blushed. I moved away from the edge, but then quickly sat down again a few feet away.

Meg came up next, and then Jake.

We walked to the center of the roof and leaned against a low wall—Jake, Meg, me, and then Matt. Still out of breath from my near-death experience, I breathed deeply as Jake opened up his backpack and handed out beers.

"Drink!" he commanded. So we did.

"The town looks so small from here," I marveled, taking in the scenery. "Like a Monopoly game, or something. I think I can see my house."

"I can't believe we only have one more year here," Meg mused. Jake got up and walked back toward the edge of the roof.

"Ya hear that, school? We're almost done with you! Screw you and your math and history and grades." Matt jumped up and ran to Jake, pulling him back to us. We collapsed in a fit of laughter and cheap beer.

"It's not *that bad*," I said.

"Says the straight-A student," Jake answered.

"I am not a straight-A student. Just because I don't get suspended every day doesn't make me a genius."

"I don't get suspended every day. Just the good days."

"Welcome to Jefferson, by the way," Meg said to Matt.

"I feel like it's already home," he replied, peering across the campus.

"Well, you're on the roof. That makes you pretty official," she said, clinking bottles with him. I knew she wasn't interested, but still, a part of me was envious. She had it so easy with guys. I never did.

"It's weird, this is the first place I've lived that my brother hasn't," he said, more to himself than anyone else.

"You have a brother?" Meg asked, raising her eyebrows.

"Yeah, he's in college."

"A college guy," Meg mused to herself, to which I added, "And apparently the ladies love him."

"Yeah, but is he in a band?" Jake inserted himself in, as he often did, and Matt just shook his head.

"No, but he plays soccer. He'll probably be captain next year," Matt said proudly, and I could tell he looked up to his brother a bit.

"Can I get his number?" Meg asked with a grin, and Jake made a *hmph* noise in response.

"He has a girlfriend, unfortunately," Matt answered. "Some girl he met at a bar. He sent me a picture. She has a neck tattoo."

"Can I get *her* number?" Jake asked, and this time it was Meg's turn to *hmph*.

"But, yeah, this place seems cool," Matt continued, avoiding their digression. "It sucks I'll only have a year here. And then, who knows."

We sat quietly, sipping from our bottles. It was true for all of us. We had no clue where we'd be in a year, or what we'd be doing. The thought frightened me. Would we still be friends, even?

"Well, I'll be a movie star, of course," Meg joked.

"Take a bow, Miss Kensey," I called out. Meg wanted to major in acting, which fit her perfectly. She had the drive and passion for the career, as well as the penchant for melodrama. Plus, she was strong and could take rejection.

"*Mrs.* Something-or-other, thank you very much," she corrected me.

"So you're married now?"

"No, but I will be by the time I'm a huge movie star."

"Oy, you slags!" Jake interrupted with a fake British accent. He jumped up and paced around in front of us, drumming with his hands. "I'll be a major rock star, headlining stadiums 'round the world. That'll show all those kids in high school who dinnit believe in my music."

114

"You'll also be British, apparently," I responded.

"O' course," Jake continued with the accent. "The best music comes from the Brits. Punk rock!"

"Didn't British punk end in the seventies?" Matt questioned. I glanced to my right and saw him smiling at me.

"Clearly, mate, you haven't kept up with the music scene," Jake continued.

"Mate?" Matt mouthed to me. I laughed at his question, coughing from the sip I had just taken. I wasn't far into the beer, but I was already feeling it.

"What about you, Matt? Any long-term plans?" I asked.

"I don't know. I was thinking of going into music production. You know, working at a music studio."

"You can produce my first record," Meg announced.

"Of course, because every great actress must be a singer, too," I added.

"Well, only the good ones." She nudged me.

"Maybe we can duet," Jake stated, walking over to Meg and putting his arm around her. She looked up at him for a second, hesitated, and then with conviction announced, "I don't think so."

I drew my attention back to Matt, who was fiddling with his watch again. "That's cool. What made you think of it?" I asked.

"Well, I can't rely on my mediocre bass playing and my boyish good looks forever," he joked. I smiled.

"Oy, I can! I'm top meat right here!"

I waved a hand at Jake, ignoring his comment. "I think it's a great idea."

"What about you?" Matt asked. "Any plans yet?"

"I'm majoring in writing," I said.

"Oh, that's cool. I didn't know you wrote," he answered, face lighting up.

"A little. I want to be a journalist. Actually, your finding-objects thing gave me an idea earlier."

"Oh yeah?" he asked, intrigued.

"Yeah. Like the photo you found in the market? I bet I could make a story from it, imagining what the people were laughing about. Kind of like you do."

"Yeah!" he said excitedly. "I guess it is pretty similar. We both think up stories, in a way."

"Exactly."

Meg gave me a pointed look and put her pinkie up. I locked mine with hers. "She's really good," she said to Matt, then to me, "I'll only allow *you* to document my highly successful career."

"It'll be the *first* thing I write about," I said, laughing.

"You should write about tonight," Jake interrupted, still in a British accent. "But give me a beard. I always thought I'd look smashing in a beard."

"That's only because you can't grow one, Mr. Peach Fuzz," Meg rebutted. He gave her a sly grin and got even closer.

"So the accent is a permanent thing now?" Matt asked, looking over.

"I'll keep going until the ladies tell me to stop."

"STOP!" Meg and I both shouted out, laughing. Our one-syllable word echoed through the trees, bouncing off nearby houses.

"But seriously, how great would this place be for a gig?" Jake asked, staring over the edge of the roof again.

"You've already played here. Battle of the Bands, remember?" I asked, thinking back to their most recent show. When they struck the last note and froze their instruments in one final flourish, I got goose bumps. They were that good.

"Well, yeah, we played *there*," he said, pointing down to the courtyard. "But I mean *here*. On the *roof*. El, when you write that book, have us play on the roof." He stepped close to the edge again and struck a rock star pose, sloshing his drink everywhere. Legs slightly bent, he held his air guitar over his head and opened his mouth. "HELLO, JEFFERSON HIGH SCHOOL!"

"I wonder why that doesn't sound as cool as 'Hello, LA!'" I asked.

Matt stood up, still next to me, and yelled out, "HELLO, ARKANSAS!" I grabbed his arm and pulled him back down, laughing. I was still afraid of attracting too much attention to us. And of falling off.

"HELLO, ANTARCTICA!" Meg yelled, still sitting down beside me.

"I hear penguins are quite the rock aficionados," I said to her.

"Dude—we're taking the band to Antarctica. You think we'd be the first band to play there?" Jake asked, half joking, half serious, as he always was.

"I think we might be the first band to freeze to death there," Matt answered.

"Touché," Jake said, pointing at Matt. I looked over and noticed Matt staring at me. Not in a calculating way, but like he was intrigued. He looked *interested*, like he was trying to figure me out. Put me together, like a puzzle. Was I that much of an enigma? I smiled back nervously and I swear he blushed.

"So what can we say yes to next?" Jake asked. He had the attention span of a puppy, always pacing around and marking his territory. The roof was his. Meg's eyes constantly followed his movement. I wanted to grab her, shake her, and tell her to stop, but I knew it was too late. She was hooked, despite her protests. I suppose I wanted to shake Jake as well, because if he was actually *good* I'd be fine with them, but he was still conflicted. He was on the cusp of being either good or bad, often jumping from side to side. And it sucked.

"Should we stay or should we go?" Meg asked, reciting the Clash's famous lyric.

"Nice," Jake said with a point to her. She looked down.

"Game?" I proposed. "It can be all middle school–like."

"So, polishing nails and calling boys?" Meg asked.

"We didn't do that *all* the time," I answered.

"I recall getting a few giggly calls from you girls," Jake said.

"That's because Shana *loooooved* you," I said. Shana had been the third member of our little group. We did everything together in middle school. That is, until Shana started cheerleading and found a new group of friends in high school. She traded headphones for megaphones and never looked back.

"Did she? I should give her a call."

Meg playfully punched him in the arm, and pulled him down to our level. "Stop your pacing. You're making me nervous."

"You know I'm always in motion. So back to the game."

"Spin the Bottle doesn't really work with four people," Matt said, bringing himself back into the conversation.

"Says you," Jake said, raising his eyebrows and nodding his head.

"No," Meg declared.

"Truth or Dare?" I offered.

"Never Have I Ever?" Matt asked.

"*Never Have I Ever!*" Jake yelled excitedly.

We couldn't say no once someone decided, could we?

"Why's he so excited?" Matt asked me in a whisper.

"We've played before," I explained. "It always ends with Jake far drunker than the rest of us."

"That's this bracelet, isn't it?" Meg asked, holding her

wrist up and pointing to the black-and-white-striped one.

"Ugh, yeah!" I said, turning to Jake. "Didn't you try skateboarding blindfolded or something?"

"Don't you mean didn't I succeed in skateboarding blindfolded?" Jake answered proudly.

"You crashed into a tree. I wouldn't call that succeeding," Meg deadpanned.

"And what about you?" Matt asked me. "How do you usually fare during the game?"

"I guess you'll see," I said with a half smile, hoping to sound cool, though in truth, I was usually barely tipsy by the end of the game. We went around in a circle and each said something we'd never done. If someone had done it, they drank. It was pretty simple. Jake passed each of us another bottle of beer, but I wasn't even done with my first one yet. I was a lightweight, so the one drink was already making everything wilder, brighter, and louder.

"Okay, me first," I said, suddenly brave. "Never have I ever gotten suspended from school." Both Jake and Meg drank. I already knew why, so no story was necessary. Matt didn't, so I turned to him to explain. "Jake was suspended for skipping class one too many times, and Meg for punching a football player who made fun of her brother."

"Why'd he make fun of her brother?" Matt asked.

"He's gay," Meg answered for me. "Which is such a shitty reason."

"Are you going to explain *every* drink to Matt? 'Cause

this game will take forever if you do," Jake interrupted, and I rolled my eyes at him in response.

"Never have I ever gotten a high five for friendship," Meg continued, to appease Jake, and get me back. I groaned and took a drink.

"Never have I ever prank-called guys," Jake said, so Meg and I took a drink.

"Are we just trying to get each other drunk?" I asked.

"Isn't that the point?" Jake answered.

"Well, never have I ever polished my nails," Matt said. Meg and I drank in unison. I looked over to notice Jake drinking, too.

"What?" he asked. "I'm a rock god."

"You wish," Meg answered with an eye roll. She was starting to perfect those.

"Oh yeah? Never have I ever moved out of the state," I said, eyeing Matt. He playfully jabbed me in the stomach with his elbow and sipped.

"Never have I ever been in a rock band," Meg said next, getting the guys.

"Never have I ever had that girl thing that happens every month," Jake countered.

"Gotten a period?" Meg asked, incredulous. "Really? You're going there?"

"Why not?" he answered with a tilt of his head.

"Never have I ever dyed my hair?" Matt asked. Again, the three of us drank, and I turned to Matt.

"Meg and I used too much dye last summer," I explained. "It was a terrible idea."

"You looked like a tiger, with those orange streaks!" she laughed.

"Oh, god, I really did," I giggled. "And Jake's gone through every color in his hair, I'm pretty sure."

"Never pink." He pointed at me and I nodded in agreement. It was something most parents would be against, but his mom was okay with it. Jake was an angel compared to his dad, who was a hardcore alcoholic. He would come home wasted every night, barely speaking to his wife and son. Jake drank too—he said he learned it from his dad—but he vowed to never get as bad. He had seen too many consequences. Instead, he channeled his anger into music. And, as it turned out, his hair.

"Never have I ever kissed anyone on a roof," I said, remembering a story Meg told me about her and Jake. Realization dawned on me as I noticed the look on Meg's face. It wasn't shock, it was just a slight raise of her brow. But that said it all. I shouldn't have brought it up. But Meg and Jake happily tipped back their bottles. We were all too drunk to care about awkwardness. I squeezed her hand to say I was sorry, and she squeezed back. It was okay. It was common knowledge anyway. I tried so hard to consciously not bring up their past relationship that sometimes little details slipped my mind.

"You haven't, that's right," Jake said, noticing that I

hadn't taken a drink along with them. "Let's remedy that. Matt, kiss El."

"Wait, what?" I spat out.

"I don't know, I think you have to. It is the night to say yes and all that," Meg added slyly. She squeezed my hand again. I knew this was her way of helping me finally get past my horrible ex-boyfriend, but it wasn't just me she was putting on the spot. My face heated up and I couldn't turn around to face Matt. Okay, I did want him to kiss me, but not like this. Not with us being forced to in front of other people. Not without any buildup or romance. Not while drunk.

"Err, I guess it's the rules," Matt said. I must have looked horrified because he quickly added, "I mean, if that's okay with you."

Oblivious to the tension, Jake started chanting *"Do it, do it, do it!"* Cheeks burning, I faced Matt. I raised my chin and looked deep in his eyes. They were wide, embarrassed, and a little scared. But they weren't hesitant, and they weren't disgusted. I could see that he wanted to kiss me as much as I did him. And that's when I was convinced.

He brushed his hair out of his face, but as he tilted his head down, it fell back over his glasses again. He looked at me and my heart melted. I leaned forward. He leaned forward. Our lips met.

I felt a spark between us, and broke away quickly. I didn't know what it meant; I barely knew him, and yet, I knew I'd remember this moment. I still felt his lips on mine. Soft, sweet. I bit my lower lip and tasted him. It wasn't until he glanced down, blushing, and I saw a smile appear on his face, that I realized I was smiling too. Beside us, we heard cheers. This time when our eyes met, it wasn't embarrassment that greeted them, but warmth. Desire. In that moment, we'd both said yes. For the remainder of the game, we sat closer to each other. Pinkie fingers brushing lightly.

"Well, I'm glad we got that out of the way," Meg said. "Back to the game. Never have I ever made out with someone at a football game."

"Shut up," I murmured, thinking of all the times Nick and I would go to games but pay more attention to each other than what was happening on the field. Our team always lost, so really we weren't missing anything. So I lifted my bottle to clear my mind, and as I drank, Matt raised his eyebrow at me.

Jake continued, "Building on that, never have I ever made out with someone at school, period." Before anyone could drink, Meg interrupted.

"Really?" she asked, staring at him with slit eyes.

"Oh shit, sorry." He realized his mistake and took a sip. We all followed his lead. This time it was my turn to be jealous as I saw Matt put his bottle back down.

"You realize this is much harder for me, since I don't know you guys that well," Matt said.

"You know Ella well," Jake said, nodding his head

suggestively. Meg laughed as I covered my flaming face with my hand. *Of course* he went there.

"Okay," Matt said loudly, moving past Jake's quip. "So . . . never have I ever been . . . skinny-dipping?" he asked, unsure if any of us had been.

Both Jake and Meg took a drink.

"I didn't know about that!" I said, then paused. "Scratch that, I don't *want* to know about that."

"Wait, you guys haven't?" Meg asked. Both Matt and I shook our heads. I felt his pinkie finger fall over mine, and a shiver went up my spine.

"So we're doing it. Now," Jake declared.

"First, where would we do it? And second, no," I said.

"Dude, there *are* no no's tonight," Jake pointed out, already up and pacing. He was determined.

My face started to flush again. I couldn't imagine *skinny- dipping* in front of anyone, especially Matt. The mere thought embarrassed me.

"She's actually right, Jake. There's nowhere for us to go," Meg added.

"Where did you guys go?" Matt asked. I whipped my head back and stared at him. "What? I was just curious!"

"Beach, but it's too far," Meg said. I shot her my best questioning look and she just shrugged. Apparently she'd done a lot with Jake that I wasn't aware of.

"Pool!" Jake shouted excitedly. He was staring off the

side of the building now, toward the gymnasium.

"None of us own a pool," I answered, assuming that was what he meant. "Unless Matt?"

"Nope, sorry," Matt answered.

"No, school pool. Down there." He pointed. The school's pool was outside, right below us. True, there was nothing blocking it—it was just a pool out in the open—but for some reason that sounded far scarier than what we were already doing. We were up high where no one could see us.

"You guys," I started to say, feeling really uncomfortable. I knew we were saying yes to everything, but this was too much. No amount of alcohol could erase my fear of being naked in front of everyone. I wasn't *ashamed* of my body, but it was far from perfect. I had larger thighs and knobby knees. I had curves. Meg was gorgeous; I was . . . me. What girl *wasn't* worried about her body?

But it wasn't just that. With the exception of changing in the locker room for PE or swapping outfits at Meg's before nights out, I'd never really been totally exposed in front of anyone. At all. Sure, I had fun with Nick, but we never went that far. I was nervous; he was all too sure. And then there was the cheating, and a part of me always worried it was *because* we didn't go further.

"This sounds kind of awesome," Meg said, standing up and walking over to Jake.

"Meg . . ." I started. Matt was looking down, finishing his drink. He realized he had no say. Jake was always in control.

Meg looked back over toward me and saw my discomfort.

"Compromise," Meg said. "We still break into the pool, but we don't have to get *totally* naked," she said, looking at me. She knew what I was most worried about without me having to tell her. A few weeks after the breakup, I'd told her why I thought it might have happened. Why he might have chosen someone over me. She pulled me in for a hug and said if that was the reason, he wasn't worth it. And while deep down I knew that, I ultimately needed someone to tell me for it to fully register.

Meg continued, looking back at the guys. "Plus, we just met Matt. He could be a gross pervert for all we know," she added with a grin.

"You never know . . ." he started. We all looked at him. "Kidding! Jeez."

I thought about Meg's compromise. It *was* better. Underwear was just like a bikini, right? It was a night to have fun, forget about the past, and move forward. Leave Nick and fear and reservations behind. Do something, say yes . . . and perhaps see Matt shirtless in the process. Which wasn't a bad bonus at all. This was a night for memories, after all.

"Okay, fine," I sighed, finishing off my beer. I needed all the help I could get.

"Operation Skinny-Dip shall commence," Jake proclaimed to the school.

CHAPTER 11

NOW
10:45 P.M.

"Ah!" I yell, and Matt pulls me close, as if that'll save me from the rain pouring down on top of us.

"Come on," he says, grabbing my hand. "We need to get down."

"How?" I think of trying to climb down from the roof while rain is falling on us. "We're going to slip and fall. We're going to die." I'm going to die on the roof of my school with my ex-boyfriend. Great.

"We're not going to die! We can't stay up here," Matt yells back, pulling me along the roof toward the edge.

"Can't we wait it out?" I ask, scared, confused, and maybe still thinking of what just transpired between us.

"What if there's lightning?" he asks, turning back to meet my face, and I realize he's right. "I won't let you get hurt," he promises, and I'm reminded of the cartwheeling that happened earlier. He stares at me, holding my shoulders tight, until I nod my head. My clothes are soaked, sticking to my body, and I have no clue how I'll be able to make it down. This was a stupid idea. This whole thing was a stupid idea.

"I'll go first, and then catch you, okay?"

I nod again, my teeth starting to chatter from the water pooling in my shirt. He throws his legs over and I watch as his whole body disappears off the cliff. My heart drums as I lean over the edge to make sure he lands okay, and he does, shakily. His feet are only just gripping the railing. This isn't a good idea. This is *not* a good idea. But he's right. Staying up here is worse.

"Okay, I've got you, I promise," he yells. I nod again and close my eyes. *Please let us live through this.* I slowly lower my legs off and wait for his touch. "A little more, El," he yells, and I cautiously lower myself a bit more, my fingers gripping as hard as they can. I keep my eyes closed, hoping the whole thing will just end and I'll open them to sunshine and warmth. I feel his hands on one leg, then the other. And then on my thighs. And then on my waist. And then my feet, too, are on the railing. I let out a huge sigh of relief as my heart celebrates. We jump down onto the stairs, onto safety.

"I've got you," he whispers in my ear, arms still around my waist, back on the staircase on solid ground. I breathe deeply in and turn around to face him. Rain covers both of us, pouring down our bodies. But his face is right there and we're right where we left off before the downpour. His glasses are so wet I can't even see his eyes, but I know he's looking at me, just like I'm looking at him. As adrenaline courses through my body, I lean in.

Thunder crashes to my right and I jump, breaking apart from him again.

"Come on," he says sadly, and grabs my hand. We race down the stairs, around the building, rain following us the entire time. It feels like I just swam. It feels just like last time.

We make it to the car in record time and jump inside, out of the rain.

"OH MY GOD," I yell. "Where did *that* come from?"

"Florida weather, the only thing I didn't miss," Matt says, turning the car's heat on high. The warm air feels fantastic. Still, my clothes are sticking to me and my hair is so wet it's dripping down my face. "Are you okay?" he asks, looking at me.

"Aside from feeling like I just showered with my clothes on, I'm fine." I smile through chattering teeth. He looks just as bad, hair matted down and clothes two shades darker. He takes his glasses off and goes to wipe them on his shirt, only to see his shirt is wetter.

"Hey, I haven't unpacked my car yet. I should have some clothes back there if you want to grab some to dry yourself off, or change," he says, turning around and reaching back.

"Awesome," I say, patting at myself. "I'd love some dry clothes right about now. Sorry for getting your seats so wet."

"I don't care." He shrugs, adding, "Here." He opens a bag full of clothes. The familiar Matt scent comes out. He grabs some shirts and sits back down in the front. He hands me a few and I take one to dry my face and then towel off my hair. I squeeze as much water as I can out of my hair, and then throw it up into a bun. It looks ridiculous, I'm sure, but so do I. I turn and see him wiping his glasses dry. He puts them back on and then takes off his shirt.

Instinctively, my hands wrap protectively around my waist, just like they did earlier when I first saw him. They're holding me together, guarding me from memories of him. My heart thunders and my breathing intensifies as I realize what's happening. He's taking off his shirt. I'm going to take off my shirt, too. With him. Here.

The last time I did that was the night before he left.

And suddenly the memory of that night rushes through my head. It was the first and only night we were together, but it was wonderful and something I held on to that gave me hope. But the memory of that night only leads me to the memory of after, and I grip my stomach harder because I don't want him to see me vulnerable like that again. I look over at the note in the cup holder. It might have been cute earlier, but now it just looks like the notes leading up to him leaving, and the note he sent me later, as an apology. It looks like the real good-bye I never received.

"What's wrong?" he asks, looking at me, scrunching down his eyebrows with concern. He's wearing a new shirt, a black one with a band logo on it, and I'm pretty sure it's the same one from the night we met. "Oh," he says, as realization crosses his face. "I'll turn around so you can change." But it's not that. It's him.

"I can't," I murmur because I can't speak any louder.

"What?" he asks, worry creeping along his forehead.

"I can't," I say louder, stronger. I feel myself breaking apart, and I have to get it all out before it's too late. "I can't pretend anymore—pretend everything's okay when it's not. At least for me it's not."

"Okay . . ." he says.

"Why did you do it?" I ask, and his mouth drops open and then closes again. He was not expecting that, but I can't just ignore it anymore. As my heart starts beating regularly again, commanding me to talk, I know I have to push on.

"Do . . . what . . ." he tries.

"Leave me," I say.

"El . . ."

"Seriously. Because I need to know now."

"You know why I left. My dad got a new job in Houston. I had to move with him," he says, looking ahead, not at me. It sounds so rehearsed, so unnatural.

"Yeah, I know that part. It's after. What happened after."

"What do you mean?"

"How you stopped talking to me? How you never

returned my calls? Jake's calls? You made us all *insane* with worry. Why did you just disappear?"

"It's complicated. . . ."

"How complicated is a phone call?" I cry out, feeling the tears spring from my eyes. It's what I've been holding in all night. It's what made me push him away when we first saw each other over the tiki bar. It's what's kept me broken all of these months.

"More complicated than I thought . . ." he says lightly, looking down, then finally facing me.

"You didn't even give us a chance."

He sighs, forcing all of the air out of his body. "There's a lot you don't know. . . ."

"Then tell me," I plead. "What don't I know?" I wonder what secrets he has hidden. What could he be keeping from me that's so extreme it's kept us apart? "Don't you think I deserve to know?"

He looks at me, and I can't recognize the look. Is it fear, worry, frustration, resignation? Sadness? Is it everything at once?

"It's just . . . I made a lot of mistakes and I'm trying to make them right with you. I really am. I don't want to go back there, to that time," he pleads. "I just want to move forward."

"So reenacting a night from our past is moving forward?" I ask, grabbing for something, anything. "I can never forgive you if you don't explain," I blurt out.

He nods, resigned, and starts twisting his watch around his wrist. Something is making him nervous, and I brace myself for the impact, hearing my heart pound in my chest.

"Okay," he says, forcing the word out as if it physically hurts him. "It wasn't my dad's job that brought us to Houston," he admits to his watch, not to me, and I raise my eyebrows in shock. He lied about that? "It was my brother. He . . . got into some trouble."

"Chris? What kind of trouble?" I ask wearily, wondering what could possibly force Matt and his family to move to another state. What could force him to stop all communication with me, and leave me wondering what happened for half a year.

"The not-good kind," he says with the hint of a smile, but he turns serious when he sees that I'm not smiling too. He breathes out, then continues. "Remember when I said he was going to be the captain of the soccer team?" I nod, remembering it. Matt was so proud. "Turns out he was kicked off the team before it could happen. He was kicked off the team, because he was on drugs."

There's silence as I process what he said. "Okay," I say. "That sucks . . . but what's that have to do with you moving? With us?" I ask, guarded, bracing for the answer.

"He wasn't just kicked off the team," he says, struggling for words. "He was kicked out of school, because not only was he taking them, he was selling them," he admits. "There

was this . . . huge scandal, and he was in the middle of it all."
He waves his hand like the situation was out of his control.
And it was, just like his many moves.

"That's crazy. So you moved to Houston for him, not
your dad's job."

"Yeah." He nods. "Yeah, it was—it was really bad. Like,
he-was-in-jail bad," he says, squeezing the steering wheel
and taking deep breaths, and I want to be there for him, I
want to reach out and comfort him, but I don't know how to
anymore. I don't know how to comfort him *for this*, because
this was not part of our history. He never told me. And I'm
not sure which hurts more—that he kept it from me, or that
he's going through this all alone.

"It was my mom who decided to move," he continues,
looking ahead. "I mean, she went crazy when she found out,
she was so . . . she stopped working, stopped going out. She
was crushed. It was . . . it was really hard." He squeezes his
eyes shut and opens them again. "She just stopped being
a mom, you know? And my dad just went on working like
nothing happened, and I hated him for it," he continues,
his voice full of emotion and malice. "I mean, our lives have
always revolved around him, and when one of us does something stupid and actually needs him, he's gone. I hated him
those days, how his life seemed so easy when we were just
falling apart." He closes his eyes and breathes deeply.

I always knew he was closer to his mom and brother than
his dad, but I never realized it was that bad. He never told

me. I'd met his dad a handful of times at dinners and stuff, but he was never overly friendly with me, like his mom was. I can't imagine how Matt must have felt. And I can't imagine how they had me over for dinner, acting perfectly normal, when all of this was happening.

I remember one time when Matt made a big production of taking me on a picnic instead of having dinner at his place, like it was planned. Was that because his mom was depressed? Was it all happening and I didn't see it?

"Why didn't you tell me?" I ask softly, because why didn't he let me in? Why didn't he trust me?

He looks at me and his eyes, though blocked by the glare of his glasses, are red and I can tell it's hurt him to go back there. I get why he didn't want to remember, but I have to know.

"At first I didn't want to involve you," he says, looking down, then back up. "It's embarrassing, you know? Having your brother in jail? Especially after everything I'd told you about him, how much I looked up to him?" He pauses, then adds emotionally, "God, I hated him *so much* for letting me down. . . ." He sniffles, then continues. "I didn't want you to see this fractured part of my life. I was already such a sad case with the moving and crap, I didn't want you to feel sorry for me. And, I mean, I'm not used to being so close with someone. It's always been me and my family, so when this all happened, I just . . . was scared."

"You were scared to tell me?" I ask, raising my voice a

little because I told him everything, *everything*. And he didn't let me in on the one huge thing he was going through.

"I know it sounds stupid, I get that now, but I was scared and so preoccupied with everything. . . . I didn't want to screw us up by bringing in my mess," he says, getting the words out quickly and leaning in toward me. I lean back a little, keeping the space between us. "I wanted us to be just the way we were. I *needed* us to be just the way we were—it was the only thing keeping me together when everything else was going to hell. You were that important to me. You still are."

"How could I be that important to you if you kept something so huge from me?" I demand, my heart racing as I realize our relationship wasn't as real as I thought it was. He never told me everything, never really let me in. "I could have helped, I could have listened."

"I know, I know," he says, his voice rising. "The thing is, I tried to tell you, but I couldn't even do that right."

"Wait, when? How?"

"At Starbucks the one day? I gave you the note?"

I think back to our trips to Starbucks. There were a few. Once, though, he gave me a note found on a recycled napkin that simply had a list of medications. "What's this?" I asked him, and he shrugged and looked down at the coffee nestled between his hands.

"You gave me a list of drugs. That you found. On the floor. At a Starbucks," I state evenly.

"I hoped it was something," he says shyly, looking back at

his hands, always at his hands.

"A list of drugs? How was I supposed to know what that meant?" I practically yell.

"I don't know! I don't know. I tried . . . you know I'm not great at . . ."

"Communicating," I finish for him.

"Right. Yeah. And then the note before I left . . ."

"Wait, the note you found at school, about going to jail for stealing lunch from the cafeteria? *That* was supposed to be a hint?" I ask. "Matt." I breathe heavily, seeing how much he tried, but didn't. "You could have just told me. A sentence, that's all it would have taken," I say. "I mean, just like tonight. You could have told me all of this at the party, but you had to make it this big production with reenacting a night. I just want you to be honest and stop hiding from me."

He balls up his fists and covers his face, pushing his glasses up. "If I could go back, I'd change everything," he says, his voice low.

"You lied," I yell. "You kept things from me and lied. You say you were happy with me, but how could you have been when it wasn't a real relationship? You can't be in a half relationship with someone. You just can't."

He removes his hands and nods his head, and he looks hurt, wounded, but I have to keep going.

"I mean, even your moving because of your dad's job was a lie."

"It was easier than telling you everything. It was

believable, so I went with it," he says, resigned.

"So what happened," I demand, crossing my arms across my chest. I want to know the end of the story.

"With my brother?" he asks, and I nod. He looks uncomfortable, but he continues. "My mom decided we'd move to Houston to be closer to . . . everything. Eventually my dad gave in. When I realized how shitty things were there, I wanted to tell you. I missed you *so* much. But by that point, my parents wouldn't let me. Seriously. I mean, it was that bad," he says, and I search his eyes for more.

"I mean, he was looking at a few years in prison, and he had people coming after him. Like, dudes trying to break into our house for money Chris owed them," he says, shaking. "So I couldn't tell you. I didn't want you part of that."

"Seriously?" I ask, seeing this as something out of a movie, not someone's life. It's horrible.

"Seriously. Everything sucked. Everything. I was constantly scared or miserable. At home my parents wanted to murder each other when they didn't want to murder Chris. At school no one talked to me. I was the new kid, and I didn't care to meet anyone, so I guess that was my fault. I never tried. . . . I was so angry, just so angry at myself for what I did to you, and at my brother, for what he was doing to us, and just . . . everyone. I couldn't handle it. He's my brother, you know? I never thought . . . I never imagined this would happen."

"I really wish you would have told me. I would have been

there for you. Jake would have been, too."

"I know, I know you would have. It's my biggest regret, not telling you. Because if I did before I left, I would have still had you. But once there . . ."

"You couldn't."

"I couldn't." He shakes his head. "My parents didn't want to get you involved, in case of anything . . . but really I think they were just embarrassed."

"Wait . . ." I pause, looking back at him. "If you knew all of this was going on, why were you okay with us trying long distance? Why didn't you just end it then? Not that I wanted you to, but . . . why didn't you?"

"I didn't want to! I thought, or I guess, I hoped, once we got there we'd see it wasn't as bad as we thought. That things could just return to normal. I mean, part of me even hoped we'd move back . . . I don't know, I couldn't do it. I didn't want to hurt you." He's twisting his watch again.

"Didn't want to hurt me?" I ask, pushing him.

"Yeah . . ." he says, combing his hair back and leaning against the headrest. His eyes are scanning the roof, possibly looking for answers there. "I didn't know how bad my brother's situation would be. Like I said, I wanted to tell you once we got there, but . . ."

"But you couldn't," I sarcastically finish for him.

"Right."

I stare at him, waiting for more, more of an explanation, because that's not good enough. Yes, he had a hard time, and yes, I feel bad for him, but there has to be more. Why didn't he just end it once he got there? Why leave me hanging? I don't know if it's his story or my pent-up emotions, but I feel my heart start pounding.

"That makes no sense, Matt," I cry out. "So you just stopped talking to me? Instead of doing anything, once again? It's such a cheap way out. Did you really think that would work? I *loved* you." I feel tears falling down my face, mingling with the raindrops, and I'm not sure which is dripping onto my shirt, and I don't know how I got from sad to angry to sad again so quickly. He drops his head in his hands and I know he feels helpless, but for once I don't care.

"I know, I know," he says, turning back to me with fire in his eyes, and I feel how close the car is around us. "Don't you think it hurt me, too?" He raises his voice. "*I* was the one being the bad guy. I had to live without you, too."

"Matt. I thought we were still dating," I yell, letting him hear the words, really hear them. "We never broke up, so I never knew where we stood, and it killed me. I didn't want to let go because I just *knew* you'd come back into my life. And then I felt so stupid when you didn't." He's silent, listening to what I'm saying. Everything hurts, everything. "So why not break up with me then? End it instead of just . . . disappearing?" I demand, breathing deep and painful in my chest.

"I didn't want to!" he practically shouts. "I *wanted* us to work, even though I knew we couldn't. And I just . . . I didn't . . . couldn't break up with you. I don't know." He exhales. "I guess I felt that if I just disappeared, you'd go on with your life and forget me. I didn't want to ruin your senior year of school with a long-distance boyfriend who had to attend court sessions regularly, and pay off debts his brother owed."

I pause. "What debts?"

He squeezes his eyes shut again. "He was selling drugs. He bought them from this guy, and the guy wanted to be paid. That's why the guy was coming after us, because Chris never finished selling them." He opens his eyes and looks at me. "This is why I didn't want to tell you. It's embarrassing and . . . insane. So, yeah, I tried to disappear from you because I didn't want to bring all of this up."

"That's crazy. People were coming after you?" I ask gently. "I can't believe . . . I can't believe you went through all of that."

"Yeah," he says. "But I know it's not an excuse."

"No," I say. "But still." I think about how different our years were. We were both angry and alone. If we had each other, it might have been better. Not perfect—especially not in his case—but better. "And the letter?" I ask, because I have to.

His face loses the intensity and he drifts back into himself. "Was really stupid, I know. I told you, I do stupid things and I can't communicate like a normal person."

"It was beyond stupid."

"Jake sent me a message I had to respond to—"

"And you didn't feel like you needed to respond to *any* of mine?" I ask. Hearing that he'd talk to Jake and not me wasn't any easier the second time.

"His was about you. He said I needed to give you closure. It was the first text he sent me that didn't threaten me, or say I was a horrible friend. He said I owed it to you."

"Oh," I say, because it's all I can. His face is open and honest, and despite being fully clothed, I feel exposed. I pull myself together closer, tighter.

"I wanted to give you closure."

I want to believe him, I want to think he meant it sincerely. But I see the letter again, not in his handwriting, but in some stranger's, and I can't help but get angry. Because it was so far from an apology, because it never gave me any sort of the closure he hoped for. "So you sent me a note you found on the ground that said some guy was sorry to some girl."

"Yes . . ."

"And you thought that would make everything better."

"It was a stupid decision."

"You could have done *anything at all* and you decided to do that," I repeat.

"I didn't know what to say!" he protests, facing me again. "What do you say after so much time? I realized how much of a mess I made. I realized how wrong I was, but I didn't want to . . . involve you anymore. And I still wasn't allowed to tell you the truth. So I thought you'd rather hear something, but not necessarily something from me. I'm sorry. I'm really, really sorry."

"This is just like the notes before you left. You could have told me. You could have talked to me. Why can't you talk to me?" I practically cry. "Why can't you *trust* me?"

He turns to me and his eyes are soft and he's holding his emotions back. "I'm so sorry. I should have trusted you, I really should have. While I was gone, I realized that it would have been better having someone I loved in my life, as broken as it was, than no one at all."

"You just realized that?" I explode. It's all been trapped in my chest, begging to be released, and now it's avalanching out. "I knew that from the start, but not anymore. I can't *trust* you. You took that away from me when you left, when you lied to me. You took everything away. I mean, look at me, I can't even take off my shirt without freaking out." I point to my wet shirt to emphasize the point. "You were the good one, the one who showed me not all guys were jerks. And then you completely changed," I cry. "You have no idea how much you meant to me, and how I felt when you left. I used to stay awake at night going over everything—over and over again—trying to figure out what went wrong. Why you weren't calling me." I pause, then face him. "I didn't even know if you were alive. Did that ever cross your mind?"

He's silent, shaking his head no. "Ella, no one has ever cared about me the way you did. I'm so sorry."

"Sorry isn't good enough," I state, because it isn't and it never will be. I want him to know how I felt then, how he left me feeling rejected and confused and just...completely alone. That was the worst, how alone it left me feeling. How I didn't feel like trusting anyone after him, after Nick. How I lost the enthusiasm and strength he helped build up.

"How's your brother?" I ask simply, because despite my anger at Matt, I'm not a monster, and I want to know. I still care. "And be honest."

"Turns out he wasn't the mastermind in the drug ring, just a participant," he says bitterly. "They caught the main guy that was harassing us . . . and my brother is out on probation for now. He's being closely monitored, obviously. . . ."

"That sucks," I say, because it does. Because, our problems aside, that whole situation is terrible, and not something I'd want anyone to go through.

"Yeah . . . My parents are still there, and they're . . . okay. My mom convinced me to come back here."

"She *convinced* you?" I ask, looking at him.

"Kind of," he admits, softly meeting my eyes. "I wanted to, but I also felt bad leaving them. And I didn't want to hurt you again. But she said it might make me happy." He looks out the window into the night.

"I would have been there for you," I say, one last time.

"I know."

"But do you?"

"Yes." He says it solidly, turning to me. I shake my head

and look away, holding the tears back. I've shed too many on him. He reaches over and tries to take my hand, but I pull it back quickly. He should know to never touch lit dynamite, and this time I'm the dynamite. He looks at my hand, and then pulls his back slowly. "I know I screwed up, and I know you owe me nothing, but I'm here now and I'll do anything to make this better. I don't want this to be the end."

"But how can I trust you?" I ask gently.

"I'm talking to you now. No notes, no hidden messages, it's just me. I don't want to be that guy anymore. I want to tell you everything. I want you and everything you come with."

"It's not enough," I say again, because it's not. They're just words. I feel trapped, claustrophobic, and I'm not sure if it's because of the car. I want to roll down the windows and let air in, but the rain will come, too. There's always rain after.

"Ella, please. Just give me another chance."

"I can't."

"El—"

"I'm really glad things at home are getting better, I really am," I say, breathing in and pushing back my tears. "But I'm leaving, Matt. It's my turn to leave. In three months I'll be gone and you'll know what it's like to be left behind."

"Where are you going?" he asks, confused, as if the thought of me leaving never crossed his mind.

"Tallahassee. I'm going to Florida State."

"Oh," he says, and the single syllable contains so much more than two letters. "I just thought, I mean, I guessed . . . never mind."

"Yeah," I say. "You didn't think about that, did you?" Though I've been looking at him this entire time, I never really *looked* at him, never met his eyes. It was too hard. But for this—for this I have to, and it breaks my heart. "Please just let me leave."

He opens his mouth to say something, but closes it again. Because he knows I'm right.

"I'll take you back to Meg, I guess," he says, turning slowly toward the steering wheel.

I nod, looking ahead out into the night. When at one time I thought the night held endless possibilities, now all I see is darkness and dead ends. The magic and mystery are gone.

Our conversation ends with a bang, and I almost expect the neighbors to wake up, turn on their lights, and wonder about the explosion that just occurred in the shadowed car behind the school. But no, no one feels the crumbling but us. The moments stretch on between our words and the engine starting, and we're left with the hollow voice of the night. The cicadas are out, but they sound more like noise than music.

And it seems only right that the same place our relationship started is also the place where it once again ends.

CHAPTER 12

THEN
10:45 P.M.

"So," I whispered, catching my breath after getting off the roof and landing, somewhat easily, on the stairs. "You lead," I said, nodding toward Jake. He smirked back and dug into his backpack and produced two small airplane bottles of rum.

"Liquid courage, eh?" I eyed Jake, wondering how much more he had in his bag of tricks. Normally I'd worry about his alcohol intake, but with skinny-dipping on the horizon, the alcohol actually looked tempting. And I hated myself for thinking that.

Jake took a swig from one bottle, and then passed the rest to Meg. He gave the unopened bottle to Matt and me.

"Well . . ." Matt said, twisting the lid open. "Bottoms

up?" He took a big gulp and then handed me the rest. I took a deep breath, held back my head, and downed the liquid. Despite it being cold, it burned, forming flames inside my body. I gagged, wanting to get the fire out, but I knew vomiting wouldn't help. I swallowed it, extinguishing the flames, but the nausea didn't go away.

"I'm never doing that again," I whispered. Meg threw her arm over my shoulders and squeezed. We were in it together, it seemed. As soon as we packed the booze back into its bag, Jake took off toward the pool, and we followed obediently.

The pool was next to the building, closer to the forest surrounding the school than the street. A thin, metal fence was around it, but it was easy to hop. We'd all hopped taller fences before; earlier that night, in fact. Lampposts on each corner illuminated the area, casting a shadow on the water. Once inside, we all stopped in front of the pool, waiting for someone—Jake—to make the first move.

"Showtime," he said, stripping off his shirt and pants, leaving his boxers on. He was pale with clothes on, but without them he was ghost white, almost translucent.

"Honey, you really need a tan," Meg said, shaking her head.

"And ruin this body?" he asked, and just like that, turned around and jumped into the pool. We remained frozen until he surfaced.

"WOOAAHH, feels great!" he said, tossing water from his hair as he broke the surface. "Who's coming with me?"

Meg took her shirt and pants off and jumped in next. I tried to remember if I'd shaved my legs. Check. I also thanked myself for choosing a black bra and matching underwear. Simple, but classic. I always wore nice under-garments to parties. It wasn't like I planned on hooking up with someone; I just liked looking good under my clothes. It made me feel more confident.

"So . . ." Matt said, looking at me. The night was dark, the pool barely illuminated. I was glad he couldn't see the redness spreading across my cheeks.

"I guess it's our turn?" I picked at my shirt, waiting to see what he'd do. To my surprise, he turned away, motioning for me to go first, and it made me smile. It was something Nick never would have done. Quickly, I stripped off my shirt, pushed down my jeans, and jumped in.

The water did feel good—warm, but not too warm. I broke the surface and swished my hair back, rubbing the water from my eyes. Meg and Jake were already on the other side of the pool talking in hushed tones and very close to each other. Secrets we weren't quite allowed to hear. Behind me, the water crashed, and I turned around to see Matt bob-bing his head up.

"So," he spit out, wiping water off his face. "This is new." Even with the alcohol coursing through my veins, I still felt self-conscious. I was underwater, but if he looked down, he'd see everything. *Everything.* I doggy-paddled by, but not too close.

"Yeah. You know—we may be the first people to swim in our underwear here," I said, trying not to blush.

"Well, I feel very honored to be among the first." He grinned. I noticed he was swimming at a bit of a distance from *me*. What did he have to be self-conscious about? I couldn't see much, but his skin looked soft and suntanned. His arms, though skinny, had the hint of muscle, probably from playing bass, and I couldn't stop staring. Goose bumps pimpled his shoulders as he bounced up and down. We made waves with our hands and the water splashed up gently against our bodies, despite the distance between us.

"As well you should. Only so many people have seen me in my bra." Did I just say that? I stopped bobbing and swam closer. He smiled in reply.

"I wish I'd known we were doing this; I would have dressed better," he said, pushing the water with his hands.

"You looked fine tonight," I answered, smiling.

"No, not that. I'm pretty sure I'm wearing Batman boxers right now."

I laughed, blushing as I thought of him and his lack of clothing. "I expect to see those by the end of the night."

"Oh no. Only a select few get the privilege of seeing my underwear."

"How does one become privileged?" I asked. The words were coming out of my mouth without me thinking. As if it wasn't me talking. With anyone else, I would have been mortified, but with the blackness of the night, the quiet behind us, and Matt's proximity—I felt unconquerable.

"Years of training. Advanced degrees. Chocolate-chip cookies."

"Chocolate-chip cookies?"

He grinned, floating above the water mere inches from me. "I really like cookies."

"I'll keep that in mind," I responded, taking him in. His face looked excited, open, and just as cute without the glasses. "Can you see okay?"

"Without my glasses? Yeah. I mean, I can't drive without them, but you're not a huge blur or anything."

"How many fingers am I holding up?" I asked, holding up three fingers above my head.

"Hmm." He paddled closer. "Eighty-two?"

"Close enough," I answered, giggling.

"I should thank you, by the way," he said, chin bobbing under the water.

"For what?"

"Taking me out," he said, completely earnestly. "I don't—I don't always do this stuff, just so you know. Like, drinking, skinny-dipping . . ."

"Oh god, I don't either. This is rare." I shyly looked down and caught him glancing at my bra. The light illuminated him just enough so that I could see the pink on his nose. I should have been nervous or outraged, but instead I felt . . . pretty. He *wanted* to look.

"I like it here. It's been a great night so far."

"Well, I'm glad you're here. It would have been really awkward had it just been me and . . . them," I said, pointing my thumb behind me.

"Speaking of . . ." He lifted his chin to indicate I should turn around. I scanned the water behind me and saw what I feared would happen.

Jake was pushing Meg's back against the pool wall and her legs were wrapped around his waist. Their faces were mashed together, not just kissing, but practically eating each other alive. It was as if they'd never kissed before. Her hands were exploring his back, searching for new territory to take over and claim as her own.

"That's . . . not good."

"I don't think they care about that right now," Matt said behind me.

"We should probably give them some privacy."

He nodded and started swimming in the other direction, toward the deeper end. We swam quietly until we reached the edge of the pool. "I can't stand here!" I said somewhat stupidly, as the water I was flailing around in was eight feet deep. None of us could stand there. I bicycle-kicked my legs to keep me afloat, trying to make it look more cool than childish.

"I've got you," Matt said, grabbing me by the waist. I yelped as his hands brushed across my bare stomach and pulled me closer. My heart was racing as I was caught in his arms, pressed against his chest. He started lifting me until I was literally thrown over his shoulder.

"Put me down!" I laughed, playfully beating my hands on his back.

"You asked for it." He picked me up and tossed me into the pool. I felt the water break against my body as I floated down, gulping in copious amounts of liquid along the way. When I reached the surface, I felt like my head was 90 percent liquid. Matt, of course, was grinning.

"You jerk," I half coughed, half laughed, trying to get the remaining water out of my mouth and nose. Seeking revenge, I swam back over and jumped on top of him, trying to push him down. It was amazing how much braver water—and, for that matter, alcohol—made me. I was in my underwear, but perfectly okay jumping on top of a guy. Who was I?

"No fair!" he yelled. He started tickling my stomach, which made me cry out. He had just figured out my Achilles' heel—I was incredibly ticklish. It was bad. Someone could just look at me and think of touching my stomach, and I'd laugh.

"Hey!" I shouted, gasping for air. I wrapped myself around his body to administer one final assault when I realized how . . . close we were. Really close. My stomach was against his, and my legs were wrapped around his waist. Our chests were rising and falling in sync. His lips were only a few inches away. He stopped too, and stared into my eyes. For a moment, I thought back to our moment on the roof.

The shock when we kissed. Our fingers touching. We were silent, staring at each other.

A beam of light crossed his face, and then another. His eyes snapped from mine to the other side of the pool, and then his body stiffened when we heard the siren.

"Are those cops?" he asked.

"What?" Jake called out, releasing Meg from his grip. "Oh shit, run."

I jumped off Matt and looked behind me to see flashlight beams weaving in and out of the buildings on campus. They hadn't spotted us yet, but with the noise we were making, it wouldn't be long. Someone must have heard us and called the police, despite that *never* happening. I felt Matt's hand close around mine as he raced to the side of the pool. I followed, pushing my arms and legs as fast as they could go. I looked back and saw that Jake was already out, and Meg was paddling by herself, almost there. I was panicked, but I still had a moment to register one fact— Jake didn't wait for her.

Matt's hand was still wrapped around mine as he led me over to the other side of the pool for our clothes.

"Just grab them and run," he said, picking up his shirt and putting his glasses back on. I grabbed my pants and shoes, and then wildly looked around for my shirt. The shirt Meg got me. I couldn't spot it anywhere. In the meantime, I picked up her clothes, just to be safe. Jake, wet, grabbed his own.

"Hey, hey you," we heard from the other side of campus. They'd seen us. I hated leaving my shirt behind, but I knew I had to. I glanced up at Matt, and he was looking in every direction, scanning the area and figuring out where to go next, so I jumped ahead and pulled him forward.

"Run," Jake said, crouched over. He led the way, once again. Interesting how the night brought us back to the beginning. At no point had I expected to escape cops not once, but twice.

We ran behind the building we had recently conquered and sprinted across the parking lot, back onto the street. The ground felt hard and rough against my bare feet. Pebbles stabbed into my soles, and I had to avoid a few pieces of broken glass. But the pain didn't make me stop. The entire time, Matt didn't let go of my hand. I was only slightly aware of the fact that we were running down the street in just our underwear. I didn't even want to think about what we'd be charged with if caught. Breaking and entering. Indecent exposure. Underage drinking. My parents would kill me. I looked over at Matt's face and could tell he wouldn't let that happen to us. His eyes held so much determination that he didn't even notice me looking. He only thought of escape. I could trust him.

We took a quick right onto the street where our cars were parked. They were still there, thankfully.

"My car," Meg called out from behind. I grabbed her keys from her pockets and threw them at her. She quickly unlocked the doors and we all jumped in. Matt and I huddled in the backseat, while Meg took the driver's seat and Jake sat next to her.

"Go, go," Jake yelled.

"Wait, no. They'd expect that," Meg said, out of breath. "Let's just stay here. They'll be looking for a car racing away. They don't know where we were parked. Let's just stay here for a while."

"And wait to get caught?"

"They won't find us here."

"Meg's right," I agreed. "They won't expect us to stay. They're probably just waiting to pull us over."

"Plus, we've all been drinking," Matt pointed out. Even though it was three against one, we still waited for Jake to answer. After a long, long pause, he finally sighed and nodded.

"Yeah, you're right. We'll stay."

We didn't turn the lights on. Instead, we sat in the dark, too afraid to talk or even move. The only light was from the streetlamp up the street and the house we were parked in front of.

"Car," Matt said. We all ducked down. It drove slowly up the street, and then passed us, not even stopping to take notice. We lifted our heads and sighed.

"We're going to do that every time, aren't we?" I asked.

"It's a good thing not too many cars come up this street." Lights hit Meg's face just as she finished speaking.

We ducked again, and the car passed quickly. "Spoke too soon." My heart was doing somersaults. It had no clue what to do—slow down, speed up. But despite everything, I actually felt safe. In Meg's car, I was where I belonged. I knew we'd be fine. I looked down and noticed that Matt's hand was still wrapped around mine. In the silence, I finally had a moment to think.

I'd never dated a good guy before. And then came Matt, who'd not only kissed me on the roof, but also held my hand the entire run back, just to make sure I wasn't far behind. Just to make sure I was okay. He never let go. He still hadn't.

I touched my lip and remembered the spark—the moment I knew we had something different. But it was all so soon, too soon. Could it just be the excitement of the night? The adrenaline pumping through us? Or real feelings?

And then there were Meg and Jake, who always showed the biggest public displays of affection, but ran apart when trouble approached. Relationships shouldn't be like that. And yet, something constantly brought them back together. What made a good relationship?

My breathing calmed as the minutes passed.

My skin felt sticky from the chlorine and I suddenly realized that I was still in my underwear. "We should put our clothes on," I suggested, feeling my face flush.

Matt looked down and quickly took his hand away from mine, realizing it was still there. He smiled sheepishly at me, as if apologizing for the mistake. My hand felt cold, empty, alone. Perhaps it was just the heat of the moment after all.

"I have your shirt, um, if you want it," he said, ruffling through his clothes. He handed me the shirt Meg gave to me earlier in the night. Relief spread through my body as I realized it wasn't lost. Of course he'd saved it as well.

I tossed Meg her clothes, and then put my own on. I hated the feeling of being wet under dry clothes. I knew wet patches would spread through my shirt, leaving marks, but at least I was covered up.

Still, we didn't talk.

Suddenly, a Flaming Lips song shouted out of Jake's phone. We all jumped as he quickly grabbed the phone out of his pocket and answered.

As he talked in one-word replies, his eyes darted back and forth from Meg to the outside. Two minutes later, he hung up.

"Who was that?" Meg asked without a pause.

"Elise."

"Elise from Wing King?"

"Yeah." He wasn't meeting her eye, staring intently at a tree instead.

I raised my eyebrow at Matt and he nodded in agreement. It was the calm before the storm. The questioning before the fight.

"Why is she calling you?"

"Because she wants to hang out. And that's okay because you're not my girlfriend anymore."

"Walk?" Matt whispered to me. Meg was already yelling her response, something about "knowing" and "not needing." I didn't want to hear any of it.

"Yeah," I answered. We quietly got out of the car and out onto the road again. Between cops and our friends' wrath, we chose the police.

"So . . . that was intense," he said once we crossed the street. I knew the road we were on well. It was small and looped around, so within ten minutes, we'd be right back where we started. At that point we could assess the situation and decide if it was safe to join them again. Small houses lined the street, each one more asleep than the last. Lights out, cars snuggled in the driveways. It seemed like we were the only ones awake.

"That's Meg and Jake."

"Are they always like that? It doesn't seem . . . healthy."

"No, they were good for a while. A long time. But their relationship was always a bit . . . much. They're both all-or-nothing people, you know? They put everything in, and expect to get everything out. And when you put that much into something, or someone, you get very . . . attached and emotional."

"They are very passionate."

"And you've only known them a short while." I bumped him with my elbow. "Wait until a year goes by. You'll be able to call their moods quicker than me."

"Yeah," he said, melancholy filling his one syllable.

"You *will* be here for a year, right?"

"Yeah, totally. I mean, I should be. We've never really been in a place for less than a year."

"Good. Because this is only night one." I smiled. He nudged me back. I wanted him to hold my hand again, weave his fingers through mine, but I didn't press.

"This has to make your wrist, right? I mean, cops were involved."

"Ha, yes, definitely." I nodded, sliding my finger along the bracelets and getting excited to add him to the mix.

"Tell me about one of them."

"Hmm," I said, looking down, trying to pick the perfect one. "Well, this one," I said, pointing to an orange one, "this one is from the other day when Meg and I passed all of our exams. We celebrated by going to the beach."

"That doesn't sound too crazy."

"They're not all crazy. It was just a really nice day. I mean, we only have one year left, so it was nice just . . . hanging out."

"I get that," he said. "I haven't been to the beach here yet. Actually, I've never lived by the beach, so I'm kind of excited to be so close."

"Where else have you lived? You don't really have an accent."

"It's what happens when you keep moving, I guess. I was

born in Virginia and we moved throughout the States for most of elementary and middle school. Then my dad got a job overseas and I spent the end of middle school and beginning of high school in various parts of Europe."

"I'd love to go to Europe," I mused.

"I'll bring you one day," he commented. Even though it was an empty promise, one said rushed after a night of magic, I still grinned at the thought. "What else would you love to do?"

"I don't know. . . ."

"Yes you do," he said, already knowing me all too well.

"I'd like to graduate high school and get into college."

"Other than that."

"I'd like to write a book, as you know." I paused. "And sing with a band."

"Really?"

"Yeah." I blushed. "I've never actually admitted that to anyone."

"Not even Meg?"

"Well, yeah, okay, Meg knows. She knows everything, though."

"That's awesome! How come you haven't? I mean, you're friends with a band."

"I'm not good, honestly. I can't really sing well. Also, I'm totally scared."

"Ella, you jumped into a pool practically naked in front of a near stranger tonight. If you can do that, you can sing onstage." He said it with such conviction, I almost believed him.

"Thanks," I said quietly. I pushed him with my shoulder. He tapped back and we both smiled, as if knowing it meant something completely different.

We walked in silence until he leaned down and picked up a sheet of paper from the ground.

"Another found object?"

"Another found object," he answered, unfolding the paper. It was scrunched up, folded into a swan. It felt almost wrong removing its wings to view the secret inside.

"So what's this one say?" I asked.

"A letter, it seems." He handed me the unfolded paper and then reached into his pocket for his phone. The light shone on the paper, allowing us to read the small block writing. Each word looked as if it were written hurriedly, as if the author wanted to get the note over with.

I'M SORRY ABOUT WHAT I DID AT THE PARTY. I DIDN'T MEAN TO HURT YOU. LET'S GIVE IT ANOTHER GO, OKAY?

"Yikes, what do you think happened?" I asked. Matt put his phone back in his pocket and folded the note back up.

"I'm guessing this guy—let's assume it was a guy because of the handwriting—did something awful at a party, and his girlfriend is not happy about it."

"Cheated on her?"

"I don't know. I'd say that too, but I don't think he'd apologize through a note if he did something that bad. You know?"

"Have you met high school boys?"

"Lest you forget, I am one."

"Well, let's just say not all are as good as you."

"You haven't seen my evil side yet," he said, tapping his fingers together with a villainous grin.

"Nice try. So no cheating. Maybe he said something behind her back?"

"That's what I was thinking."

"It's that whole macho thing. Guys say things to other guys to sound cool, but they rarely think about how their words will affect others."

"You've been through a lot, haven't you?"

"You're talking to the girl who was high fived, need I remind you."

"Guys really do that, don't they?"

"One of the problems with Jake and Meg. He's very much a guy in front of other guys. You know, bragging and all." It's one thing I hated that he did. Nick did it, too. I couldn't take it—I didn't get how Meg could.

"We're awful."

"Not all of you." I looked at him, hoping he got what I was saying. "I wonder what he said."

"Exaggerated about how far they've gone?"

"That sounds about right. Maybe it was something off the wall, like they had sex on the moon."

"That seems logical. I mean, I'd believe it," he said.

"Or at school."

"Or on the school's roof. Wait. Ewww."

"I don't want to think about that," I said, dismissing the thought. "I will say, this guy's really good at folding notes."

"Yeah, seriously. I've never gotten a note folded as neatly as this."

"Clearly you've dated the wrong girls," I said. "That should be another requirement next time you date someone. No pets or houseplants that might destroy the relationship, and must be able to fold notes into swans."

He laughed, looking over at me. "Right. I just need to find the perfect person now." I snuck a glance at him as we continued to wind down the road.

"Why do these notes and random objects mean so much to you?"

"I don't know. I guess . . . they remind me that people have stories, you know? I mean, I do, too, but they don't really go on after I move. I just start over. And, yeah, starting over can be cool, but when there's no history involved, it's also kind of . . ."

"Lonely?" I asked.

"A bit, yeah," he said, looking down and mussing up his wet hair. Bits of water splashed around.

"At least you have your brother," I tried.

He shrugged, then answered. "Yeah, we're pretty close. We've been through a lot together, with all the moving and stuff."

"Does he collect things, too? Other than ex-girlfriends."

"Nah, he adapts a lot easier than me. He's quicker at finding his group, or, more so, becoming the leader of a group."

"So he's one of those guys? Center of attention?" I asked.

"Well, let's just say he would have been able to get us the drinks at Shop & Shop," he said. "I go out with him sometimes, but his friends are a bit too wild for me. Like, this night is tame comparatively."

"Details," I pushed.

"Um . . . once he called me to pick him up from a field. I seem to recall him not wearing pants," he laughed.

"Oh wow," I giggle.

"But, I mean, he's not always like that. He just likes to fit in. So do my parents—my mom's big into entertaining, so she meets people easily. And my dad just really gets into his work."

"And then there's you," I said, seeing how different he was from his family. Maybe that's why he needed notes and memories—so he had a way to fit in, too.

"And then there's me," he repeated. "So, yeah, the notes and pictures I like picking up to see other snippets of the world. Like, see that people are happy and have all of these memories and lives. I guess it makes me feel closer . . . more involved." He paused. "God, I've never told anyone about this stuff. I'm sorry."

"No, no, don't be sorry. It's interesting," I said, but it was more than interesting. It was sad. He found his place in the world through other people's memories, not his own. How did someone live like that? "What do you do with them?"

"I have a shoebox of them. That's right, I'm classy like that," he fake joked. "I keep all these memories in a box." He paused, then said, "I don't know. Maybe it's time for me to stop."

"Well. For what it's worth, I'd like to see the box."

"Okay," he said, nodding. "You can be there when the swan note joins it."

I smiled and hoped, truly hoped, that Orlando might be the home he was looking for.

<><><>

When we got back, Jake was leaning against his truck, holding a lit cigarette. The smoke was dancing around his body as he sighed deeply. I knew nothing good was going to come from this. Jake only smoked when he was stressed or upset. Clearly his fight with Meg had gotten to him. And the fact that Jake was there and Meg wasn't worried me.

"You, come on, we're going," he said as soon as he saw us.

"You, who?" Matt asked.

"Matt, we're leaving."

"What happened? Where's Meg?" I asked.

"Ask your best friend. She'll tell you." I glanced over and

saw Meg still sitting in her car. She was staring ahead, visibly fuming.

"Jake, you can't drive. You've been drinking."

"El, seriously, I don't want to be lectured right now. So stop being the mother you always end up being, and leave me the hell alone." The words hit me hard, vibrating through my body. I stopped walking and just stared at him as I let his words sink in.

"Jake, leave her alone," Matt said.

"Screw you, Matt. You want to stay here with your new girlfriend? Fine, see if I care." Jake threw his cigarette on the ground, stepped on it, and got into his truck. Two thoughts battled in my mind. On one hand, I didn't want Matt near Jake at a time like this. I'd seen Jake angry before, but never mean like this. But on the other hand, I wanted someone to look after him, make sure he didn't hurt himself. Jake revved his engine, presumably waiting for Matt.

Matt looked at me and then back at the truck. I spoke before he could, effectively deciding for him.

"You should go."

"Screw him. After what he said about you? And how he's acting?"

"I know, but . . . he's Jake."

"Yeah, and I don't know him as well as you do. I don't have to take care of him."

"But you're not the kind of person who'd just let him drive away," I said, turning around to look at him right in his eyes. He blinked, and then lowered his face.

"I'll . . . I'll call you later."

"Thanks."

"I . . . um . . . yeah, I'll see you." He turned around and ran to the car, making Jake go to the passenger side. No hug, nothing. Watching him go, I realized that he didn't have my number.

CHAPTER 13

NOW
11:00 P.M.

Matt and I are silent during the car ride back to Evan's party. I have nothing to say. I'm numb. Matt puts on music to fill the void, but it doesn't work. I know something is playing, something melodic with voices and instruments, but I can't concentrate on it. I'm focused on him. I'm conscious of every move he makes, every breath, every frown. I'm sure he's just as aware of me.

I text Meg to let her know that we're on our way back. I don't give her any details—I'd rather not get into them over the phone. It's as if she already knows, though, because she just responds Okay, I'll be outside, and leaves it at that. My phone vibrates again and I pick it up, expecting something else from her, but instead I see Jake's name.

Where r you?

Heading back to Evan's

I hope he gets what that means and leaves it at that. But of course he doesn't, because as soon as I put my phone down, it vibrates again.

What happened?

I take a deep breath and out of the corner of my eye see Matt looking at me, watching me. I'm sure he knows who I'm talking to, or at least can guess. And it's awkward thinking about him, writing about him, when he's right there. And I have that always-present urge to tell him everything, but I can't. Especially now.

As I raise my thumb to start typing to Jake I realize that what I say will affect him, too. That without me, there won't be a Matt and Jake reunion. That I'm this strange building block that's deciding if our group can once again become whole.

I can't be that. Everything can't revolve around my decision. He left me. And while what happened to his brother and family is terrible, I still can't get past the fact that he lied to me. So it's his fault. Jake will have to understand that.

But still, how am I to compose all of that into one simple text? I shake my head and simply type:

Will call later.

And I hope that's enough. I look over at Matt and see him staring out at the road in front of us, watching the lights as they pass by. The rain has stopped, but everything looks slick, wet. He's so close and still so far away. I feel like this is it—this is the conclusion, the closure, I wanted. But I still feel a little piece of me breaking off, and a little part of me wanting to cry. Because once I get out of the car, it's officially over. The feeling of that washes over me—as soon as I'm out, I'm free of him.

But am I?

I think about when he left, about the good-bye we had the night before. It feels so different now, knowing he wasn't just leaving because of his dad's job. That the sadness he was holding back had to do with his brother, too. Did he know when he kissed me good-bye how much my heart was breaking? I know his was. I remember the tears in his eyes.

Even so, this good-bye seems much sadder.

We pull up to the house, and Meg's outside waiting for me, frowning. Her foot is tapping, her hands are on her waist, and I can tell she's using every ounce of energy she has to not run over to the car and punch Matt in the face. I almost let her.

When he parks, I look over and don't know what to say. There isn't much left to say.

"Ella . . ." he starts, looking down at his knuckles clenching the steering wheel. "I'm sorry."

"I know," I answer, because I do. Deep down I do believe he's sorry, that he regrets everything, but that isn't enough to make up for how I felt, for what I went through. *I'm sorry* just isn't enough of an excuse.

"It's just," he continues, turning to me, and I see the fear and hope in his eyes, "you're here for three more months. Just give me another chance. I'm not leaving this time, no matter what. And here would be a hell of a lot better if you were with me."

And now it's my turn to open and close my mouth and find no words coming out. Because it sounds so rehearsed, but still. He means it. "Matt—"

"Please," he cuts in. "At least think about it. I mean, even if you don't want to date or anything, at least let's try starting over. Like, as friends."

"We never were friends," I respond meekly, tugging at my bracelet. "I mean, not really. We were always more than that."

"So let's try, okay? Just . . . say yes."

My heart leaps from his pleading, from his question. We're back there. We're back to the beginning of the night, to the game we started. But saying yes was so much easier a year ago when I didn't know I could be that hurt. When

I didn't know how much each yes meant. This time it just seems like a pale comparison, a reminder of what once was and can never be again.

"I can't do that," I say, turning away to see Meg waiting for me, beckoning me.

His head slumps down, but he jumps back up, ready to try one more time.

"Just don't judge me for what my brother did. I'm not him."

"I know you're not," I say.

"And I won't be. Ever."

"Okay," I say, noticing the resolution in his eyes. I know he won't be—he's too good for all of that. But I can also see how everything he's gone through affected him. "I should go . . ." I say, feeling myself wanting to stay and talk more. I can't do that right now.

"You almost kissed me tonight."

"Matt—"

"That's it. That's all I wanted to say."

I take a deep breath and remember how it was on the roof. How close we were. How, were it not for the rainstorm—

And it is enough. I *did* want to kiss him. But it was before. Before I knew everything. Before I realized the closer he got, the harder it was. And we can't go back to before; this much was proven by everything going wrong tonight.

But I did want to kiss him. I really, really did.

"Okay, that and I really missed you," he admits, and I can't help but smile. His words are so simple now, so uncomplicated, and I kind of wish we started here instead of under this whole facade of re-creating the night.

"I missed you, too," I respond, giving him one more look before unbuckling my seat belt and opening the door. Enough.

I shut the door before he can say anything else, but I do stop to look back. He's staring at me, and even though it's dark, just like earlier in the night, I know his eyes are shining.

"What was that all about?" Meg asks, instantly by my side. She shoots him a look that could kill a weaker animal, and then pulls me away.

"We said some things that should have been said a long time ago."

The next time I look back, he's gone.

CHAPTER 14

THEN
11:20 P.M.

In the car, Meg let out all of her aggression on the steering wheel. "He's such an asshole," she yelled, slamming her hands. We were still parked on the street beside the school. We hadn't left yet; we weren't ready. With the mixture of alcohol and anger, I knew we'd be in trouble once she started the ignition. So I opened a bottle of water, handed it to Meg, and let her vent.

I sat in the passenger seat, looking out at the houses in front of us, sometimes glancing at her. I knew she just had to get everything out of her system, let it all pass before I could offer any sort of advice. Not that I had any, really. Jake was an asshole in so many ways, but she wasn't helping when she decided to kiss him. Not that I'd say that to her.

Meanwhile, I hadn't heard from the guys. I didn't let on, but I was worried. I was worried something had happened when they were driving. I was worried they were hurt. And part of me, a small part, wondered why Matt just left without anything more than a wave. No hug, nothing. But I decided not to dwell on that since there was other drama going on. There was no point in doubting something before it even started.

"I mean, he comes back to me, as if nothing happened, and promises to change. Promises to be someone different. And then he goes off with someone else."

"What?" I was lost in my own thoughts and had missed a bit of her rant. She'd been yelling for a while.

"Nothing has changed," she continued over my question. "He's still the same asshole he was before, despite his promises."

"What promises?"

"Just . . . stuff he's said."

"When? Tonight?"

Meg was silent as she stared down at her hands. "Things are complicated. This wasn't the . . . first time we hooked up since the breakup," she said quietly, not meeting my eyes.

"What?" I spat out, finally looking at her. "How could you do that, after everything you'd said?"

"It's hard! I mean, it's Jake. I hate him, but I love him. And every now and then, he calls me."

"But you broke up with him," I pointed out. "And for a good reason, don't forget."

"I know, and I'm glad I did. He was a crappy boyfriend, but . . . it doesn't mean I stopped loving him," she sighed. She looked defeated, dead behind the eyes, as if it hurt her to admit this. "He's dated a few girls since . . . you know. They only last a couple of days. Every time they break up, he comes back to me. And I let him. Every. Single. Time."

"But why? You know it's not going to last. You're better than this, Meg."

"I know, it's just . . . how do you think it makes me feel every time I see him with a new girl? I hate him. And then he comes to me, all cute and sweet, with these promises about changing. I know he won't, but . . . I can't say no."

I took everything in, letting the quiet steal our words. "I just . . . I don't see how a relationship like that could make you happy." She simply shrugged in response. "I couldn't handle it," I admitted. "I mean, I get that it's you guys, and that's how you work, but . . ." I trailed off, not ending my thoughts, because I knew they'd hurt her. How could she still trust him? And if she liked him so much, why live in a secret? So I settled on a different question. "Why didn't you tell me?"

"I didn't want you to be upset with me."

"Meg, I'll never be upset with you." But I was. What else didn't I know?

"It's also—I just didn't want to admit it. I hate myself for getting into this situation, for going back to him. And it's like . . . if I admitted it, said it aloud, it meant I was actually doing it. You know, becoming someone I hated."

"Don't hate yourself; hate Jake, if anyone. You deserve better than him." She looked sad, hopeless, and I couldn't handle seeing her like that.

I knew why she liked him. It wasn't just the looks or the attitude. He was just so . . . in control so often—it was like you wanted to be in on whatever joke he was thinking about. Go on whatever adventure he schemed. But still—that was all he could give her—a fun time and a small claim to fame. Nothing substantial, nothing emotional.

I didn't know what to do, so I hugged her tight and felt her body shake. I knew she was crying. We'd all been there. We'd all had those moments. She didn't have to hide from me. Her secrets washed away with her tears.

We stayed in the car for about half an hour. Having lived in the city my whole life, I knew there was nothing to fear. The biggest danger to us was bad boyfriends, not predators who lurked in the dark. That knowledge kept me protected, and happy. Especially in times when we were too drunk to drive.

Clucking interrupted our silence.

"Chickens?" Meg looked at me, surprised.

"What the— Oh wait, it's my phone. It's Barker." A few days prior, Jake and Barker had stolen my cell phone and decided to change their ringtones to something annoying so I always knew when they were calling. Jake picked an old locomotive sound; Barker decided on clucking chickens.

My heart skipped a beat as I pulled my phone out. Was he calling about the guys? Were they okay? Did he know anything? Why else would he be calling so late?

"Hey Barker, is everything okay?" My body literally slackened when I heard everything was fine. Okay. Good.

"Hey, I'm with Meg, I'll put you on speaker." I put my phone down and turned the speakerphone on.

"Hey Barker," Meg said.

"Hey guys. So, here's the deal. A bunch of people went over to One Spin after the party broke up, just to hang out." One Spin Records was the only remaining local indie record shop. It still sold CDs and records, as well as books and DVDs. To make up the money they lost after everyone started downloading music, the manager built a stage in the back for local bands to utilize, and for touring bands to host secret shows. He also had a small recording studio put in that most local bands took advantage of. It was significantly cheaper than most other places, and added a neat authentic (as in, kind of tinny) sound to the recordings. "I guess word got around about what happened, and the manager invited all the bands to play tonight."

"Oh cool!" I answered, and then looked over at Meg. She wasn't as pleased. "When?" I asked tentatively.

"That's the thing. They want us on tonight. As in, right now."

"Right now?" I questioned.

"Well, like in a half hour, but you know. Anyway, I wanted to let you two know. I just talked to Jake and he said he wasn't with you all anymore. Should I ask what happened?"

"Jake was Jake," Meg said, her words full of venom.

"Not surprised," Barker groaned.

"Yeah, um, I don't know if we can make it," I started. I wanted to, I did. I really wanted to see Matt again, but my allegiance was to Meg. I'd do what she wanted. I couldn't leave her now.

"No, no. We'll be there. Give us half an hour. We wouldn't miss it," Meg said.

I looked at her wearily, wondering why she'd want to go, why she'd want to see him again. She said she was a masochist when it came to him, but this seemed to be going too far.

"Sweet. Okay, see you soon. Gabby's glad you're coming; she doesn't want to be the only girl there. For some reason, she thinks no one else will show up. *But they will.*"

"Of course they will," I reassured Barker, although I really wasn't sure. It was late, after all. "See you soon."

"Later." I hung up the phone and stared at Meg. She knew what it meant.

"It's the night we said yes," she sighed.

"So? We don't have to do this. Also, didn't the game end when we all broke up?" She flinched at the words "broke up."

"Yeah, but I'm not turning back now."

"Are you sure?"

She pushed her hair back and then looked at me. "You like him, don't you?"

"Who?"

"Matt. I saw you with him tonight. And I saw your face light up when Barker said they were playing. I've known you for how many years? I've never seen you so . . . excited . . . over a guy."

I didn't know how to react. I did feel differently about him, I just didn't know what it meant yet. It was so soon; I still barely knew him. But when we were walking, or swimming, I felt free to be who I was. I felt safe.

"He makes me feel like me."

Meg smiled to herself, I'm sure remembering a time she, too, felt that way. I wondered if that was how Jake made her feel. "It's decided, then. We're going. And, hey, Gabby's glad we're coming, apparently."

"So I heard," I sighed. It's not that I didn't like her, I did, I just still felt a bit off since finding out she'd known about Nick cheating. I hated how she'd betrayed me. But I loved Barker; I didn't want it to get in the way of our friendship. I'd lost the guys once—when Meg and Jake broke up—I really didn't want to lose them again.

"She's trying, that's for sure," Meg responded, referring to the numerous attempts Gabby had made in trying to get me to forgive her. The multiple texts with sweet messages that I deleted. The "I'm sorry" cake that, okay, we did eat.

"She makes it hard to hate her." I sighed.

"Do you ever think of what you'd do in that situation?" Meg looked over to me with one eyebrow cocked.

"What, like if I saw Jake cheating on you?" I asked.

"Yeah."

"I'd tell you. I'd call you right away," I answered automatically, but when I thought about it, I realized how hard it would be. Telling Meg that Jake was with someone else? It would have killed her. Could I have been the one doing the murdering? For the first time, I started to see Gabby's side.

"Same here, of course, but I bet it is hard. Telling someone that their boyfriend is cheating."

"I know. And I know that's why Gabby didn't tell me," I said, for the first time honestly. "It's a touchy situation; I get that. But still." I mulled Meg's question over.

"I saw her yesterday, and *again* she told me to apologize to you for her. Listen, she also said, and I found this interesting, she said she feels bad that she struck gold with Barker. Like she doesn't deserve it or something. I don't know." Meg paused and fiddled with her water bottle. "We always give her and Barker such a hard time about them being so cute and sweet together . . . maybe she felt bad because she *does* have it so good, and we, well, don't."

"Maybe." I pondered this. While all of that might have been true, it still didn't make the situation any less awkward. "I guess we'll see tonight."

"And I guess we'll see what happens with you and Matt."

She nudged me with her elbow. "If anything else, this night deserves a bracelet," she said, lifting her wrist up. I matched mine to hers and smiled, feeling a bit like a superhero. "Oh, hey, we should get going. I'm good to drive now."

"Okay," I said, erasing Gabby from my mind and replacing her with happier images of crooked black-rimmed glasses, random notes, and hands being held.

As Meg put the key in the ignition, she looked down at her wet clothes. "Ummm . . . we should probably change first."

"Yeah." I looked down at my shirt. "My wet bra is kind of peeking through this shirt. We've had some amazing ideas tonight, might I say."

"Can we go back to your place? Grab some clothes?"

"My parents think I'm spending the night at your place. How about yours?"

"Oh. My parents think I'm spending the night at yours."

"So . . . wait. If both . . . where *are* we supposed to spend the night?" I questioned nervously.

"Oh shit." She paused. "We'll think of that later. Let's just get a move on," she said, waving off the question.

"Where to? Everything is closed. And I really don't want to go to One Spin in wet clothes."

"Well, there's one place that's still open."

I looked at her warily as she started the car.

CHAPTER 15

NOW
11:15 P.M.

Inside Evan's house, Meg and I crash on the couch. By now, most of the people have left his party, save one guy playing a video game, and a couple of people hanging out in the corner. Evan pulls up a chair to join us.

After I tell them about the night—in mostly full detail—they just stare at me.

"So what are you going to do now?" Meg asks, not giving me any indication of what she'd prefer to hear me say.

"Nothing?" I ask, but they stare at me until I'm more honest. "I don't know. I hate this." I lean back and close my eyes, hoping the answer will magically appear on my eyelids. "And I feel like I'm letting everyone down."

"Letting who down?" Meg asks, angling herself to face me.

"You guys? Jake? I don't know."

"Let Jake worry about Jake. Right now this is about you," Meg says, taking my hand. I squeeze hers back in appreciation.

"And it's clear you still like him," Evan points out, stretching his arms over his head.

I turn to face him and furrow my brows. "I'm not sure how you came to that conclusion from my story. How I 'still like him'?"

"Ella, I've done this whole act before, trying to convince yourself you're over someone when clearly you're not. Hell, for half my life I convinced myself I didn't like people I really did. It sucks. So don't lie to yourself."

"I'm not lying to myself," I say defensively, "I just don't know what I want right now. He did a crappy thing, and I'm not exactly ready to say it's all okay."

"Good, you shouldn't be," Meg interjects.

"I just don't know if it's all worth it, especially with me leaving," I admit, thinking about the look he gave me when I left the car. He was so disappointed.

"Are you willing to risk finding out?" Evan asks.

I think about what he asks, and honestly, I don't know. He's Matt.

"Hey, where'd the boyfriend go?" Meg interrupts, realizing the absence.

"Asleep. Actually, I should go check on him." Evan stands up and frizzes my hair. "Let me know what happens. And El, don't do anything I wouldn't do."

"Like kiss a girl?" Meg jokes.

"Love you too, sis," he says, his back to us as he walks to his bedroom.

Meg stares at me, squinting. "I wanted to wait until he was gone to yell at you."

"I knew you'd have an opinion on this."

"It's bullshit, you know."

"Excuse me?" I ask, stunned.

"Everything. Him keeping secrets, lying to you. About something so big, too. And, seriously, is it really that hard to make a phone call?"

"That's what I said," I point out.

"And, like, coming back here and hoping you'd take him back? After everything? Come on. You're not that stupid." I nod my head but her words kind of strike a chord. I'm *not* that stupid, but neither is she. And she's taken back Jake loads of times.

"I mean, I'm glad you got your closure and all, but it's over now, right? Just leave it there. You're leaving, anyway. College guys are in your future." And even though I'm listening to her, and even though she's saying the same things I said and thought earlier, it just feels different. Perhaps it's because it's coming from her. Perhaps it's because it's okay for her to go against her rules, but not me.

"But what if he *is* really sorry? I mean, we all make mistakes."

"El, he's *so* not worth it."

"And Jake is?" I cautiously ask.

"What?" she asks, taking her hand away. "What does Jake have to do with this?"

"Jake's made hundreds of mistakes and it's okay to take him back each and every time?" I'm not sure why I'm questioning her, but I need to know.

"Jake and I have nothing to do with you and Matt," she says quickly.

"I know, but still. Why with him is it okay, but with Matt it isn't? It's not like I'm considering taking Matt back, but why *can't* I, if I choose to?"

"Then why are you even asking?"

"I just want to know," I say, standing up for myself.

She straightens up and tilts her head to the side, a snake waiting to attack. "Jake's different and you know it."

"Is he, though?" I ask, turning to face her, crossing my legs on the couch.

"Yes. He's part of us, part of our group. And he's never done anything to hurt me *on purpose*."

"Meg," I reason, "he's flirted with other girls. In front of you. That's okay?"

"So what you're saying is it's not okay to flirt, but it *is* okay to just disappear and leave you worried for, like, a year?" she stammers.

"No, I'm just trying to figure out how they're different," I continue, pushing her. My cheeks are heating up. I know people are watching, but I don't want to stop. "Every time Jake does something stupid, you forgive him, and I never stand in the way. Because I want what's best for you, and what makes you happy. But Matt makes one mistake and we're quick to toss him out?"

"I thought you didn't want him back," she snaps, and she's mostly right. I don't even know *why* I'm arguing with her. But I just *need* to. I want to yell.

"I don't," I say strongly, "but I at least want the option. I feel like you're saying no without even giving him a chance. I'm *always* behind you every time you go back to Jake . . . I just want you to support me if I want Matt back."

"No, not when I think it's a stupid idea. Not when I think you'll get hurt again."

"Yeah, maybe I will, but maybe you will with Jake."

She presses her lips together and squints her eyes. Here goes.

"Fine, do what you want. Go say yes to him, or whatever. But next time he disappears, don't tell me that I was right. Because I'll already know." She sneers, and then stands up.

"Meg—"

"No, if you want to go back to him, go ahead. You value his opinion far more than mine, clearly," she yells, throwing her bag on her shoulder and stomping toward the door.

"What's that supposed to mean?" I ask, turning around to follow her.

"I spend *months* making you feel better, and then he says two words and you listen to him?"

"Meg, it's not like that." I'm used to her anger, I've seen it before, but it's never been directed at me.

"Then what is it like, Ella? Huh? Explain it to me."

"I *always* take your side, I *always* agree with you. I'm just trying to make my own decision for once, and I want you to be okay with it."

"Because I made all of your other decisions? It was my decision that you date Nick? And Matt?"

"No, it's just—"

"Was it my decision that you move away to college?"

"No!" I say, then pause. "Wait, is *that* what this is about?"

"No, of course not," she says, but I think it is. I think there might be more.

"Meg . . . you know I'm not leaving because of you, right? I just wanted—I just *want* to get away. To start over somewhere new."

"So? Go ahead and make your new life. Mine here will be just fine," she says with a cross of her arms.

"Meg—"

"I'm going to find Jake," she interrupts me. "Who'll never just disappear. Who will tell me if something is up with his family. Who cares too much to do shit like that," she yells before slamming the door behind her. I'm pretty sure everyone in the state heard her. I slouch back on the couch and crumple. A lump is forming in my throat, but I don't want to cry. Not here.

Does she think I'm going to disappear like Matt?

Raking my fingers through my hair, I sigh. This was not how I wanted the night to go. This is not what I wanted to happen. Why was I fighting with her? Why did that just come out of me? Was it because I meant it, or was it something else? She is right, he did a crappy thing. But so has Jake, and she knows it. And now I've lost all of them.

I don't think my heart can handle any more of this.

And I think back, again, to Matt leaving, and all of the secrets he held. I can see the truth behind Meg and Jake's relationship, but how could I not have seen what was going on back then? How could I have been so blind to how Matt was feeling? There was the time at his house when his mom was in the kitchen, but didn't even say hi. She just walked back up to her room, and Matt assured me she was feeling sick. He knew about Chris then, didn't he? And when he said that, I knew I saw something else in his face, something more, but I didn't want to ask because it seemed private.

I should have asked.

"Play?" the guy on the other side of the couch asks, handing me an Xbox controller. I eye him, wondering why he thinks I'd be interested in playing when my best friend just stormed out on me. When the love of my life is back and I can't stand to be by him. But unlike them, this guy, this stranger, isn't even looking at me. He's not expecting anything from me. And for once, that feels kind of good. So I take the controller and press the Start button.

He's playing a game where a zombie invasion has taken over Earth. My job, as Player Two, is to kill all the zombies until only humans are left. I love video games—it's sort of my guilty pleasure—so I figure, what the hell, and start. It might feel good to lose myself in something else.

And it does. I concentrate on the zombies, not my thoughts. I click the button intensely and know my score is rising. I'm in a trance, seeing only the game. My hand is one with the controller.

But I'm not that good, and the zombies fight back. They're biting and scratching and teething. They're all over me, like ants crawling up my body. I try to push them off, but I can't. I shoot madly with the gun, but it's not working. They keep multiplying, taking over.

While I'm getting chewed on, giant yellow letters appear on the screen: **YOU'RE DAMAGED!**

The thing is, I already know that.

It started early, when I was the third wheel and the side-kick to Meg and her relationships, a role I never quite grew out of. And then there was Nick and the high five and the cheating. My relationship with him layered me with experiences I didn't want to make a part of me. I hated that he had a say in who I was becoming. I hated that I let his actions affect me. Then Matt came along. I had some notion of him being sort of the anti-Nick, but he hurt me too. And I started to worry they all would.

I didn't know who—or what—to trust anymore. Even Gabby let me down, so I started to wonder who would next. Jake? Meg? I started doubting myself, going back to where I was more comfortable—going along with the stream instead of creating my own tide. I stopped daring myself to live. Even tonight I followed Meg to the party when I would have preferred to stay home. I followed Matt even when I wasn't sure if I should.

So what do I do now? I have no one to follow—I just have me.

It feels weird and lonely, but also . . . new. And real.

I feel the strength return to me, the one that came when I confronted Matt, and, just now, Meg. If I can stand up to them, maybe I can do more. Maybe I can dare myself to say yes. I've been living through Matt's found objects habit for so long; it's time to let go of that and leave my own mark. Stop writing about people and write about me.

I can keep going the way I was, keep ignoring everything that's happened and just move away. I can continue going with the flow. Or I can change. I can make decisions for myself. I revamped my plan once, I can do it again. I can start creating my own future again and move forward. I can stop dragging my baggage around. I can be strong. I can laugh.

I tug the bracelet on my wrist and know what I have to do.

I watch my video game character get eaten and stabbed. And instead of flinching or mourning, I accept his damage and move on, as I should have half a year ago when Matt left. I put imaginary bandages on him and let him continue killing zombies, just as I'll keep fighting. I'll move on to my next stage without the sorrow and pain I've held on to for so long. Whether it's with Matt or not, we'll see. But it's my decision. I may be damaged, but I'm okay.

The yellow letters flash on the screen again, signaling that my game is over. I didn't win, but I did beat the first level. Tomorrow I'll beat another and then another until one day there won't be any zombies in my path.

CHAPTER 16

THEN
12:00 A.M.

"Walmart!" Meg shouted proudly as we pulled into the parking lot. It was only about a mile away, so the journey was a quick blast of loud music and fast driving. We needed the escape. The chance to feel like we were flying.

"I can't believe we're actually getting new outfits for the night," I grumbled as we got out of the car. The parking lot was mostly empty with a few straggling cars here or there. They probably belonged to employees and insomniacs.

"Why not? We've done it before."

"Yeah, but never at midnight."

Inside it was freezing. I shivered as we walked through the doors, passing the spot where an employee usually greeted us. It was always the same white-haired man; he was there so often, I almost thought he lived there. It seemed like a boring, monotonous job to me, but he seemed to love it, constantly offering smiles and conversation. He wasn't there tonight, though. As familiar with the store as we were with our own homes, we walked to the right, toward the women's section. We came here often for odds and ends—pens, hair ties, snacks for movie theater excursions.

"Remember when we played hide-and-seek here?" I asked as we walked past some clothes.

"And that lady yelled at Barker for hiding under the women's clothes rack. That was hilarious."

"Not as hilarious as finding you and Jake making out in the camping section. I'm pretty sure that didn't count as hiding," I said, shaking my head.

"You were taking too long to find us!" she protested, just as she had back then, and I laughed.

We walked through the aisles, touching clothes here and there. We'd feel the fabrics, as if they'd answer our prayers and say, *Yes, we are the perfect shirts for tonight's adventures.*

"So what are you thinking?" I asked Meg, holding up a blue shirt to my body.

"I don't know," she said, putting back a skirt. "Something nice, but not *too* nice."

"Too nice, like we went out of our way to go to Walmart to get new clothes."

"Exactly."

"Oh my god, look at this." I held up a pink taffeta dress that looked like something my mom wore in the '80s. It had long sleeves, small shoulder pads, and very bright, shiny fabric.

"You *have* to try that on."

"No way. It's terrible." Meg pouted until I relented. "Okay, fine, only if you try on something equally as heinous. You have to say yes," I taunt. We quickly forgot our original mission, and instead concentrated on finding ridiculous ensembles. We were wasting time, but we needed the distraction. Meg was active again, out of her melancholy funk. I wanted to keep her that way, so I didn't mind spending a few minutes looking for ugly outfits. And besides, I *did* kind of want to look nice for Matt.

"How about this?" she asked, picking up a brown-and-black leopard-print jumpsuit.

"*Yes.* Who would wear that?" I asked, touching the horrendous outfit.

"A backup dancer for Lady Gaga? Anyway, have you seen the red carpets? I mean, celebrities wear some ugly things. And yet they manage to get away with it." Meg paid attention to award shows and red carpet galas as if they were sporting events.

"I wish I was like that sometimes."

"Right?" she said. "I think the difference is self-esteem. They wear something ugly, and act like it's the most beautiful thing in the world. And it ends up looking that way to everyone else. I'll wear something ugly and cower in fear. So I just wear something nice to feel nice. It's an odd circle, I guess."

"*You* cower in fear?" I asked, eyeing her.

"You know what I mean."

"I know, I know," I said. "So, essentially, you don't have to dress pretty to look pretty. It's a matter of . . . conviction or something like that."

"Yeah . . ."

"Which sounds so much better in theory. Because I'd just as easily wear pajama pants to school, then."

"You already do sometimes," she pointed out.

"I did on pajama day! You'll never let me live that down, will you?"

"Nope! Although you did give me a great idea."

"What's that?"

"We don't have to dress nice to look nice. So let's not dress nice."

"Meg, if you suggest wearing these outfits we're currently holding to the record store, I'm walking out and leaving you here."

"No, not that. Let's just wear something comfortable rather than something nice. You know? Go low-key. As if the event isn't that important."

"So, head games."

"Sort of. Only it'll leave us more comfortable than we are now. What I wouldn't give for a sweatshirt."

"It's like a hundred degrees out," I argued.

"That's beside the point."

"Okay, so let's grab some comfortable clothes, and try those on with our ugly outfits."

"Sounds good."

We scoured the store and came up with options. I settled for a plain black racerback tank top, as I needed one anyway. Meg picked up a loose-fitting plain black T-shirt. Our jeans, despite previously being soaked, had dried by that time, so we didn't need to replace them.

I came out of the dressing room in my pink ensemble and laughed. Just laughed. I couldn't believe someone would not only try on, but purchase, the dress. I waited patiently for Meg.

"Introducing . . . Megdonna!" she shouted from her dressing room. She came out strutting, as if she were on a catwalk, and I cracked up. Not only was the jumpsuit hideous, but she paired it with oversize glasses and a wide, bright gold belt. Her hair was piled on top of her head in a huge knot.

"That . . . is . . . amazing," I said, catching my breath.

"Isn't it? I can totally rock it."

"Of course you can. Megdonna?"

"Like Madonna," Meg said matter-of-factly, before belting out the chorus of "Like a Virgin." I joined in, offering backing vocals and laughing the entire time. "El, you should totally join the drama club."

"And hang out with people more dramatic than you? No thank you," I declared.

"But you love singing!" she continued.

"With you. Here alone. Not in front of people." Which was mostly why I never tried. I did love singing, I loved how it made me feel, how I could express myself not with words, but with notes. But the thought of someone judging me felt wrong. Which was why I never asked Jake if I could sing with them. Despite part of me wanting to, I was too petrified.

"Whatever. You'll get over your little stage fright sooner or later. By the way, why aren't you strutting around in your amazing dress?" I took my cue from her and performed a full-on twirl, letting the dress puff out all around me.

"Six-year-old me would have loved this," I said, watching the fabric shine under the lights. Meg laughed loudly, covering her eyes from the sparkle.

"El, I think we found your prom dress."

"Oh man, yes please. I'll get all the guys in this." I laughed. "Okay, change?"

"Yeah, I think I'm getting a wedgie," she admitted. I laughed, shook my head, and walked back into the dressing room. I put on the tank top, along with my worn jeans, and felt . . . like me. It was an outfit I'd normally wear, normally feel comfortable in. Not like a dolled-up fancy version, or even lazy-on-the-couch version. Just like . . . myself. I walked out and waited for Meg.

What was simply a plain loose black tee on the hanger

was now stunning on her. Her body transformed it so instead of just looking frumpy, it fell perfectly off her right shoulder. Even low-key for her was fantastic. We wouldn't have had it any other way. That was how she dressed. And this was how I dressed. I looked down at my black flats and felt ready to go to the show.

"You were right, you know. These are good choices," I said to her.

"Yeah, I think so, too," she said, twisting and turning in the mirror. The light hit her hair and she started to glow. She always glowed, though; she was always the star. And though sometimes it scared me, I still hoped some of her light would cast off onto me.

◇◇◇◇

After paying, we walked back to the car. By Meg's tire there was a small scrap of paper. I instinctively leaned down and picked it up.

Milk, Yogurt, Eggs, Orange Juice, Bread, Nacho cheese

I laughed, thinking of someone getting the essentials, and then a huge, economy-size jar of nacho cheese. I stuck the note in my pocket, folded up as it was found. I knew Matt would like it, and I couldn't wait to give it to him.

CHAPTER 17

NOW
11:35 P.M.

I put the Xbox controller down on Evan's couch and realize that my new plan has one large problem—I have no mode of transportation. Meg left with her car and I'm stuck here with the video game guy. Great.

I know she's already with him, but I feel compelled to text Jake. As I pick up my phone, I feel it vibrate and realize he's beaten me to it.

Meet @ Kikis.

Are you w/Meg?

Yes. She's pissed.

It's my fault.

Yep. And you're gonna make it better.

I sigh, realizing, yeah, he's right. Right now it's my job to calm her down, not his. But at least he's telling me to meet her. At least he's bringing us together. I need to end this before it gets bigger.

Just as I'm about to ask video game guy if he has a car, Evan walks out of the bedroom.

"EVAN!" I shout, and he balks at my excitement, raising an eyebrow in confusion. "I need your help."

"What's up?" he asks, then, "Where's Meg?"

"Um, that's why I need your help. Meg kind of left."

"She left?" he asks.

"Yes."

"She left you here?"

"We kind of had a fight."

"You had a fight?" he asks, even more surprised.

"It's a long story, but anyway, she left."

"It must have been bad if she deserted you."

"Well—"

"But she gets like that. You know Meg, kind of overemotional at times."

"Right, so I was wondering—"

"Do you want me to call her or something? Get her back over here?"

"No, actually—"

"Because I will. I'm sure she's calmed down by now."

"Evan, *listen*," I yell. Just like Meg, he has a tendency to bulldoze over everyone else when he's on a roll. "We got into a fight. It's not bad. But she did leave. She's going with Jake to Kiki's right now. Can you take me there?"

"To Kiki's?"

I sigh in frustration. I know I shouldn't take it out on him, but I'm impatient and he's making it too easy. "Yes, to Kiki's. It's, like, down the road."

"Yeah, I know where it is. Sure, hold on," he says, turning around back toward his room. I love that he understands without me needing to expand any more. I look over and see a photo on the table. Unlike the one Matt originally found in Italy, I know the people who are in it—Meg and Evan. It's from a few days ago, at graduation. I smile, remembering how we had to take it five times because Meg's hair looked off, or Evan's tie wasn't straight. And even though I just saw her, I miss her.

He comes back out in a few minutes, swinging his keys on his index finger, and I walk with him to the door. My mind is made up, and I have to follow it before I'm too chicken to leave. I know I have to figure out Matt and what I want, I know that's going to come up, but right now I just want to talk to Meg. She was right, in a way, but so was I. Maybe we need to be a bit more honest from now on.

But before leaving, I turn back and look at the guy playing video games. He's still there, engrossed in his epic battle. He made it farther than I did in the game.

"Thanks," I say, hoping he knows why.

He just nods in response, as if to say *No problem. It was my pleasure.* As if to say *Good luck.*

◇◇◇◇

"So what was the fight about?" Evan asks once we're in the car.

"Matt. Jake. College. Everything," I sigh.

"College?" he asks.

"I think she's upset that I'm moving away."

"Of course she is. You're her best friend."

"Yeah, I know, and I'm not looking forward to leaving her, but we talked about it. I thought she was cool with me leaving. She knew how much I wanted to. . . ."

"You know Meg. Sometimes she says one thing and thinks another."

"But never with me," I admit. I didn't know me leaving was hurting her so much. "It's not like I'm going to disappear on her, I'm not going to just stop talking to her once I'm up there—she'll still be my best friend."

"I know. Tell *her.* I love my sister, but she can be a bit melodramatic at times," he says, and I nod because, yeah, she can be. "And let me guess, she doesn't think you should get back together with Matt, either?" he continues.

"No, and I kind of told her it was hypocritical to say that, considering Jake and all."

"She has a tendency to see things one-sided," he says, nodding.

"I feel bad pointing it out."

"Eh, she probably needed to hear it."

"But it's my job to cheer her on and support her." It's always been my job. I've always been in her corner. I pull on my bracelet, thinking of the millions of nights we've had together. I might have cut a lot of them off, but they're all still a part of me. She's a part of me.

"No, it's your job to make sure she's being smart. I like Jake and all, but if he messes with her again . . ."

"You'll . . . ?"

"I don't know what I'll do." He grins because he's Evan and he's not one to fight. Meg's the fighter, after all. "But I'll do something."

I smile at him and shake my head. My purse vibrates and I figure it's Jake texting, again, to see where I am. He's impatient like that. But when I pull my phone out, I see that it's an unknown number.

What do you call cheese that isn't yours?

My heart jumps, and I almost stop breathing. It's Matt—it has to be. I deleted his number after he left, but only he would ask me this, after everything. He's daring himself to say yes, too, by continuing to try.

My fingers hover over the letters, but I hesitate. I practically just got out of his car; he can't expect me to decide so quickly. I have no idea what I want yet. I look over at Evan and think about what he said, realizing that, well, maybe I do know. I type back Nacho Cheese and wait for his response. I can picture him at home—wherever his new home is— leaning over his phone waiting for my answer. I can picture his fingers perched over the phone, too. I can picture his hair falling over his glasses, which more than likely are still spotted from the rain. We might have left on uncertain terms—we might still *be* on uncertain terms—but we'll always have that stupid nacho cheese joke that started with the piece of paper I found in the Walmart parking lot.

And sometimes just one thing is enough.

CHAPTER 18

THEN
12:30 A.M.

After leaving Walmart, Meg and I arrived at One Spin Records in just under five minutes. We'd taken longer than the thirty minutes we initially said, but we didn't care. We didn't want to look too eager, but we were. At least I was. We got out of the car and looked at the shop, preparing ourselves for the rest of the night.

"So, once more," Meg said, twirling in front of me.

"You look great. Me?" I had pulled my hair into a low, messy bun to hopefully disguise the frizz. It wasn't a permanent fix, but it worked.

"Marvelous, darling."

"Are you ready?"

"As I'll ever be," Meg sighed.

"We don't have to go in," I reminded her. "We can just leave. Right now," I said, though there was hesitance in my voice. I *wanted* to go. I *wanted* to see Matt.

"I'm not letting him control my life. I *want* to go. I want to see the band for Barker and Matt. And I want you to go. I know what will happen anyway. We'll see each other. Fight. Make up—"

"And more than likely make out."

"And be totally fine until the next time. The end."

"Well, it seems like you've got it all figured out," I said.

"We're not going to make out," she stated, referring to my interjection.

"Of course you won't." I grinned and we both laughed, knowing that, with their history, it wouldn't be odd if they did. We turned around and walked toward the store.

The building was old, weathered but resilient. It took hits each time a band played there, but still stood strong. It also had amazing soundproofing, because while outside it sounded like another quiet night, inside it was an explosion of music. A band wasn't even playing; it was just an extremely loud recording.

"We couldn't have missed them, right?"

"No way, it's too early," she answered. "Unless they decided against going on. Let's find them." I followed her into the rather large store and through the people, toward the stage in the back. Album covers, gig flyers, and old movie posters covered the walls. There was hardly a bare spot left, as posters overlapped posters. Customers flipped through rows of used CDs and vinyl.

The place was remarkably crowded for midnight, but then, it always was. It became a second home for many, a place to hang out when everything else was closed. About half the people from the party had come. While everyone was hanging out and talking, there was an energetic buzz vibrating through the room. It was the anticipation of what would come next.

The stage was set up in the back. Relief washed across my face as I saw Barker adjusting his cymbals. He tightened each onto its stand, and then hit them in succession to test the sound. The bass drum thumped along as well, filling the room with a meaty undertone. We hadn't missed them after all.

"Well, there they are," Meg said, nodding to the stage. Where were the other two? I tilted my chin in his direction, and she nodded.

"Hey Barker," I called over his thumping. He was wearing the same thing he had on earlier, though small patches of sweat had started to form under his arms.

"Hey!" he called over his drum set. He threw down his drumsticks and crossed in front. "You made it!" He jumped off the small stage and gave us each a hug.

"Of course. Where's Gabby?" I asked, trying to be nice.

"Right behind you."

Gabby came running up to us, arms open. She was small and sprightly, with a black bob that ended at her chin, and blunt bangs.

"Hey guys!" she squeaked cautiously. Excitement was bubbling in her voice, but she was restraining herself, unsure, I guess, of how we would respond.

"Hey Gabby," I said, smiling. She brightened at my look.

"Hey Gabby!" Meg said beside me. All the sunshine in our voices was awkward and made it obvious that we were all trying to ignore the space between us.

"I'm so glad you guys made it. I was getting sick of being the only girl," she said a little too perkily.

"Are the rest of the guys here yet?" I asked, moving on to a comfortable subject.

"Yeah, they're in the back. Jake wanted one last cigarette, and Matt was on the phone. I swear, if Jake doesn't stop chain-smoking, his voice is going to be shot. I know he likes that gravelly sound, but it's getting ridiculous."

"Is it that bad?" I asked, glancing over at Meg. She, too, looked surprised. Barker let us talk, and walked back to his drums. The beat continued under our conversation.

"It's worse tonight. I mean, he just keeps smoking. I get it, it's a habit, but it's not healthy. And of course he won't listen to me," she sighed.

"I'll try to talk to him," I said, again looking at Meg. She was the reason for his smoking, of course, though it wasn't exactly her *fault*. Meanwhile, I wondered who Matt was on the phone with. The mere mention of his name sent my heart spinning, but I was still wary. He hadn't contacted me. We'd left on uncertain terms. Would he even be happy to see me again?

I looked behind Gabby, as if willing him to walk through the front door, and saw someone I definitely didn't expect. My heart thumped in my chest and I became, of all things, nervous.

"You've got to be kidding me."

"What's up?" Gabby asked, turning around. Meg didn't have to, though. Seeing the shock on my face was enough.

"He's here?" Meg asked. I nodded, quickly looking at her in order to not meet eyes with high-five-for-friendship Nick.

"*Why* is he here?" I whined. I didn't want him here. Not now. He ruined my night before; he wasn't going to do it again.

"Who's here?" Gabby asked.

"Nick," Meg spit out, not wanting to even taste his name, as if it was poison inside her mouth. Gabby turned pale. Meg looked at me, studying my reaction. "Well, hey, you knew you'd see him. Now is fine. You look great. Feel great. And don't need him."

"Yeah, maybe, but . . . uggggghh," I groaned.

"What's up?" a voice said behind me. I spun around and there was Matt. He stood on the stage with his hands in his pockets, rocking back and forth on his heels again, just like the first time I saw him. He was just as good-looking, with mussed-up hair and glasses askew. And for a moment, all I could think was *mine*. Not that he was mine, but after the night we had, we at least had a connection. A memory. We had kissed only hours ago. Our lips touched. Other girls could look on and swoon all they wanted, but for a few minutes he was mine. And as my smile broke out, I realized that I did hope he'd be mine again. Just seeing him again made me want to forfeit my plan to avoid guys, the one I made just before the night started, scratch it out and reconstruct a new one with him. It was crazy, and made me terrified, but I knew what I wanted, and for once I didn't need someone else's approval or push.

"H-Hey!" I stuttered, my face a flash of red. He looked down, grinning, and then back up at me.

"You changed," he said, nodding at me. I instinctively touched my new shirt and felt good about the choice. It was representative of me—it had personality and, perhaps, it had the power to shine on its own. At least a little bit.

Matt, on the other hand, was wearing the same thing. The wet patches had mostly dried, but there was still a mark on his jeans by his knees and on his shirt by his waist. His waist, which I had previously attacked while in the water. I blushed again.

"Oh, yeah, well, we were all wet." In my peripheral vision, I saw Gabby give Meg a look. Meg nodded to the book section and Gabby followed her gaze before shooting a knowing look and a smile my way. Despite everything, I loved how we all could still communicate without words. An understood quietness.

"You look nice." He paused, and then rushed to say, "I mean, I liked the other you too. That one was nice, but you look nice now, and oh god, never mind." He slapped his face with his hand and I started laughing. I grabbed his hand and pulled it down. Only I didn't let go.

"You look nice, too."

"Ella?" My face flushed instantly because I knew the voice. I knew who it was before I turned around and dropped Matt's hand. I didn't want to; it was an automatic reaction.

"Oh, hey Nick," I said. I felt a shudder go up my spine. I was literally shaking. Why was I so nervous? I'd seen him since the breakup, even since hearing that he cheated. But with Matt there, I felt different. Nick was just a couple of feet away from us. I vaguely recognized the clothes he was wearing. He had on his signature cocky grin, which I hated. The one he wore when he broke up with me.

It dawned on me that I was between my ex and my crush. My hopeful future and my painful past. Right in the middle. That's why I was nervous. I now knew what purgatory might feel like. "Um, Nick, this is Matt. Matt's the new bassist for the Pepperpots. Matt, this is Nick." I looked up at Matt in time to see recognition flash across his face. His mouth went from serious to smirking. He was thinking of the high five.

"You're the new bassist, eh? Good luck. I heard the band just plays birthday parties now after losing so many bassists." Nick was jealous, of course. He'd always been jealous of the band because not only was it better than his, it had an audience. His band didn't. As I watched the words come out of his mouth, I wondered why I even liked him in the first place. He was cute enough, but underneath he really was a jerk. As I was told numerous times after he ended it. I'd never felt more ready to push off my past and race into my future than I did right then. I knew it was time to let go of whatever anger or confusion or regret I felt about him and just . . . start new.

"The Pepperpots just lost one bassist. Plus, they have a gig tonight, here, and this is clearly not a kid's birthday party," I said, rolling my eyes.

"You guys are playing here tonight?" Nick asked, surprised.

"Yeah," Matt said. "They called us about an hour ago."

"Oh, backup band, eh? It happens," Nick said.

Oh my god. I rocked back and forth as the two guys officially started to hate each other.

"To be fair, we were invited to play. And I'm pretty sure you weren't. So I guess that says something," Matt retorted. I stopped. Just, stopped dead in place. This was the first time I had heard him say anything negative. Sure, I had just met him, but the change in tone was kind of appealing. He smirked at me, and I couldn't help but shake from concealing a laugh. It was amazing.

"At least we have a real name. The Pepperpots? Really?" Nick asked. Barker had suggested it originally, because it was a Monty Python reference, and Jake loved it because it was also the name of, in his opinion, the hot chick in *Iron Man*. Oddly, it worked perfectly.

"No Signal isn't a better name," I said, shaking my head.

"Whatever," Nick said, "at least our lead singer isn't such an egotistical ass."

"Aren't *you* the lead singer?" Matt asked, challenging him and defending Jake.

"Yeah, and?" Nick answered, then added to me, "Hey, Ella, if you want to hang out, I'll be over there." He nodded toward the book section, where Meg and Gabby weren't anymore. "Maybe we can . . . catch up."

I breathed in and remembered when I would have said yes, when I would have jumped at the offer because I just wanted *someone*. But not anymore. I'd seen what a good guy was like, and I didn't want to go back. I couldn't let myself. And finally, I didn't want to. I was done with Nick, and ready to dismiss him. See how he liked it.

"No," I said strongly, finally. "I think I'm going to stay over here, thanks." I turned back to Matt and grinned.

"Suit yourself." He shrugged and started to walk away.

"Oh, hey, Nick," Matt said. "High five for being in bands?" Matt watched my face as it burned in both humiliation and admiration. I couldn't believe he said that. He'd seemed so . . . quiet up until now. Where was this Matt coming from? I liked him.

"Whatever," Nick said before walking away, clearly missing the joke. Once he was out of earshot, I started cracking up. Matt joined in, finally jumping off the stage.

"I can't believe you said that," I said, catching my breath.

"I'm so sorry, I'm usually not that . . . um . . . mean, but I just had to. Come on, he made fun of the band and Jake, and then tried to get you back? No way."

I stopped laughing and smiled at him. He was standing up for me.

"Err, yeah," I said, suddenly realizing that he had just witnessed my terrible taste in guys. I didn't want him to think I only dated jerks. "I've made some bad decisions."

"So I've noticed. You did run from the cops in your underwear tonight."

"I'm trying to forget that, thank you very much," I gasped. He was okay. He didn't mind. "Speaking of, where did you and Jake go after you left?"

"Oh god, yeah. That was interesting. I pulled over on the next block. I was okay to drive, but I still wanted to wait it out. And Jake . . . I mean, you could smell the alcohol coming off him. It was bad. He wasn't really happy with me. And then . . ."

"What?"

"He just kind of shut down. He punched his door, and then just stared ahead for a long time. It was . . . kind of weird. We stayed there until I got the call from Barker and drove us here."

"Jake was re-wiring."

"Huh?"

"That's what we used to call it," I explained. "I've seen him do it after fighting with Meg. Whenever Jake gets really angry, he shuts himself down. It's a natural reaction. His dad is kind of . . . forceful, and Jake doesn't want to turn into that. So instead of letting his anger take over, he shuts his body down. I guess it's good, you know, because he doesn't get out of control, but I'm just worried that one day he won't shut down. Or that all the shutting down is hurting him more."

"That's tough."

"That's Jake," I admitted.

"He didn't tell me about his dad, but he did talk about Meg a bit when we drove here. I think he's conflicted," Matt said, scratching the back of his neck. "I think you're right, though—he's a pretty good guy."

"Yeah," I said, nodding. "He is. Sometimes he just needs to let it out and talk to a friend."

"Yeah," Matt said, looking a bit proud, looking like he was happy to be that friend. "What did you guys do?" Matt asked, changing the subject.

"Similar to you, really. Meg sat and took her anger out on her steering wheel. And then we just . . . talked." I left out the trip to Walmart, of course. "Oh, that reminds me, I have something for you." I reached into my pocket for the slip of paper I'd found in Walmart's parking lot. "Here," I said, handing it over.

"What's this?" He unfolded it with a wary look. And then, almost instantly, recognition. "Nacho cheese?!"

"I suppose it *is* essential for any household," I answered. He smiled and put the paper in his pocket.

"Hey, I have a joke for you. What do you call cheese that isn't yours?"

"Nacho cheese!" I yelled. "That's the worst joke in the world, but I love cheesy jokes so it's okay."

"Cheesy jokes? I see what you did there. So I guess I turned you on to picking up trash now?"

"Maybe," I said, looking him right in the eyes. I wasn't sure what I was feeling, but I knew bubbling inside me was hope and excitement and intrigue. I noticed the look Meg had mentioned earlier. The shine she said I had; he had it too. There was something there. I held his gaze. "It is pretty fun."

He smiled, genuinely smiled, and then pulled a piece of paper out of his back pocket. "Well, I've got one for you." He handed me the paper, and I opened it up. It was a poster for a band, an album release party that happened at One Spin a few weeks ago. He'd probably found it discarded while setting up. I read it over, trying to figure out why it was interesting to him, until I saw the name of the band's album. *"She Has a Pretty Smile,"* I read out loud, and grinned. Was he telling me I had a nice smile through the flyer? By the look on his face, the shy, bashful turn away, I thought maybe. And I couldn't help but feel special, because he was communicating in his own way with me.

He grinned back and looked down. He opened his mouth to say something, and I held my breath, waiting for a response, but before any words came out, there was a tap on my shoulder.

"Um, El? You better go out back."

"What's up?" I asked in a daze, still distracted by the flyer. Gabby looked drained, and I quickly snapped to. Whatever had happened had wiped the previous smile off her face. I had a hunch I knew which two people were to blame.

"Meg and Jake are fighting behind the building. It's getting . . . heated."

"Oh god. Okay, thanks." I sighed, folding the flyer to put in my pocket for safekeeping. I knew this would happen. I knew it would be a bad idea for her to go to him so soon. "I should go—"

"I'm coming with you," Matt said. He already understood the importance of me being with Meg. And the need for another bystander. I nodded, and then led the way past the stage and out the back door. It banged shut loudly, but no one seemed to notice.

There wasn't much outside. Dumpster; some trash littering the street; an old, beat-up Volvo that belonged to the owner of the store. Meg and Jake were staring at each other, screaming over the loud buzz of a radiator.

Words were flying out of their mouths, seeming to forcibly hit one another. Meg's face was red, blotchy, and her hands were balled into fists. I knew that look; she wouldn't be calmed down easily. Jake was more relaxed, but still spitting out his words, and I was sure his flippant attitude only added to her anger.

"I don't get it, Jake. What do you *want*?"

"I don't know. How many times do I have to tell you that?"

"If you don't know, then leave me out of it," Meg said.

"I would if you'd let me."

"You're the one who keeps coming back to me. Every time you're bored with another one of your girls, you come back to me."

"Because you tell me to!" Jake yelled. "You're always *there*. Always telling me what I'm missing out on, or whatever. What if I'm not missing you, huh?"

"It sure seems like it, with the amount of times you've tried getting back with me."

"Yeah, because it's easy."

"What's that supposed to mean?" Meg asked, aghast.

"It means I know you'll be there, so I might as well go back to you. Why do you think I always leave again?"

"You leave because I tell you to," she yelled at him. "I'm

sorry I let you back in, but I'm not sorry for letting go again. I can't *do* this anymore. I can't keep being your backup."

"So stop making it so easy for me. Let me get by on my own," he yelled back.

"I've tried!"

"Whatever," he said dismissively.

"No, I'm sick of this, Jake. I'm sick of everything. What do you want from me?"

"I don't know!" he yelled again.

"Do you want me to just disappear? Leave town?" Meg asked.

"Meg—" I started, knowing this wasn't going to end well.

"That would be great. Could you just do that?" Jake responded.

"Jake—" Matt tried.

"Fine. Consider me out of your life. It's over. Done. Just don't come back to me when another one of your girls decides you're too boring or too stupid."

"MEG—"

"And don't come back to me when you're lonely and desperate for affection. It's not my fault no other guy wants you."

"JAKE—"

But he continued. "It's not my fault you're a bitch."

Meg paused, visibly shaken by his last insult. Her mouth hung open slightly. I wanted to run to her, hug her, but I knew not to yet.

"Shit, Meg, I didn't—" Jake started.

"No!" she yelled, her voice shaking. It was loud, vibrating across the alley. Despite being hurt, she stood taller, straightening her back. "You don't get to talk anymore. We're done. I don't—I don't even know why I thought you cared." She turned around and started walking to the door. She didn't see us standing there; it was as if we were invisible. Spectators to a movie unfolding before our eyes. I didn't know what to do, so I stayed where I was. It was safer.

"Don't you get it?" Jake yelled back. "I care about you too fucking much." He let it all out, all of his pent-up anger, all of the shutting down, it all came out in that one sentence. Years of emotions and letdowns and heartaches pulsated from his words. She paused, her back still to him. He looked down, and then walked toward her. His voice was lower, less angry. "I go back to you because I need you, but I can't do that anymore. I can't go through another round, knowing that I'll eventually hurt you again."

Tears streamed down her face. She wiped them away before turning around. "What are you talking about? How do you know?" Her voice was soft, barely audible.

"Because it's me. I'm a fuckup. I mess everything up. I've messed you up enough; I can't do it again. You were right to be done with me." They'd broken up before, but his honesty made this time different. I could see his words still crossing Meg's face.

"But I didn't want to be done with you," she admitted finally.

"I didn't want to be done with you, either, but I just . . . can't keep screwing you around. I know what I'm doing, and it kills me."

"Then don't do it," she said simply.

"It's not that easy. . . ." He messed up his hair, pulling at bits until they stood up. "I can't be this perfect guy for you, as much as I'd like to. It's just not me. I'll always do something to fuck it all up, just like my dad. It's in my blood."

"You're not a fuckup," she said, sniffling.

"I am," he said, moving closer to her. "And you're my ultimate weakness."

She nodded, understanding, then took a step toward him. "So let me help you."

He paused for a second, and then visibly thawed as they collapsed onto each other. Tears kept coming, but they were okay.

A white flag was waved. They had a mutual understanding. Finally. I looked over at Matt, remembering he was beside me. He put his arm around my shoulders and squeezed. I leaned into him, resting my head on his collarbone. He might not have known them well, but he understood perfectly.

"We'll get through this, you know. It's not over. You're not over," Meg said gently.

"I know." Jake shook his head. "You're the only one who gets it."

The door opened behind us, but only Matt and I seemed to notice.

"Hey, guys? It's time to go on," Barker said cautiously. He stayed concealed by the door, only poking his head out. The sight of Matt's arm around me, and Meg's fresh tears, made him balk. Realizing just how much he was interrupting, he shook his head and ducked back into the store. Within moments, Gabby popped her head out too, to take us all in. She gave me a wink before shutting the door yet again. I knew we'd have some explaining to do. I looked back at Meg and Jake and sighed. They weren't over. They never would be over, and there was something oddly comforting about that.

"Come on," Matt said, leading me back to the door. Meg pulled Jake, and he stumbled behind her. For once he wasn't leading.

CHAPTER 19

NOW
11:45 P.M.

It's about seven minutes from Evan's door to Kiki's, the bar/karaoke place where I'm meeting Jake and Meg.

"Thank you," I say to Evan, giving him a big hug. "I promise to take care of Meg, even though she definitely doesn't need taking care of."

"She does," Evan says. "She just doesn't like to admit it." With a wave, he drives off, and I'm left to face the night alone. I take a deep breath in, squeeze my hands tight, and head inside.

After Kiki's Bar opened about five months ago, we quickly became regulars. There's karaoke on Friday and Saturday nights and they never card. If you look old enough, you can drink. And, because it opened after Matt left, it's one of the only places around town that doesn't remind me of him. He left no trace here; our relationship isn't written on the walls. It's a safe space, which is kind of why I'm glad Jake suggested it.

The entrance is above ground, but the bar is actually below. I slowly walk down the flight of dirty steps, careful not to touch the handrail. My shoes stick to the floor, squeaking with every step. Inside it's small, dark, and smoky. One bartender manages the dark wooden bar behind which mirrors hang, all in differently sized black frames. It's neat seeing yourself at different heights as you order a drink. It's there that I find Jake.

"Hey," I say, coming up beside him.

"Oh, thank god you're here," he says, pulling me in for a hug, then leaning back up against the bar. He has that laid-back rock star thing down: mussed hair, casual pose, black jacket despite the heat. He already has a drink in one hand.

"That bad?"

"I can't handle her when she's like this."

"I'll make it better," I promise, patting him on the arm. He takes a sip and then eyes me.

"You better, otherwise we're in for a long night." I give him a sad smile and then turn to leave. I feel him pull on my arm, so I turn back around. "You okay? With Matt and everything?"

"I will be. I think," I say. He nods, a silent promise that

we'll talk more about it later.

I turn around toward the tables. In the back of the room is a small stage where, right now, a lady wearing a pink feather boa is doing her best, singing an old song my mom likes. And at a table not far from her is Meg, sitting alone and typing on her phone.

As soon as she sees me, her eyes go wide and then squint into thin lines. Clearly Jake did not tell her I was on my way. She lowers her chin, tilts her head, and with her best annoyed voice, she asks, "What are *you* doing here?"

If Jake wasn't already at the bar, this would have been his cue to leave. Actually, if this was a year ago, it would have been mine, too. I'm not big on confrontation. And I definitely don't want to fight with my best friend. But I know this is worth it, so I pull out a chair and sit down across from her. She crosses her arms over her chest, but doesn't protest, doesn't tell me to leave. That's a good start.

"I wanted to talk," I say, keeping my voice calm.

"Wanted to tell me that I'm wrong for dating Jake again? That all of my decisions are totally stupid?"

"No, it's not that—"

"Then what is it? That you're better than me because you're moving away? That your relationship is better than mine? Because here's something—Matt left you. He's no better."

Her words strike a chord, and my heart jumps in response. "You're right, he's not." But I can't let that small fact defeat me as it has before.

"I'm glad we agree on something." She sneers, still glaring at me. So I proceed, breathing in deep. I want to stop, I want to just give in and tell her she's right, I'm wrong, let's move on. But I can't. It's still the night, so right now I'm saying yes to speaking my mind.

"But I'm not going to take back what I said. Jake's done some crappy things and you always return to him." She opens her mouth to protest. "WHICH," I yell, overpowering her for once, "I've always stood behind you on. And I still will. I'll *always* support your decision, even if I don't necessarily think it's the right one."

"So you don't think getting back with Jake was right? He's your *friend*, Ella."

"I know, and I'm not saying that I don't totally think it was right. I'm *glad* you guys are together *because* you're my friends. Because I know it makes you both so crazy happy. Because you really do work well together. But sometimes—" I pause. "There were times I didn't think you should take him back."

"Why?"

I was dreading this question. There are millions of reasons, but I'm not about to list all of them. "Because he's Jake? I mean, I love him, but he's . . ." I pause, thinking of a good word. "Everywhere."

"Everywhere."

"Yeah. I mean, he likes you—obviously—but he's just

all over the place. And I want him to only focus on you."

"But I understand his situation; I mean, he's the lead singer of a band—"

"I know, I know," I say, sighing. "It's just, I hate that his desire to be this rock star means you have to be okay with him flirting with other people."

"I'm only okay with the flirting because I know he won't do anything else," she clarifies, but it still doesn't make perfect sense to me. "And he never has. He's never cheated on me."

"I know, and I know he won't. It's just . . ." I pause again, leaning in. "You're my best friend. I want the world for you. I want a guy who will bring you everything you ever wanted and more. And he doesn't always live up to that."

"But I like what we have. It's why we're together. I don't need everything in the world."

"I know. Believe me, I know. If you want something, you'll get it for yourself."

"You better believe it," she says with a raise of her eyebrows.

"I just don't want you to be hurt," I finally say. "So whenever he does something stupid, I'm upset for you."

"You don't have to be," she says.

"I know. I just care about you."

"Really?" she asks, after a moment.

"Meg. Duh." I grin and she smiles back, dropping her arms. A wave of relief washes over me; this step is complete.

"And about college . . . I'm not leaving you."

"Well, you are."

"Okay, I *am* leaving you, but I'll still be here for you. You can still call me at midnight with crazy ideas like, oh, how to sneak into the back room of a club so we can meet the band playing."

"You have to admit, my plan worked."

"We have the pictures to prove it." I grin, but she doesn't. "Seriously. I'm not running away from you. If I could pack you up and bring you, I would."

"I know . . . it's just . . . sometimes when you talk about leaving, it feels like you want to be rid of everything here. And I'm sometimes afraid that means me, too," she admits, and it hurts me that she thinks that. Meg rarely shows signs of weakness.

"Never, Meg. I'm coming back on weekends just *for* you."

"You better," she says, her posture loosening, relaxing. "And no making new friends."

"None at all," I say, and we both know it's a lie, but it's a good lie. One I don't mind saying.

Meg sighs and says, "I don't like being mad at you."

"And you think I do? God, you really are scary." I shake my head and she laughs. Her moods are a hurricane, and this one is finally passing on.

"Maybe I was a little harsh on Matt earlier," she admits, glaring at me to let me know that she doesn't admit she's wrong very often. This I know.

"Nah, he deserves it," I say, waving her away. "And maybe I was harsh on Jake."

"Well, he *definitely* deserves it," she jokes, and we laugh. "He has done some crappy things, and it does make me upset . . . but I don't know. He's so much better now, and there's something about him. . . . Do you really think we work well together?" she asks, a glimmer in her eye. For once she's relying heavily on my answer. So I can't let her down.

"Absolutely. Dysfunctional at times, but always great," I say because I can't just say they're perfect. They're far from perfect, but they're perfect enough. And that's all right. She smiles in response and lays her arm on the table, pinkie out. I link pinkies with her and we grin like crazy people because, sometimes, it's more fun to be crazy.

"So," she says, taking her hand away, "any thoughts on the Matt situation? I won't freak out this time, I promise."

"Har har. No, not really. It's still . . . confusing."

"But you're still *thinking* about him."

"Yeah, of course," I say.

"So the answer isn't no, then."

"Hmm?" I ask.

"If you didn't want to see him again, you wouldn't still be thinking about it."

I open my mouth to argue, to say no, that's not the case. But she's right. She really is. If I didn't care what would happen, I wouldn't still be thinking about it. "Can I admit something?"

"Of course," she says seriously.

"I feel bad that I didn't know about his brother."

"Why would you feel bad about that? He didn't tell you—you couldn't have known."

"I know, but I should have. I saw him every day. I saw how some days he was off, not his usual self. Like the time we road-tripped to see that band in Tampa?" I say, remembering the day as I say it. "He was so quiet on the way there, and then tried to overcompensate once when got to the show, jumping around and stuff. It wasn't . . . exactly him. I asked if he was okay, but he said he was fine. . . . I should have pushed him," I admit.

"El, you had no reason to suspect something so crazy was happening to him at home. If he already decided to keep it from you, he wasn't going to blurt it out at a concert."

"I know, but . . ."

"And anyway, you had no idea what was going on, so wouldn't have even known the right questions to ask. You shouldn't feel guilty about this."

"I know, and you're right, but I guess . . . I just feel bad that he went through all of it alone."

"And that was *his* decision. Remember that," she says, staring at me, and I listen to her. Because this time she's right. It's just a lot to take in for one night.

I don't want to think about that, about not knowing, anymore, so I give her the latest update. "He texted me on my way here."

"He did? What did it say?" she asks, leaning in.

"Nothing, really. Just an old joke we had."

"Hmmm." She flicks her eyes up, staring at the ceiling. Contemplating. Picking her words so they don't hurt me. But she won't censor herself. She never does. Music fills the void as I wait for her to continue. "Let me ask you a question. Why did you like Matt?"

Why did I like Matt? It's such a simple question, but it means everything.

"Back when we were dating, we went to this pizza place for lunch. It was when we were still getting used to each other, when we were new, so our conversations were endless. We never had awkward pauses, and never ran out of things to say. So as we're talking, a waitress interrupts us to get our order. Thing is, I completely forgot we were in public. I was in this . . . daze, and I know he was too because we both jumped. The same thing happened tonight at Wing King. It's like—when I'm with him, nothing else matters. He makes me feel like I'm the most important person in the world. And I know you don't need a guy to make you feel that way, but it's just . . . nice. He makes me feel nice. With us, nothing is ever forced." I pause, remembering her original question. "I guess I never really thought about why we worked, we just did."

I look up at Meg and see her smiling. A warm and fuzzy smile, one that's usually reserved for first date reflections or love letter rereads. "Honestly?" she asks, leaning closer. Her words are hushed. "I think him coming back is crazy, and I think you wondering about him is crazy, too. But, as we *previously* discussed, I'm not one to judge," she points out. "That's the thing, though. Most of the time I thought I was crazy, too, for going back to Jake. I thought I was completely mental. But something inside me said it was okay, told me to do it, despite what others thought. I knew it was right. Clearly it didn't result in the healthiest of relationships, but I feel like everything had to happen to lead to where we are now. I feel like we're right. Are we right? Who knows. But I'm happy, and isn't that what matters?"

It's the first time I've actually heard her say that she's happy with Jake, with where they are, despite the ups and downs. I know she is—I can see her face when he's around—but it's nice to hear her say it. Just like it's nice to see Jake being, well, Jake—and not rock star Jake.

"I liked Matt. I thought you guys worked well together. You were so happy with him. And, honestly, I was a little jealous."

"You were?" I ask, surprised. "What were *you* jealous of?"

"Did you guys fight once? Did you even bicker? I mean, seriously, it was obnoxious how cute you were. Jake and I, on the other hand . . ."

"Gotcha." I nod, knowing what she means.

"So, I'm not saying you should take him back or anything—I mean if you do and if he hurts you again and then disappears, I'll kick the shit out of him—but I'm saying you should do what feels right . . . whatever that is. So do you feel it's right with Matt?" she asks.

"So am I late for the fire and brimstone?" Jake cuts in, appearing behind Meg and giving me an excuse not to answer. He sits down, brushes his fingers through his hair, and then throws his arm around Meg. He pulls her in for a kiss, disregarding the fact that I'm mere inches away. It's not everything she's ever wanted and more . . . but it's right for her.

"Hi to you too, Jake," I say. He pulls away and smirks. Grinning, Meg links her fingers together and rests her chin on them, elbows on the table. He keeps his arm around her. They really are good together when they want to be. She's the only one who really understands him, and he's the only one who really makes her happy. And as I watch him absent-mindedly rub her shoulder, I think maybe Meg is onto something. She's crazy when it comes to relationships, she really is, but she always knows what she wants and goes for it. Nothing holds her back. Maybe I need a little bit of her in me now.

"Where's Barker and Gabby?" Meg asks Jake.

"They had to go home, something about a family reunion tomorrow. But Barker said to call him if we need backup, and Gabby sends a hug, or something like that." I smile, thinking of Barker running in to save the day, and Gabby in the corner protecting me from danger. After Matt left, she kind of became my savior, along with Meg. She baked me "screw him" cakes and let me vent throughout the day. I'd thought it was because she was still upset about the Nick situation, but really, she was just being a good friend.

"So, where's the man of the hour? Late? That doesn't bode well for his execution," Jake continues.

"Hm?" I ask, wondering who he means.

"You didn't tell her?" Jake asks, turning to Meg.

"I didn't exactly have a chance to yet," she says to him, then turns back to me. "But I guess the cat's out of the bag."

"What cat . . . ?" I ask the question cautiously because if she says what I think she might, I'm not sure I'm ready.

"Matt's coming."

"WHAT?" I practically yell.

"At least he said he would. Jake invited him," she continues.

"Why would you do that?" I turn to him, still yelling. I feel the familiar flush coming to my face as my mouth goes dry. This is not happening.

"Hey, he's my friend, too," he defends himself, but I'm not taking that.

"Friend? Since when are you friends again?"

"We're not," Jake says, crossing his arms in front of him, doing the exact same pose Meg did earlier. "I just wanted to test him."

"Test him how? See how much he could make me go insane?"

"It's not that," Meg cuts in, trying to rescue Jake, and I know she's in on it, too. Why would they do this to me? My heart is racing again, just as it was earlier in the night when I first saw him. Just like then, it doesn't know what to do. Should it be excited? Should it run away in fear? "You said he's sorry. We want to make sure he is."

"By making me face him again."

"No, by making him face *us*," she clarifies. "It's one thing to be all apologetic to you—you're, like, the nicest person in the world—but to us?"

"We're not as nice," Jake says, pointing out the obvious. "And he still has a lot of explaining to do. To me." I calm down a bit—just a bit—when I remember Jake's right. He's in this, too.

While Matt was here, they became good friends. Closer than he and Barker ever were. They just got each other without any explanation. So when Matt left, it hurt Jake, too. I didn't even know Jake was trying to contact him so often until he told me he got through. Sure he was trying so hard for himself, but it was also for me, and I'll always remember that. And when I told Jake about the letter, he was livid. I had to stop him from driving to Texas to beat Matt up. To this day, I'm pretty sure he would have gone had I not stopped him.

"So what happens if he passes the test?" I ask tentatively.

"He can hang out again, and you're allowed to date him, or whatever," Jake answers.

"If you want," Meg clarifies, cutting in.

"Allowed?" I question, raising an eyebrow.

"Permitted?" Jake counters, and I shake my head.

"And if he doesn't pass?"

They turn to each other and share a private smirk reserved for lovers and criminals. They're both, I suppose.

"This should be interesting," I sigh, tracing my finger over a napkin left on the table.

"I'll say. The four of us together again," Meg answers, leaning back on her chair.

"Listen, I'm all for him coming back and being in our lives. I liked the guy a lot. But if he pulls that disappearing crap again, I'm going to beat the shit out of him," Jake announces, and I shake my head.

"Hey, that's what I said!" Meg interrupts.

I smile, looking at my friends. It's interesting—as a child you think your parents can solve anything and make the world a better place. But slowly, unexpectedly, that belief transfers over to your second family, your friends. My parents don't know about any of this, but if I go a day without talking to Meg, I feel lost. When does the transfer of power happen? And why does it feel so good?

Suddenly, Meg raises her eyebrows, and Jake straightens up in his chair. I don't have to look behind me to know that Matt's just walked into the bar, and he's heading in our direction.

CHAPTER 20

THEN
12:50 A.M.

One Spin Records was just as crowded as earlier, but for some reason it seemed louder. As if everyone was screaming, trying to cover up the fight outside. Once we approached the stage, Barker ran up to us, with Gabby tagging along behind him.

"Um, I hate to ask this . . . but what are we playing?" Barker asked. Jake had his arm draped over Meg. Matt and I weren't touching, which I noticed every single second.

"Same set that we were going to do at the party?" Jake asked.

"Sounds good," Barker answered, twirling his drumstick through his fingers.

"Wait, I have an idea," Matt interrupted. "You know how we're doing the cover of 'Bad Reputation'? Why don't we get a girl to sing it?"

Oh no.

"What girl?" Jake asked.

No, no, no, no, no.

"I was thinking maybe . . . Ella?"

NO, NO, NO, NO, NO.

"What? You want to sing, El?" Jake asked, a curious smile on his mouth. My face was the color of a tomato. I felt it spread down my neck. I was sure my stomach even looked sunburned at that point.

"No, no, it's not that," I quickly answered, trying to figure out what to say. I glanced over at Meg and saw her beaming, visibly brightened by this prospect. Besides Matt, she was the only one who knew, who'd been pushing me to break out all along. So of course she was thrilled. Her eyes softened as they darted back and forth between Matt and me. She approved of him, of us.

"I just . . . I told Matt earlier I'd always wanted to do it, but not now. I can totally do it another time. It's no big deal, go do your show. Don't worry about me." I kept rambling, hoping someone would cut me off. Of course, it took them a while to put me out of my misery. I loved that Matt remembered, I loved that he wanted me to do this, but at the same time—I really hated him. I wasn't prepared at all.

Jake and Matt exchanged glances, and then looked back

at me, grinning. Actually grinning. This was not happening.

"Um, I think you have to do it. Let me reflect for a minute . . . what's tonight again?" Jake asked, crossing his arms.

Matt checked his watch. "He's right, you know. I'm pretty sure you have to say yes."

"It's past midnight!" I interjected. "It's technically tomorrow."

"The night doesn't end until we go to sleep," Matt said authoritatively.

"His game, his rules," Jake added, nudging Matt.

I was going to kill them.

"Oh, come on, guys, she doesn't have to." Gabby jumped in, trying to save me. I gave her a look and mouthed "thank you." She was trying to prove that she was on my side, and at that moment I was extremely thankful.

"What's this yes thing you're talking about?" Barker asked.

"Long story," Meg answered, waving him off.

"What do you say?" Matt asked.

And then I looked at him. His eyes were shining, daring me. Full of light and hope and everything I wanted in life. He believed in me, he actually believed in me. I didn't have to plan this, prepare for this; it was actually here. Why shouldn't I believe in myself? Why should I be afraid?

"I . . . okay, fine," I relented. The guys high fived in response, and then laughed at their action. Because *of course* they were high fiving. Despite hating them at that moment, I also loved these guys. For a multitude of reasons, but mostly because they were helping me do something I wanted to do.

"Okay, we're on, guys. El, we'll call you up when it's your turn. Good luck?" Barker asked, still confused.

I shook my head and watched as Jake took Matt to the side ever so slightly.

"Hey, thanks for tonight."

"No problem," Matt answered, shrugging his shoulders.

"Seriously, I know I was an ass. But . . ."

"Hey, I know you've got me next time," Matt said, and Jake nodded and they both did that guy thing where they patted each other's shoulders instead of hugging. And I smiled because I was pretty sure I had just witnessed the start of a real friendship, one Jake needed. Even with his many conquests, he didn't really have anyone else besides us. He needed someone for when he and Meg were, well, being him and Meg.

They turned around and took to the stage. Matt looked back and flashed me the rock 'n' roll hand gesture, then closed his eyes and mouthed "Wooo!" I laughed, shaking my head, and when he opened his eyes we shared a smile. I was still shocked by what was about to happen, but I took in his grin and let nerves and excitement take over.

Meg grabbed my hand and pulled me over to the side of the stage. Gabby followed us after giving Barker one last kiss. He placed his hand on the side of her face and kept it there as they had a whole conversation with a single touch. I turned away; their moment was too private.

"Are you okay?" Meg asked, grinning.

"I think so. What's going on?"

"All of your dreams are coming true, Cinderella." She smiled, bringing me into a big hug. I held on tight, not wanting the moment to end.

"Are *you* okay?" I whispered in her ear.

"Yeah . . . sometimes I just need to yell." We broke apart and took our place by the stage, staying off to the side while everyone else made their way to the front, crowding around to get the best view. "By the way, what did I miss when I was outside? Are you guys in love yet?"

I thought back to our conversation, the hugs, the hands, the looks, the touches. I thought of the moments we shared. When I opened my mouth to answer, I realized I didn't want to tell her what happened. Not everything, at least. Not because I wanted to keep things from her, but because they were our moments, mine and Matt's. They were private, special, and I wanted to remember them as such. Our own little scrap of paper. My heart leapt every time I thought of his eyes. Now I understood why Meg never told me everything about Jake. Sometimes you just have to keep secrets.

"We talked a lot. And I have hope." She linked her pinkie with mine and gave it a squeeze. We weren't perfect, far from it, but we were picking up our pieces and assembling our own puzzles.

"I like that boy," she said, nodding toward Matt. "You should keep him." I nodded in agreement, basking in her approval.

The lights dimmed and the stage was illuminated in blue and red hues. The guys looked great onstage, like superheroes emerging from our daily lives. Barker was excited, jittery, bouncing his leg repeatedly and twirling his sticks in the air. Jake stood tall in the front—shoulders back, head high—smirking at the audience's cheers. And Matt stood next to him, tapping the strings of his bass as he looked out into the oasis of faces. Barker lifted his sticks high in the air, the universal signal for starting a show. He hit them three times and then . . .

An explosion of sound hit the crowd and bounced off the walls. They played a few covers at first, to get the crowd excited, and excited they were. They were singing along, jumping to the beat. When the band switched to their own music, no one noticed. A few people even continued singing. The music flowed out, filled the store. It felt full.

Jake sang with emotion I'd never seen before. He closed his eyes when he yelled, and *felt* the music as it came out of his mouth and fingers. His hand easily slid up and down the guitar, hitting the strings repeatedly and making the song come alive. Sweat beaded by his hairline, slowly dripping down. Girls gathered by him, staring longingly as he played. I side-glanced at Meg, but she looked okay. She was smiling, laughing and cheering.

Barker, in the back, was just having fun. His eyes were wide and mouth agape as his arms moved wildly, hitting his drums and cymbals with an amazing amount of force and speed. He was a blur, all motion all the time. He was obviously enjoying himself, which was the most exciting thing to see. Gabby stood by us, looking at him proudly. She flailed her arms in the air, and didn't care who was looking. She was dancing just for him.

Matt stayed on the side, not making a big deal of himself. I could see why Jake knew Matt would be a perfect fit. He was *good*. It looked like playing the bass came as naturally as breathing to him. His fingers moved wildly along the neck, adding rhythm to the song. He bit his lower lip when hitting certain chords and jumped during off beats. It was exhausting and exhilarating to watch. I knew the girls would notice; they were already crowding around. Soon we'd hear the murmur of wondering who he was and who he was with.

I let the music take over and danced next to Meg, bumping hips with her and flailing my arms in the air. It might have taken all night, but the guys were finally playing. And it was worth it. The wait, the struggle, the games, the running. After their last bassist moved, we didn't know what would happen to the band. But they never gave up. And for one night, newly formed, they were together again, doing the one thing that made all of them happy. And we were there, too.

And then the moment I was anticipating came.

"For our next song, we have a special guest," Jake said, raising his eyebrows suggestively, voice low and hoarse. "El, let's go."

As soon as I heard my name, I was thrown back to reality. There was cheering, and there was yelling, but my feet weren't working. Planted on the ground, they did not want to move. There was a buzz in my ear. My heart was racing. And everything seemed muted.

"El, El." Meg grabbed my hand, tugged on my bracelets for support, and spun me around. "You've got this." I blinked, seeing nothing and then . . . everything. She came into view. And the music amplified. And I was there in a store, about to sing. My heart beat loudly, I took a breath in, and I smiled.

"Okay . . . okay." I squeezed Meg's hand, and then raced up the stairs. One foot in front of the other. And everything came into focus. The lights, the instruments, the guys. Especially *him*.

I walked to the front of the stage and stood behind the microphone. Matt was behind me to the left, Jake on my right. Barker was directly behind me. Knowing they were all there, that they all had my back, made it easier.

"You all right?" Matt asked, raising his eyes in my direction. I stood there awkwardly, rigid. A buzz circulated the room; I couldn't blink. I flexed my hands, releasing the tension, as my heart pounded. I wanted to do this, I really did, but could I?

"You've got this," Jake said on my other side.

Matt reached over to adjust the microphone to my height. Head bowed, his shaggy hair fell down, hiding his face. He looked over and our eyes met. I grabbed the microphone just as he was taking his hand away and for a moment, we touched. That same spark I felt on the roof reappeared, and a shudder went through my body. He was smiling that proud smile that nothing could destroy. I wanted to kiss him, but instead I took a deep breath.

They could push, they could support, and they could all tell me to do it. But only I had the power to actually open my mouth. And I was ready to do that.

The microphone was warm in my hand, used and wet with sweat. It smelled like cheap beer and sour-cream-and-onion potato chips. I gripped it tightly to steady my shaking hand.

The room looked dark, save for the stage. A throng of people was spread out around us. They must have been chatting, cheering, and murmuring. They must have been rowdy. But I didn't hear a thing. It was just me and the mic and the guys behind me.

I suddenly felt the ground thump, thump, thumping with the bass drum all around me. The music was full, loud, hugging my body. All at once I heard the cheering, clapping, drums, and guitar come together. I felt the blood in my face drain and my palms start sweating. My eyes widened in shock and horror and excitement and glee. And then it was my turn, my moment in the spotlight. My moment to do what I wanted. I couldn't even remember how I got there. I closed my eyes, opened my mouth, and let go.

CHAPTER 21

NOW
12:15 A.M.

"Hey guys," Matt says, walking past Kiki's karaoke stage and taking a seat next to me.

It's awkward, as expected. It's obvious he's nervous, as his normal charm doesn't shine through. It's like we're back in the car and he's playing with his watch again. Nothing is more interesting than his watch. But this time, he's looking at us, darting his eyes between Jake and Meg. Asking the parents for permission to date their daughter. A part of me feels bad, wants to grab him and tell him it'll be okay. But another part wants him to feel the shame, the exposure. I want to test him, too.

"Matthew," Jake greets him, ever so properly.

"Jacob," Matt says, a glimmer of a smile poking through.

"Hi again," Meg says.

"Hey Meg," he answers.

More silence. He hasn't quite met my eyes yet, but I can feel him next to me. I can feel the air between us, both pushing us apart and pulling us in. And I can see the nervous looks everyone is exchanging.

"Well, this isn't awkward or anything," Matt finally says, breaking the ice. As I let the relief wash over me, I laugh, giddy with the feeling of confusion and exhaustion and just . . . everything. Finally, he looks over and catches my eye. And he smiles. I feel our same old spark, that electric shock, between us. It somehow feels new every time.

"So I hear you're back?" Jake asks, finally giving in to the conversation.

"Um, yeah, just moved back. Going to UCF in the fall." I can feel the table nudge from Matt's leg repeatedly tapping.

"So are we," Meg says politely. She's restraining herself. For me.

"So I heard. It'll be nice to have familiar faces around." He pauses, and I can almost see the realization form on his face. He doesn't know if they actually want to see him around. "I mean, if we hang out or anything. The school is big, so bumping into one another won't be easy. . . ." He fades out.

"We have a new bassist. Just FYI," Jake continues, I'm sure still reeling at having to find a replacement on such short notice. And, while he won't fully admit it, losing a friend.

"I heard," Matt says softly. "I'm sure he's better than me. Remember how much I messed up?" He acts nervously self-deprecating as he did the first night I met him. It makes me want to smooth things over, start from scratch.

"We've had some awesome gigs, too. Big shows," Jake says, and I watch Matt almost visibly shrink.

"That's great," Matt responds, his voice low and unsure. "I'm glad the band's still together."

"Not for long, with everyone moving away. But whatever," Jake announces, glancing at me, and then back at Matt. Jake's challenging him. I stare at Meg, and thankfully she can pretty much read my mind.

"Jake's starting a new band soon," Meg cuts in, easing the tension. "Maybe you can join him, if you're still around." Jake shoots her a look that says *We'll talk later*, but she just grins in response. She doesn't have to ask him for permission; this we know.

"Yeah!" Matt answers excitedly. He leans forward, and his leg stops tapping. "That would be great! I mean, if Jake wouldn't mind having me."

"We'll see. I'm having auditions, so . . ."

"Jake," I cut in, fed up with his ego.

"What? I am," he answers me.

"Well, I mean, I can audition," Matt offers. "I haven't played in a while, so I hope I'm still okay."

"Shit, you were a godsend." Jake waves him off. "But if you pull that disappearing crap again—"

"I won't," Matt says, quickly, as if he expected the threat. As if he was prepared for it to be brought up. And it was, and I can actually feel it hanging in the air. The thing that broke us all apart. And the thing that's oddly bringing us back together tonight. The fact that he disappeared on us all—not just me, but everyone—is out in the open. Not everything I learned tonight, but this part. This is the part that affects us all. "I won't," he repeats, looking at me this time. It makes me a little nervous the way he's looking at me, like he's trying to prove what he's saying, but they're just words. I think seeing Matt look at me like that makes Jake nervous too, because he barges right in, as if to warn Matt not to look at me that way if he doesn't mean it.

"It really sucked how you left," Jake is saying. "And, yeah, Ella, I know you said not to mention it, but I have to." Matt stares down again, hand on his watch, and I don't know how to feel. They're hurting him, just like he hurt us. I don't really want to be a part of that.

"What Jake is so eloquently trying to say," Meg joins in, and I shoot her a look that begs her to stop mentally kicking him. I did it enough to him tonight. ". . . Is that we like you, but we don't want you to leave again."

"I won't," Matt says, a boy scorned. "I just got back. Give me a chance." The strength in his voice surprises me, though I suppose it's warranted. They were hard on him. They were testing him.

A silence fills our table as the music in the background

plays on. "So . . . where are you living?" I ask, the only thing that comes to mind. I want to change the subject, not discuss the past. I learned enough tonight.

"Oh, an apartment complex right by the school," Matt answers. The lines on his forehead even out, and I can tell he's grateful for the change in topic. "Jackson Point? It's all right, I guess. My roommate Anthony is . . . special."

"He hit on me at the party," Meg says, mostly for Jake's ears.

"Is that so?" Jake asks, eyeing her.

"He's all right," Meg answers. "We just talked."

Matt looks at them, confused, clearly wondering if they're together or not. "Yeah, I'm glad that's all you did with him. I've been there for three days, and each night he's brought back a different girl. On the plus side, I've met new people."

I visibly glare at the thought of him and his new friends; I can't help it. I can't stand the thought of girls spending the night at his place. I can't stand the thought of him seeing them first thing in the morning, even if they're not there for him. As the jealousy seeps through I realize one important thing—everyone was right, I'm clearly not over him. If I was, I wouldn't be feeling this, I wouldn't be wanting to kick girls I don't even know. And I certainly don't want to think about the fact that I won't be here in three months, and what will happen after that.

"They're all pretty gross, though. And they hate cheesy jokes." He eyes me quickly.

"How are the girls in Texas? I hear they don't live up to ours here in Florida," Jake interjects, spoiling the moment.

"Jake." I glare at him.

"Ah, yeah. They're fine, I guess," Matt answers. An expression passes across his face that I don't quite catch. It's gone before I can register it. "But nothing like the ones here."

I glance down, trying to hide the redness spreading across my face. I notice Jake staring at me, and his face softens for the first time since Matt got here.

"So, do you guys come here often?" Matt continues, changing the subject. "I've never been before." And there it is, another separation between him and us. Between the time he was around and the time he wasn't.

"We found it a while ago," Meg answers. "We've been a bunch since. Celebrated Gabby's birthday here last month. God, what was that song she sang? It was awful."

"It wasn't as awful as Barker's backup dancing," I add, laughing at the memory of him attempting to do the robot.

"Or Jake thinking he could take two shots at once," Meg adds.

"It was an experiment!" he protests. "A quicker way to get drunk, am I right?" he asks Matt, and Matt just shrugs in response. Of course he doesn't remember Gabby's party or the robot or the shots. He missed every party, every birthday. He looks down at the table, waiting for the conversation to pick up again, but making no attempt to start it.

"Hey, remember when we got El to make it to three

drinks?" Jake keeps going, laughing more comfortably. "Dude, Matt, you should have seen—" Meg lays her hand on his arm, interrupting him. "What?" he asks, looking right at her. She raises her eyebrow in our direction, and he gets it. "Oh. Yeah. Well, you didn't miss much. I mean, she was El, but like, ridiculously happy. Anyway."

Anyway is right.

"If you're here for her birthday this year, you'll see it," Jake continues. Despite it being backhanded, it's an invitation to hang out. The iciness in Jake is thawing.

"I'll be here," Matt says, at once forceful and irritated. He's not sensing that Jake's easing up. I'm sure he's tired of defending himself by now, tired of being tested.

"So, wait, are we going to do karaoke or not?" Meg asks, clearly excited to skip to the end of the story. Solve the problem and move on. Will Matt join our group again or not? My stomach churns, but this time it's not from the idea of singing in public.

"Yes," I answer, a bit too enthusiastically. I'm just glad to be talking about something else, something that hopefully doesn't make Matt want to crawl under the table. And it's in that moment that I realize how funny it is, that tonight I'm going to end up singing again. Just like last year.

"Yeah, okay," Matt says, a bit apprehensively. "Although, I'm terrible at it. That's why Jake always took lead. That is, when you didn't," he adds, staring at me, reminding me of one of the best memories we do share. Despite the time apart, we still have that. Under the table, I feel his leg come closer to mine, almost touching it. Jeans against jeans. A small contact, but one nonetheless.

"Let's be honest—Jake would have taken the lead even if you were the best singer in the world," Meg says, and we laugh.

"I'll get the book." I get up and rush over to the karaoke DJ, and bring the book full of songs back to the table, eager to see what happens next; if it ends the same way it did last year.

"'Living on a Prayer.' Boom. Done," Jake announces, pointing to the Bon Jovi song he always sings. He does a great punk cover of it during shows.

"No surprise." Meg rolls her eyes and playfully nudges him. "I've got 'Like a Virgin,'" she decides, writing it down and eyeing me from across the table.

"I know for a fact you're not that," Jake says, wiggling his eyebrows and leaning into her.

"Shut up," she says, pushing him away.

"What are you thinking?" I ask Matt, leaning over the book with him.

"I don't know." He's twisting his watch around his wrist again, looking at the words, not me. Maybe he just needs to be pushed, awakened. He dared me to sing once, it's my turn now.

"You know, I'm pretty sure it's still tonight, so I think you *have* to say yes to singing something. . . ." I say, egging him on.

"How could I forget." He shakes his head.

"They don't have a great list, really, unless you like songs older than our parents. . . ." I joke, trying to ease the mood. I turn the page of the book, looking for a song for me to sing as well, when a piece of paper falls out and onto the floor. Matt grabs it first.

"Well, it looks like the last person here was a Green Day fan," he says, handing me someone named Scott's song choice, "21 Guns."

"And was too chicken to sing," I agree. If the song is here, it wasn't submitted to the DJ. I know the song, I know it well. Meg and I went through a Green Day stage a few years ago, and then it reemerged when she learned they turned their songs into a Broadway musical. It was so weird it worked. We screamed out the lyrics to "American Idiot" regularly. And it all clicks instantly. Another found object that somehow perfectly dictates the night. And though I don't believe in his notes and photos anymore, I think this one might work.

And once again, I know what I'm going to do. Looking at Matt, I'm ready to take a leap. I'm ready to move without being pushed or prodded. I'm ready to sing.

"I've got my song," I say, crossing out *Scott* and writing in *Ella*.

"Really?" Matt asks, eyeing me. He knows the song, too.

"Really."

CHAPTER 22

THEN
1:10 A.M.

Standing on the stage at One Spin Records, I was reminded of my past. When I was young, I'd put on all of my mother's fake plastic jewelry, paint my lips red, and stage elaborate spectacles just for myself. I'd sing along with the radio, pretending I was Madonna or Britney Spears. With no understanding of the lyrics, I'd belt them out as if I were performing at Madison Square Garden. I learned later that my mom would sometimes hide behind the wall and watch. She knew I'd stop if I realized she was there, but she loved seeing me perform.

I thought of that as the first few lyrics left my mouth. As my guard came crashing down and I was left exposed. But as the lyrics came, I realized that I was okay. That there was no one yelling at me, or saying I was bad or wrong. And that I was . . . fine. I was glowing.

My voice wasn't perfect, far from it. I would never be a rock star, or a famous Broadway actress. But I kept singing because it *felt good*. I thought of my mom hiding, secretly cheering me on. Even when I stopped letting her into my life—when I found a friend who understood me better—my mom still was always in my corner. Much like Meg was earlier, in the dressing room. And Jake, and Matt, and Barker, and even Gabby. They were all hiding in plain sight so I could let that little kid become a star. That knowledge was all I needed to let loose.

I shouted, screamed, sang the lyrics. I closed my eyes, let go, let the music flow from my body. I danced along onstage, weaving in between the guys. I looked at the crowd and threw my voice at them. I wouldn't have known if they were cheering or booing. But it wouldn't have mattered. It was my moment.

And it ended all too soon.

I powered out the last few lines, giving them to the crowd. As I knew the last lyrics were coming, I finally brought myself back to the stage, back to myself. I saw the guys behind me, all smiles. I saw Meg screaming her head off to my right. I saw the microphone, the lights. I saw it all. And I was a part of it.

And then it ended.

I crashed back into the reality I was used to, and prepared myself for feeling embarrassed or shy . . . but as I looked out into the audience, I didn't feel any of that. I felt *alive*.

The cheers came in and they were raucous and loud. No one expected me to do something like that, no one. After all, I wasn't *that* girl. I wasn't loud, I wasn't the girl you'd expect to see singing with a band. I was Ella. But that girl was in me, and now she was in the world.

I'd never felt so in the moment, so in control of my present.

I took a bow, adrenaline pumping through my body. I couldn't stop smiling.

I looked over at Matt, who was beaming. He flipped his bass over his shoulder and charged toward me. My heart jumped as he got closer, closer. Right in front of me, he grabbed my face and brought it up to his. And we were kissing, only this time without someone daring us to. It was as if an electric field brought our lips together. I felt his body move into mine, and I pressed mine back. I couldn't get enough of him. He moved his arms down and wrapped them around my waist. I threw my arms around his neck as he lifted me off the ground. My heart was thumping, as I thought only of him, and his lips and his arms and his touch.

The microphone slipped out of my hand and landed with a loud thud. We jumped as the noise brought us back to Earth. He put me down and leaned his forehead onto mine. Our cheeks became a hotter pink, Matt's face echoing mine. We were both grinning madly at each other.

"Oh, don't worry about us. You keep making out. We don't need to finish the gig or anything," Jake said. Embarrassed, we broke apart. I couldn't look at anyone; my face was on fire, and I threw my hands up to cover it. I couldn't believe what had happened with me, and between Matt and me, and in front of everyone. My pulse was pounding and I couldn't stop beaming, despite the embarrassment. I turned around and stepped off the stage and into Meg's embrace.

"You, my dear, are a rock star," she loudly whispered into my ear.

And for once, I actually believed her.

CHAPTER 23

NOW
12:35 A.M.

We write down our song choices and I bring them up to the karaoke lady. She nods, barely offering a glance in my direction, and sighs at our selections. I suppose she does hear them often. Matt kept his a secret, and I was too good to peek.

Our conversation stifles as we await our turns. The place is pretty empty tonight, so we know it's only a matter of seconds before she calls our names.

"Who'd have thought that two musicians who play in front of hundreds of people would be so nervous about karaoke," Meg jokes, and I smile.

"Not nervous," Jake rebuts, but he obviously is. He

shuffles in his chair, playing with everything on the table. His napkin is torn, his chair won't stop moving. Meg puts her hand over his calmly. The simple gesture makes him stop.

"And you?" I ask Matt.

"Nah," he says, but I think I hear his voice crack. He's still twisting his watch and looking straight ahead. His eyes are wide, intense. I'm not sure what he's more nervous about—singing, or being here with us. Or perhaps he's thinking back to last year. It makes sense that we're here, singing, after a night of reenacting. We both know how the story goes. But will history repeat itself? I glance over at him and think of us on the roof again. Of him so close. And him so close right now, back in my life. He's so cute when he's nervous.

I don't have much time to deliberate, though, because I'm called up first.

"WOOO! GO ELLA!" Meg yells, thrusting her fists in the air.

"You've got to be kidding me," I groan, hiding my face behind my hand.

"ELLA!" Jake joins in, knowing it will further embarrass me.

"I hate you all." I glare at them, knowing I was in for this. Just knowing that this would happen.

"You've got it," Matt says, while placing his hand on my shoulder. I look over at him and he removes his hand, quick to react. But instead of wanting him gone, I finally feel the absence of his touch, and how that empty space will be left unfilled were he not to be in my life. I want his hand—and everything else—back.

I grab his hand and squeeze it, just as I did one year ago. He jumps, just as he did then, and then squeezes back. His mouth twitches as if to ask *Dare I smile?*

I nervously walk to the stage, thinking of my friends behind me and how ridiculous I'm going to sound. Yes, I've sung more since that one night, but I'm still not comfortable.

But—it's always memorable.

I take the microphone from the stand and step up onto the stage. Everyone's looking at me, and I can feel my heart racing in my chest, beating over and over again, as if creating a musical beat of its own. I look over to Matt and suddenly I'm brought back to that night. I can see the crowd. Hear the murmurs filtering through the shop. I squint at the lights hitting my face. My hands go clammy.

But at the table, Matt's there, looking at me like no one has before. As if all the belief in the world is coming from him. As if he's offering me everything in the world and more. He's not leaving. He's staying. Maybe it's worth taking a leap. Maybe we can start fresh, ignore the past and move on. Make memories of our own again, ones that'll be truly remembered, and not just scraps of paper for others to pick up. Maybe it's time for us to start living instead of planning or re-creating or avoiding what we really want.

As soon as the song starts, the millions of voices fighting in my head are silenced. Out of many, one survives, and I hear it. And I know what I want.

As I sing out the lyrics, letting them do the talking instead of me, I think back to the time in the pizza place when we were new and light. And also to the time at the record store one year ago when we were still tentative and unsure. And while these memories are great, I realize that I'd rather make new ones. I want to create a new story that doesn't already have an ending. I'm ready to forgive.

We as a couple were far from the perfect memory I had imagined and relived in my head over and over again. I know that now. I also know that this night was far from perfect, and trying to reenact the past won't change anything. Why try bringing back the past when it's far and gone and possibly not quite how it was remembered? Why not shoot for more or better or what might happen next?

My heart races as I realize I want my future to be with him.

Lay down your arms
give up the fight . . . you and I.

CHAPTER 24

THEN
1:15 A.M.

The Pepperpots played one more song, which I more or less paid attention to. I saw them moving, and I heard the music, but I was mostly focused on Matt, wondering what would happen next and waiting for him to put down his guitar. My adrenaline was fully charged; despite the late hour, I was ready for the night to continue.

Finally, with one last chord and one last "Yeaaah," the song was over. I hopped in place, my heart racing. People swarmed around, going back to the CD racks, or waiting to greet the band. Meg and I stayed where we were; we didn't need to look eager—we were with the band, after all. Or, in my case, I was kind of in it.

"You're amazing," Gabby yelled, hugging me again. She'd repeated the compliment at least seven times already, and I let her because it was time to move on. "And the kiss? Is there something I should know?" She smirked, eyes sparkling.

"Yeah, yeah, yeah," I answered, giggling, and not nearly as embarrassed as I would have been had we kissed in front of everyone prior to the show. Singing onstage was so exhilarating that at that moment I felt like I could do anything, including let her back into my life. Nick was in the past, I saw to that earlier, and Matt was my future. And, like Meg, Gabby would be with me through it all.

"Seriously, it was adorable! Matt's a million times better than Nick," Gabby continued.

"Right?" Meg piped in, eyeing both Gabby and me. I nodded in agreement, eyeing Meg right back so she'd know I was also telling her that it was all okay, that I had finally forgiven Gabby.

"Definitely," I said, and Meg grinned and grabbed us both in a hug. "And we're back," she announced triumphantly, over our heads, and Gabby and I just giggled in response. Because yes, yes we were.

When we released I just stood there grinning stupidly, with one eye on my best friends and one on the stage. Matt looked over and smiled, ducking his head down. My pulse sped up as he started walking in our direction, but then he stopped by the microphone and mouthed, "Striking." Of course, they had to pack up the instruments first.

"So, what's next?" I asked.

"Well, we know what's next for you," Meg said, making a kissing face.

"I'm never living this down, am I?"

"Nope," they both answered.

"I think some girls are jealous," Gabby clucked, eyeing a group of girls behind me. I turned around and noticed them all staring at me, eyes squinted and mouths pursed. I turned back to my friends, feeling a bit alarmed.

"Of course they are. Cute guy taken? It's heartbreaking, really," Meg commented, faking a swoon.

Jake jumped off the stage, and walked—no, strutted— toward us.

"Can we for a second discuss how our set turned into a porno halfway through?"

"Ugggh," I groaned, rolling my eyes and feeling my face heat. But before I could get too embarrassed, he pulled me in for a big, sweaty hug and I knew he was proud. After pulling away, he walked over to Meg and threw his arm over her.

"Ew," she said, pushing him off. Sweat had already seeped onto her shirt.

"What? I thought girls loved it."

"Your sweat? Not so much."

"Then perhaps it's just my beautiful smile."

"Jake, ladies and gentlemen," Meg said. He threw his arm over her again and rubbed his hair on her face, attacking her with his perspiration.

"ACCKKK," she laughed. "GET OFF." She tried pushing him, but he just held on, squeezing her tight. He was laughing, too, really laughing. It was the first time I'd seen him that happy in a while. I guessed she was right—sometimes you just needed to yell.

"What?" he said, back in his faux-British accent. "When I'm a famous rock star, you're going to remember this day."

"Oh, not the accent again," I sighed dramatically.

"When you're a famous rock star, I'm going to prove to everyone that you're not British," Meg snickered. He stopped wiping, and, instead, drew her in for a hug. She let him, leaning in. She turned around to face me, but kept his arms around her waist, resting on him as he supported her—something she didn't often do. He placed his chin on her head and drummed his fingers on her stomach. Clearly the epic saga of Jake and Meg was far from over.

"Hey," I heard behind me. I turned around to see Matt sitting on the edge of the low stage. His glasses had slid down his nose, and he was looking at me over them. He looked . . . shy. His hair fell on his face delicately, and I wanted to touch it, push it to the side. I felt myself walking toward him without even telling myself to move.

"Guys, let's get out of here. I don't want to witness another make-out session," Jake said. I didn't see it, but I knew Meg hit him in response.

"Hey, we had to see yours earlier," Matt responded

over my head. I didn't know what to do other than smile awkwardly at him. So close. Apparently, he didn't either, because he just played with his watch, rolling it over and over his wrist.

"And I'm going to go help Barker with his drums," Gabby said, making an excuse to leave.

"Yeah, I should go greet my adoring fans or whatever," Jake added.

"Or whatever is more like it," Meg answered, following him away. Just Matt and I were left. In a crowded room. Right by a stage we previously kissed on. No big deal.

"So," he said, amused.

"So." Silence. Silence. Silence. And then, laughter. A lot of it.

"Come here," he said, grabbing my arms softly and pulling me to him. I stepped in between his legs, which were hanging off the stage, and hugged him. Breathing in his scent, one I had just met earlier that day, I leaned my chin on his shoulder and my cheek against his. We stayed like that, content in the moment, as our laughter died down.

"I should apologize for, you know, ravaging you onstage like that. It was a bit much."

"A bit?" I answered, leaning my face away from him, but keeping my body where it was.

"Okay, a lot." He smiled. "It was just . . . our first kiss was on the roof during a game. I wanted our second to mean something a bit more."

"And how'd you know there'd be a second?" I asked, grinning.

"I didn't. I hoped, though. So, you know, onstage in front of everyone—what would be more memorable than that?"

"Hey, would you look at that—you have a memory of your own now!"

"I do, don't I? I guess I can't use my loner speech on girls anymore."

"Well, you have a ton of candidates lining up, in case you're interested." I nodded toward the crowd, who were mingling, only slightly aware of our presence. Some of the girls were still staring, watching our whole interaction, but instead of feeling scared or embarrassed or alarmed, I felt . . . proud. Standing there in Matt's arms, I didn't care what anyone thought.

"So I saw. They were undressing me with their eyes."

"Were they?"

"No, I just wanted to see what it's like having Jake's ego." With each sentence, we were leaning in again. An inch at a time, our faces were getting closer.

"Never try to have Jake's ego." And closer.

"Deal." And closer, until his lips found mine again. This time he was gentle, careful. My body filled with adrenaline again. I felt like I could fly. I pulled him closer as the kiss became more intense, more electric.

I heard a cheer bellow out, and turned to look. Of course it was Jake.

"You think there will be a time when Jake doesn't interrupt us?" he asked, laughing.

"Nope." I sighed. "We should go before he wants to join in." Matt pushed himself off the stage and started walking toward the crowd. But first, he reached back for my hand. I grabbed for it, as if it was the most natural thing in the world.

We caught up with Jake, Meg, Barker, and Gabby in the middle of the store. They were leaning against racks of CDs, recounting the night. Matt and I walked up, still holding hands.

"What'd we miss?" Matt asked.

"What did *we* miss, you mean," Jake answered.

"See? Never living it down," I pointed out.

"You guys can keep making out if you'd like. We'll just watch."

"Jake—" Meg said, slapping him playfully.

"Hey." He grabbed her around the waist, pulling her to him. "So, what's up now?"

"What time is it?" I asked, realizing I had absolutely no clue.

"After one a.m.," Meg answered, pulling out her phone. "Crap, what can we do?"

"I gotta go load my drums and get out of here," Barker answered. "If I don't get Gabby home in the next few minutes, her dad will kill me."

"No he won't," Gabby responded, then turned to us and

mouthed "yes he will" while nodding. I muffled a laugh.

"Good show, guys," Barker said, high fiving Jake and Matt.

"Lame," Jake responded. "Go home with your woman."

"Don't mind if I do," Barker responded. Gabby shook her head, rolling her eyes at Jake. Before leaving, Barker came over to hug me good-bye.

"I did not see that happening," he whispered into my ear.

"I didn't either," I whispered back. "But I'm glad it did." He stepped back and grinned, saluting me as he always did when he was happy. Gabby ran over and gave each of us a hug as well.

"Seriously, you were great," she said again, and I smiled because I just couldn't stop.

"Come on," Barker said, slinging his arm over Gabby's shoulders. She reached up and intertwined her fingers with his. As I watched them go, I thought of their relationship, which was all stability and sweet touches, which always seemed private. And then there was Meg and Jake, who were all impulse and passion, and shared it with the entire world. I suppose I fell in the middle somewhere, not quite on solid ground, but far from outrageous.

"Hey Meg," I asked, suddenly remembering our big problem we had conveniently ignored earlier, "where are we staying tonight?"

"Oh god, you're right."

"What do you mean?" Matt asked.

"Meg said she was staying at my place. I said I was staying at hers. Our parents never check because we're at each other's houses more often than we're actually home. But now we're not. So . . ."

"And we can't just go back because then they'd know we lied and were out until one a.m."

"Come home with me," Jake answered, reaching his hands into the front pockets of her jeans.

"Not helping."

"How about me?" Matt asked innocently.

"Don't you think we're moving fast enough as it is?" I joked, smiling, even though the suggestion enticed me.

"No, really. My parents won't care. I was on the phone with them earlier and they suggested it since it was late." Oh, so that was who he was on the phone with. He paused and exhaled. "I've never really . . . brought people home before. I mean, here or there when I was little, but not much. I just always went to their places. My parents were always on me about it, but I didn't want people to see our temporary lives. So, despite it being so late, I know they'd be thrilled I actually have friends. They practically threw me out the door when I said I had plans tonight. I realize how awesome I sound right now, by the way. Feel free to run away."

"You're a real winner, aren't you?" Jake asked, still holding on to Meg.

"I think they just worry about me, since we move so often. It's hard to make connections." I put my arm around his waist and leaned my head onto his shoulder. He needed a hug. "So, my place?"

I looked at Meg and she answered with a shrug. "We have no better option. Just promise us your family isn't, like, made up of vampires or anything."

"Nah, just zombies. Let me call them, hold on." He walked a few steps away and got out his phone.

"I'm coming too. I'm not leaving you girls alone in a house of zombies."

"I think we'll be fine, Jake," I said, smiling. But really, I was nervous. I was excited to go back to Matt's house, was excited to meet his family. But I didn't know anything about them. What if they were crazy? What if they didn't like me?

"I know, but I'll still come. I've met his parents already, they're cool, but they'll probably be wondering why he's bringing home two random chicks. Also, more time to do this." He continued wiping his sweat on Meg.

"I'm going to kill you, you know that, right?" Meg announced as Matt came back.

"Yeah, they're cool with it. Jake, you want to come, too?"

"What are your parents doing up so late? They are vampires, aren't they?" I asked.

"Yeah, mate, I'm coming too. To watch out for the ladies. You know how they get," Jake answered.

"Um, sure? As for my parents, I just woke them up. Like I said, they're fine with it. A little too eager, actually. My mom is getting the sheets out now . . . and putting in a pizza. She's weird."

"We're going to die," Meg said. "They're going to eat us."

"At least we'll have fresh sheets to die on," I added.

"Matt, take my keys and lead the way," Jake said, tossing his keys at Matt. "You take El. I remember where you live, so I'll direct Meg." He looked at her suggestively as he said it.

"Really?" she said, punching him in the stomach lightly. He pulled her away, and she mock resisted as they moved toward the back of the store.

"Okay, I guess we should go," Matt said, squeezing the keys in his hand.

"You okay?" I asked, noticing the tension in his grip.

"Yeah, fine. I'm just . . ."

I looked at him seriously, wondering what was going through his head. Wondering if he didn't want me to meet his parents. It was too soon, I figured. Panic started bubbling in my heart.

"Do you want to go out with me? Like, on a date sometime? God, that sounds ridiculous. I'm terrible at this."

I laughed because I didn't know what else to do. "Of course!" I said, pulling him in for a hug. His body relaxed as he wrapped his arms around my waist. "We've kissed, Matt. I kind of feel like we're past dates."

"Okay, good." He chuckled nervously. "Because when I introduce you as the girl I'm dating, I don't want to be lying."

"You're going to introduce me like that?" I asked, look-ing up at him.

"Why wouldn't I? I know we just met, but . . . you're amazing. You're funny and kind and passionate." He pulled my face up to look at him. "I really like you."

"I really like you too," I said, bringing my lips back up to his. Old Ella wouldn't have done this—but New, singing-onstage Ella didn't care. She still felt the adrenaline from the performance, still wanted to stand out. It was crazy and exciting and I didn't know what it all meant, but I was there, living it. It wasn't Meg shining this time; it was me.

We were in the middle of the store, with people all around us, but we didn't care. We embraced each other, embraced the moment, and fell into a new one together. Arms around arms, lips pressed together. And this time, Jake didn't interrupt.

CHAPTER 25

NOW
12:45 A.M.

I leave the karaoke stage while Meg and Jake are still cheering like crazy. They're making me blush, but I love them anyway. When I get to the table, Meg wraps me in a hug and I close my eyes to take in the moment. The feeling where everything will fall into place.

When she lets go, I finally let myself look at Matt. He's smiling, but it's not reaching his eyes.

"Hey," I say, offering a meek, stupid wave. What else do you do after publicly announcing—through song—that you're okay with starting over.

"You were great, really, great," he says, and instead of looking excited or anything else I would have imagined, he almost looks sad. "I'll, um, I'll be right back." And with a simple sentence, he gets up and leaves the bar. And I'm alone as I feel my heart cracking.

"What was that all about?" Meg asks me, and I shrug because I honestly don't know.

But I'm going to find out.

"Give me a second," I say. I follow the way he went, up the stairs and out the front door, finding him pacing in the gravel parking lot.

"Matt," I yell, and he whirls around at my voice. "What's going on?" I walk over closer to him so I don't have to yell. He's stopped pacing, but he's still avoiding me. I need him to look at me. Once again, I need him to explain.

"I get it, it's okay," he says quietly.

"What do you mean?" I ask. If he gets what I was singing, wouldn't he be happier? Isn't this what he wanted? Am I completely wrong?

"I just thought . . ." he says, mussing up his hair. "I don't know. It would have been nice."

"Nice?" I ask.

"To be back. I mean, when Jake invited me and you . . . never mind," he says, going back to his pacing.

"Matt. Seriously. *What* are you talking about?"

He faces me again and he looks lost, alone, and I still don't know why. "El, I get it. What you sang? I'll leave you guys alone. You don't have to be nice about it or anything."

"What are you *talking* about?" I ask, grabbing his

shoulders to stop him from moving. He lifts his head to look at me and this time doesn't look away. He didn't get anything I sang, anything. "Are we . . . are we fighting because of a misinterpretation of lyrics?" I ask, a weight lifting off my chest. It makes me want to laugh. It is easier talking through notes and songs, but never, never worth it. And I find the irony of the situation amusing.

He cocks his head to the side, and though he's still guarded, light is coming to his face again.

"Matt . . . when you came back tonight, I wasn't ready. I was just so . . . surprised, and still—" I sigh, finally allowing myself to admit it. "—not over you. Despite how much I tried to convince myself otherwise. But I wasn't *ready* to just . . . go back to what we were."

"We don't have to, I just—"

"But the thing is," I cut him off, "I don't want to. I don't *want* to reenact the past anymore and remember it by papers or bracelets," I say, holding up my wrist. "The past is gone and I'm ready to have a new beginning. I can't be mad anymore." He looks up, raising his eyebrows as a question. As awkward as it is, I meet his eyes for my confession. "I like you too much."

"You do?" he asks, breathing out the words, as relief shows on his face. I nod in response because it's all I can do. I'm done staying in the dark; I'm finally letting myself shine. "But what about the song?"

"It was my way of saying I didn't want to fight anymore. I

was ready to just . . . give up and be happy." I shake my head. "I guess that wasn't conveyed, was it?"

"Not so much," he laughs. "Now I know how you felt with the notes. . . ." he says, suddenly looking forlorn. Then he adds, "But you're leaving soon. . . ."

"I know," I say, and then, "But we do still have three months. And I think they'd be a hell of a lot better if you were in them." I smile.

His face is full of a *really?* he doesn't dare ask. I grin and start to laugh, answering anyway.

"Wait, this is what I came here to give you tonight," he says, reaching into his pocket and handing me a piece of paper. My stomach seizes up because I thought we were past this.

I open it up and see that it's blank. "What's this?"

"It's nothing. I don't want to communicate that way anymore, or live through memories. Chris and I had different ways of adapting after we moved, and neither worked. I want to just try . . . living now."

"I'd like that," I say, putting the paper in my pocket. It's the most honest thing he's ever given me.

"So what do we do?" he asks, still standing a few inches away from me. I look at him and find myself wanting to run at him, hold him in my arms. Not because I did it in the past, but because right now, it's all I want to feel.

I hold out my hand to him, ready to take the next step. Or the first. "Hi, I'm Ella. I enjoy breaking into schools, telling cheesy jokes, and occasionally singing with a band."

He laughs and takes my hand. "I'm Matt. I also like cheesy jokes and playing in a band. And I just moved back here for a girl I couldn't get out of my mind. Thankfully, she doesn't think I'm a complete idiot."

"She seems nice," I say, feeling his thumb rubbing the back of my hand.

"Oh, she is. Even if she's afraid of climbing off a roof during a thunderstorm."

"Hey!" I laugh as I feel him slowly pulling me toward him.

"But she makes up for it by being really cute." He keeps pulling and my heart beats with anticipation.

"Better," I answer, liking where this is going. Wanting to be closer, wanting to close the gap forever.

"And she has a pretty smile," he says, raising his eyes, and I get what he's saying. It's the gig flyer from last year. Back then, and in so many other moments, he gave me these pieces to read what he was thinking and feeling. Something was always holding him back. But now . . . now he's taking the risk. He's jumping in, opening up and actually talking. And I feel myself leaning into him, and his words, because he broke down the barrier, and nothing stands between us anymore.

"Maybe I'll get to meet her someday."

"Maybe," he says, finally bringing his hands to my face. "But I'm going to keep her to myself for a bit."

He leans down and just when my pulse beat thinks it can't take it anymore, I feel his lips on mine. And it's soft and sweet and feels like home.

He pulls away smiling, but still tentative, holding me as if I'm glass that might break. I respond by wrapping my arms around his waist and gazing up at him. But before we kiss again, my mind manages to make sense out of one question.

"You moved back here for me?" I ask, face so close.

He blushes slightly, but doesn't pull away. "Of course. I didn't lie earlier—the school here is good . . . but . . . I've spent my life on the road, trying to find home, when really, you were always home to me."

As the hole in my heart fills and beats and breathes again, I reach my hand up and bring it behind his head, curling my fingers into his hair. His body sighs, collapses at my touch, and then we're kissing again.

They're not small or sweet exploratory kisses, like the one before. They're passionate and deep, making up for lost time. His arms wrap around my waist tightly, bringing me close to him. I throw my other arm around his neck. Our lips refuse to leave one another, not wanting to be separated again. Even moments to breathe feel like too long apart. The entire planet is moving and time is passing, but we're staying in this one spot. We're not leaving.

I want this. It's a decision I'm making.

Gasping for breath, we break, parting our faces ever so slightly. He leans his forehead onto mine, playing with the hair around my face, and I know he's feeling the same way I do. He can't even control the goofy grin plastered on his face, just as I can't control mine. We laugh, because what else is there to do?

"Ahem." We were so absorbed in the moment, I didn't realize that more cars have pulled into the parking lot, that music is filtering up the stairs with someone doing a terrible rendition of Weezer's "Buddy Holly," and that Jake and Meg are a few feet away, staring. We jump at their interruption, breaking apart to face them. But Matt still pulls me close, an arm attached to my waist. I put mine around his, not wanting to let go ever again.

"I guess our job here is done," Jake says, crossing his arms in front of his chest. Next to him, Meg is looking at me, grinning wildly. All is forgiven, apparently. To be fair, no one can argue with how happy we look.

"It feels only right that Jake interrupts us. Again," Matt whispers to me, squeezing my waist. I giggle into his shoulder. It *does* feel right. Everything about this does. I feel his lips on my head and I memorize the touch. We don't need to pick up a scrap of paper to remember tonight; we just made the perfect memory ourselves.

CHAPTER 26

THREE MONTHS LATER
7:00 P.M.

I see the lights first, extremely bright against the night sky. Whites and reds and blues flashing, announcing the fair's presence. Calling everyone to attend. The Ferris wheel is tall, high in the sky and rotating continuously. A roller coaster stands next to it, all loops and drops.

"The fair!" I exclaim, thinking back to the amazing day we had a year ago when we went and he dared me to ride the roller coaster.

"Of course," Matt says with a smile. "I thought it would be a fun way to spend your last night in town. Meg and Jake will be here in a bit."

"You're the best," I say, hugging him as he drives into the

lot. It *is* my last night in town before going away—it wouldn't be right if we weren't doing something ridiculous and scary with Meg and Jake.

He parks in a grassy lot, and holds my hand as we walk in. Since the night in Kiki's parking lot, he's barely let go. And though we don't know what the future will hold for us, we don't plan on letting go anytime soon.

He buys us tickets for the rides, and we walk inside. Instantly, we're hit with the smell. It's a mixture of sawdust and sugar, ponies and funnel cake. Cotton candy piled high in pink and blue is sold to the left of us; loud games with blinking lights and bottles to topple over are on the right. Straight ahead are the rides.

"There's something I want to do before the others get here," he says, giving me a secretive smile.

"And what's that?" I ask, raising an eyebrow.

"You'll see," he answers, before leading me toward the games.

"I don't know if I'll be able to fit a giant stuffed unicorn in my dorm," I say as we keep walking past the stands. He squeezes my hand and gives me a quick kiss on the cheek.

"We'll play the games after. I can be your own personal strong man."

"I think the strong man is supposed to have muscles," I joke.

"Ouch!" he laughs. "It should be over . . . here," he says, in front of a generic photo booth.

"Picture?" I ask, not exactly sure where he's going with this.

"Work with me," he says, and I just nod and follow him into the booth. We close the curtain and it's so small I practically have to sit on top of him. I snuggle up close and as the light flashes we make ridiculous faces, trying hard to make the other laugh. The last one is just that—a blur of us laughing.

When the photos print outside, I grab the first row of four. While waiting for the second set to print, we look at our faces and laugh. Much like in the photos still saved on his phone, we look so happy.

"I look ridiculous," I say.

"You look cute," Matt adds just as the second set of photos prints. But he doesn't make an effort to get them. When I bend down to, he stops me.

"What's up?" I ask.

"Let's leave them."

"Why?"

"A nice memory for someone else?"

I smile at him, remembering how the first object he picked up was of strangers laughing. It made him curious, and gave him something to hold on to until he stopped collecting these scraps earlier this summer, after coming back. He doesn't need them anymore, and neither do I. I think of someone picking up our photo later tonight, and wonder what they might think. Maybe our photo will do that for someone else, show them that there's happiness in the world. Perhaps they'll start collecting things, too.

"What next?" he asks, snaking his arm around my waist.

"Roller coaster?" I dare to ask.

"I thought you were scared of them?" he asks, surprised.

"I'm done being scared," I say, giving his hand a squeeze and leading the way. I don't need a bracelet or a cheer to let me know I can do it. Though they're great reminders, I can dare myself to live.

We approach the ride and find ourselves at the front of the line. There are tons of people here, but they all seem to be at the games and Ferris wheel. The roller coaster isn't nearly as popular. Which, of course, scares me.

"Tickets?" a man wearing a striped red-and-white shirt asks. His expression is weary, his tone bored. He's clearly tired of watching the fun and not being a part of it. White hair pokes out of his matching red-and-white cap.

Matt hands him our tickets and we walk up to the iridescent green dragon we'll be riding. I glance at the sign above our heads: **DRAGON RACE**. The tracks look old, weathered; not quite silver, but a muted, worn gray. The dragon shakes as we sit down.

"I hope our weight isn't too much for it," I say, worried.

Instead of answering, Matt reaches over and gives me a kiss. We then pull the harnesses over our heads and get ready to go.

"WOOOOOOO!" I hear to my right and see Meg

running with Jake slowly following behind. "GO ELLA!" she shouts again, always cheering me on, and I wave and smile because even though I'm terrified, I'm glad they're here.

"Ready?" Matt whispers, and I grab his hand again.

This is the part I hate the most. The anticipation before the ride. It's like how I felt before singing. But I always love the rush. Always.

We start out slow, heading up the track for the first drop. We hear the click, click, click of the wheels, taunting us before the fall. It's as if they're counting down the seconds until our demise. And as we approach the top, I think of that first night Matt and I met.

It was much like this, a slow incline to the top. Small gestures click, click, clicking. And then, whoosh, we fall, fall, fall for each other. The first loop comes, and it's like that first kiss that left me light-headed and faint. Then we're rushing steadily along, then we suddenly drop, leaving each other. But after that, an incline, another go, and we climb, climb, climb to the top. We talk and feel each other out. And then we fall down again, and before we know it we're outside Kiki's kissing madly. We don't care who sees or who hears as we're screaming with the next loop, and the next fall. And I know there will be more. I know there will be ups and downs and corkscrews and loops, but I don't care. I keep my eyes closed and enjoy the ride, hearing Matt scream right beside me. Knowing he's with me through everything makes it so much better. I know we'll make it.

As the harnesses rise, Matt jumps up, looking wild, excited, pumped full of adrenaline. It's how he looks after a gig. It usually takes about an hour for the feeling to wear off, and in that time, he's unstoppable. As am I when I sing with them, which from time to time I still do. He grabs my shaking hand as we walk off the ride. I'm giddy, jumping, thrilled, and my smile won't stop growing. It only gets bigger when I see Meg holding a tiny bear Jake won her, and Jake pretending it wasn't a big deal. It gets bigger when I remember I'm here, with them, and though this is my last night in town, I know it's not the end. Heart pounding, wind in my hair, laughing crazily. I don't care what happens next, but I'm ready for it. If I can face a roller coaster, I can face anything.

So when Matt leans over to kiss my cheek and asks if I want to go again, of course I say, "Yes."

ACKNOWLEDGMENTS

Thank you to my editor, Karen Chaplin, for taking a chance with *The Night We Said Yes* and me. For your enthusiasm, editorial notes, and love of my characters. You helped shape my book into what it is today. And to the entire HarperTeen team, including Abigail Tyson, Erin Fitzsimmons, Heather Daugherty, Bethany Reis, Kim VandeWater, Lindsay Blechman, Olivia Russo, the whole sales team, and anyone else who has touched this book—you're all amazing.

To Michelle Andelman, the best agent in the world. Thank you for believing in *TNWSY* from the start, for knowing exactly how to get the best out of the story, for advice and thoughts, and for not minding my endless emails (right?). I couldn't have done all of this without you. And to everyone at Regal Literary, thank you for embracing my book.

So much love to my original readers, from when *TNWSY* was just a baby: Colure Caulfield for a keen eye, Katie Harding for plot thoughts, Joe Chandler for a guy's point of view, and Misty White for psychoanalyzing Ella. And thank you, Megan Donnelly and Michelle Carroll, for your undying support and demands to read more. I love you all.

Every writer needs writer friends. Thank you Jessica Martinez and Jenny Torres Sanchez for advice, support, and awesome vent sessions.

To the original Pepperpots: Joe Davenport, Dan Lugo, and Ben Grey. I'm still convinced you were the best high school band ever.

To everyone at the Alafaya Library for embracing my enthusiasm for YA books (and everything else). This book must stay in the collection forever.

To all of my family members, but specifically Justin Gibaldi—my baby brother who's twice my size. Continue being a tattooed mechanic with a heart. To my parents, Paul and Tami Gibaldi, who never doubted me for a second. Thank you for believing in me. And to Jetta, just because.

To Samir Mathur. Thank you for listening to me even when I ramble on and on. Thank you for challenging me and believing in me and being my biggest supporter. I love you and I like you.

And to my love, my Leila—if there's anything I want to teach you, it's this: always believe in your dreams, because if you work for them, they just might come true.

JOIN THE
Epic Reads
COMMUNITY

HE ULTIMATE YA DESTINATION ///////////////

◀ DISCOVER ▶
your next favorite read

◀ FIND ▶
new authors to love

◀ WIN ▶
free books

◀ SHARE ▶
infographics, playlists, quizzes, and more

◀ WATCH ▶
the latest videos

◀ TUNE IN ▶
to Tea Time with Team Epic Reads

  Find us at **www.epicreads.com**
and **@epicreads**

JUN - - 2015